T0063084

Spirit of the Law

Written by
Darla J. Vasilas

Order this book online at www.trafford.com
or email orders@trafford.com

Most Trafford titles are also available at major online book retailers.

Printed in the United States of America.

ISBN: 978-1-4907-4848-1 (sc)
ISBN: 978-1-4907-4850-4 (hc)
ISBN: 978-1-4907-4849-8 (e)

Library of Congress Control Number: 2014917834

Trafford rev. 10/08/2014

www.trafford.com

North America & international
toll-free: 1 888 232 4444 (USA & Canada)
fax: 812 355 4082

Dedication

I want to dedicate this book to my husband, Steve. He put up with me when I would bug him when I would have one of those writer's block moments and graciously created the illustrations herein. I would also like to thank my mother-in-law, Mrs. Lillian Vasilas, for all of the support she has given us over the years.

Prologue

It was May 1878, in the small Texas town of Rio Madre located in the southern part of what is now the Texas panhandle. Forty-two year old Marshal Bill Raines was six feet tall, had slightly graying hair, brown eyes and a medium build. He had been hired three months before and was still getting to know the folks around the area. Most of them he found to be normal, law-abiding citizens. That is, until it was payday and the area cowhands would come into town to spend their hard-earned money. Now he saw nothing wrong with that, not at all. They were supplying a livelihood to the local merchants, saloon keepers, and any number of travelling gamblers that might be gracing the town with their presence at the time. The problems came when these law-abiding cowhands would have a few too many drinks at the saloon and suddenly think they were God's gift to the women in the town, especially the saloon girls. They also seemed to take a dislike to any gambler that would try to 'cheat' them out of their hard-earned money. It never occurred to them that just, maybe, they were just not good poker players. Also, recently, some of the local ranchers had been missing some of their stock. Not a lot, but it was becoming more than a suspicion that there just might be a rustler problem developing in the territory. Therein lies our story.

Chapter One

November 1878. The holidays were approaching and Marshal Bill Raines knew that he was going to need hire some help, soon. That Monday morning he placed a sign on the office window saying that he was looking for a deputy. The pay wouldn't be great, but it would be a steady job. Early that afternoon he was visited by young Corey Hansen. Corey was 5 feet 10 inches tall and had sandy brown hair, green eyes and had been working at the local livery stable; but he wanted to do something else…something meaningful.

"Hello, Marshal," Corey said as he entered the office.

"Can I help you?"

"Yes, I saw your sign, and I'm the man for the job."

"How old are you, Young Man?"

"Nineteen, Sir."

"Can you use a gun?"

"Yes, Sir. Growing up, my Pa and I didn't have a lot of money, so we had to fiend for ourselves. I got real good at shooting rabbits, quail, anything that would put meat on the table."

"Shooting at game is one thing. It's a totally different thing when you have to point that gun at human being."

"Well, Sir, I guess if someone is shooting at you, you don't really think about it, do you?"

"That's the whole point, Son. You have to think…you have to know what you're doing. You have to know that when you pull that trigger, someone may die!"

"Look, Marshal…"

"No, you look. I need someone I can depend on to back me up, in ANY situation. Someone a little more experienced."

Corey knew he wasn't getting anywhere and turned and stormed out of the office.

The next morning Marshal Raines was in his office when Pete Reed, one of the local shopkeepers came running in. "Marshal…they're robbing the bank!"

"Who?"

"Three men….I saw them when I walked by the window."

The Marshal grabbed a rifle from the gun rack and went outside. He was running up the wooden sidewalk across from the bank when the three men came running out and jumped on their horses. "Hold it!!!" The Marshal called out as he fired a warning shot. The three men all turned, firing at the Marshal as he took cover behind a watering trough. The Marshal was able to take down one of the bank robbers but the other two had already started to ride out of town when a shot suddenly rang out, knocking one of the men off his horse. Marshal Raines fired again, hitting the lone remaining robber. When he turned to see who had fired the shot that took down the second robber, he saw Corey Hansen coming toward him, holding a smoking rifle in his hands while he ejected the empty cartridge.

"You all right, Marshal?" Corey asked, as the Marshal walked over to retrieve the bag containing the bank's money.

"Yeah…do I have you to thank for that?" He asked Corey, pointing to the second robber.

"Saw what was happening, didn't think, just reacted." Corey said, then grinned.

The Marshal raised an eyebrow, then, "Anyone here know who these guys are?" The marshal asked as a crowd began to form around the scene. Nobody responded. "Okay, you men," he pointed at some of the men closest to him, "take these three over to the undertaker. Have him bring me any identification he finds on them. You…" he pointed at Corey, "come with me."

Moments later they entered the office and Marshal Raines went to his desk and pulled out a box of cartridges and began reloading the rifle. Meanwhile, Corey just stood there...waiting. The Marshal put the reloaded rifle back into the gun rack and turned to look at the young man who began to nervously shift his weight from foot to foot. "Just reacted?"

"Uh…yes, Sir. When I saw them come out of the bank and you started shooting, I kind of surmised that they were up to no good and you were out-numbered, so I figured it wouldn't be a good idea to let them get away with the bank's money…so I took the shot. Then you shot the other one, and then…"

"I know what happened then," the Marshal interrupted him. He sat back in his chair for a minute just looking at Corey, then reached into the desk drawer and pulled out a deputy's badge. "Still want to give it a try."

"Yes, Sir!" Corey said, happily.

"You willing to follow orders?"

"Yes, Sir."

"There will be long nights, long dangerous rides escorting prisoners… think you're up to it.?"

"Yes, Sir!"

"Raise your right hand…" Corey did so. "Do you swear to faithfully execute the duties of Deputy Marshal of the town of Rio Madre?"

"I do," Corey said, smiling.

"Welcome aboard…Deputy. Now, as your first duty…make me a pot of coffee, then second, go on down to the livery stable and tell Abe you found another job…."

"Yes, Sir. I will do that right now." Corey hurriedly put a pot of coffee on the wood stove to brew, then left the office as the Marshal leaned back in his chair.

"What have I done?" He thought to himself. A few minutes later he poured himself a cup of coffee, took a drink, and almost choked as he tried to swallow.

When Corey returned to the office the marshal was sitting at his desk looking through the latest bunch of wanted posters that had come in the morning mail. "Here," he said handing a bunch to Corey, "familiarize yourself with these faces. Oh, by the way, from now on I'll make the coffee around here."

"What's the matter? I made it just like my pa always did."

"He must have had a cast-iron stomach," the marshal said under his breath, then he clarified himself as Corey just looked at him. "Just never mind…I'll make the coffee."

Marshal Bill Raines

Chapter Two

Over the next few months Bill tried to teach the young man the fundamentals of being a town marshal. Corey seemed to catch on quickly and was soon patrolling the town, watching for anything that might be out of place. One morning in mid-March, he was just returning to the office after lunch when one of the local ranchers, Ken Harris and his daughter, Peggy pulled up in a buckboard in front of the Marshal's Office. "OK, Peggy," Harris said, as he got down from the buckboard and started around to help his daughter down, but Corey got there first.

"Allow me, Miss Peggy," Corey said as he took her by the waist and lowered her to the ground.

"Thank you, Corey," she said, smiling at him. Suddenly Corey seemed to get lost in her blue eyes and long blonde hair. He just stood there with his hands still on her waist.

"As I started to say," Ken said as he got to them, "I'm going to be in the Marshal's Office for a little while. You go on over to the store and the dress maker's and I will pick you up there in about an hour."

"OK, Papa," Peggy said as she again smiled at Corey and turned to go down the street.

"How's your new job going, Corey?" Ken asked as Corey opened the door and they went inside.

"Great, Mr. Harris. At least I think so," he said as he saw Bill looking at them as they came inside.

"Hello, Mr. Harris, what can we do for you today?" Bill asked him.

"I think we have a problem, Marshal."

"Oh, what kind?"

"I've noticed a few head of cattle missing. Not a lot, but more than one would expect…you know, those that stray and keep going, so to speak."

"You're thinking rustlers?"

"Yeah…I do. I've heard some of the other ranchers have also had some of their stock counts come up short."

"Have your hands seen any sign of anyone being around the herds that shouldn't have been there?"

"No…that's just it, Marshal, I'm thinking that whoever is doing this is only taking a few head at a time. Hoping we wouldn't notice."

"How long have been you aware of the disappearances?"

"On and off over the past couple of months, but we couldn't be sure. But, now, I'm thinking that, in total, I'm missing probably around fifty head."

"Have you been posting any guards on your herds?"

"Not yet, but I think I'm going to start tonight. I wanted to let you know what was going on and see if you had heard anything from any of the other ranchers in the county. I don't get to see a lot of them on a regular basis."

"I haven't been approached by anyone else. But, I think it's time I got out and introduced myself to some of the outlying ranchers again. See if they want to open up and tell me if they're having any problems, as well."

"Thanks, Marshal, you will let me know what you find out?"

"Of course. I'll get back to you in a couple of days, how's that?"

"Sounds good, Marshal, thank you." Ken got up to leave and started to the door, then turned back. "Thanks again."

"No problem….I'll get back to you."

Corey waited until Ken had left and then went over to the Marshal. "Do you think there is a problem with rustlers?"

"Could be, Corey. Let's ride out to the Randall place and see what he has to say." He walked over to the gun rack and took out two rifles, handing one of them to Corey. Both men checked to make sure the rifles were loaded and ready then left the office.

When they arrived at the Randall ranch they saw Martha Randall working in her flower garden.

She looked up when she saw the two riding up to the ranch house. "Hello, Marshal, Corey."

"Hello, Mrs. Randall. Is Bob around?" Bill asked her.

"No, Marshall, he's out in the north pasture. We've had some of our stock come up missing, and he's trying to figure out what's going on."

"That's one reason we're here, Mrs. Randall. It seems that other ranchers are having similar problems."

"Oh, my…you don't think it's rustlers, do you?" Martha was suddenly very concerned that her husband might run into trouble if he started digging too deeply.

"That is one thing we're going to be investigating, Mrs. Randall. But, don't you worry, we'll find the culprits."

"I know you will, Marshall."

A little while later, they spotted Bob Randall as he was sitting on his horse and talking with one of his ranch hands. Bob looked around as he heard the other horses approaching.

"That will be all for now, Sam. Just keep your eyes open."

"Yes, Sir." Sam said as he turned his horse and cantered away.

"Hello, Marshal," Bob said as they pulled their horses to a stop beside him. "What brings you out here?"

"I've heard that some of the ranchers have had some of their stock come up missing. Your wife just confirmed that you have, as well."

"I can't account for about 30-40 head. I was just telling Sam that I want to start posting some guards on the main herd at night."

"Can you pinpoint when you realized that some of the cattle were missing?" Bill asked him.

"I did a head count about a month ago and noted that we were missing about twenty head. At the time, I thought that could have been from the fact that they just strayed away from the main herd, but now there's at least ten to twenty more gone."

"Have you seen any strangers hanging around?"

"No…not that I recall. Come on, Marshal, you can't think it's someone from around here? I've known most of these people for years."

"You can never count out everyone, Mr. Randall. Come on, Corey, let's check out some of the other ranches before it gets dark. One more thing, when do you usually do your main round-up? And do the ranchers join their herds together to get them to market, or does everyone do their own drivers?"

"We usually start the main round-ups and branding in the last part of April and band all the ranches together into one big drive around the middle to end of May."

"So you probably wouldn't normally start doing a major head count for the next few weeks. That's probably what these guys were counting on. They wanted to get what they could and get out before you did your roundup and realized how many were missing."

"That sounds logical, Marshal."

"OK, Corey, let's get going."

Chapter Three

When the Marshal and Corey got back to Rio Madre the Marshal began sending out telegrams to the law in nearby towns to see if they were also experiencing any stock missing. Bill had a feeling that it was not a localized problem. When he got back to the office he saw Corey going through a bunch of the wanted posters. "See anyone you know?" Bill asked him.

"No...not yet."

"Corey, how well do you know the area around Rio Madre?"

"Pretty well, I guess. I grew up near the mining camps in the mountains."

"Are there any canyons, any area where a large herd could be kept without anyone knowing?"

"Not that I can think of, right off. Wait, there are a couple of dead end canyons on the east side of the Pecos Ridge, north of here. I guess if you blocked them off far enough back you could hide a herd there. It would also give you time to use a running iron to change the brands. But Marshal, once you start moving a herd like that, you're going to draw attention."

"Yes, but think about it….if you wait until the other ranches start to do their round-ups, and start moving their cattle out from the winter grazing areas and down to the main ranch pastures, you just might be able to get away with it."

"I see what you're getting at…just another rancher moving his herd."

"Exactly. Another month and the ranchers will be moving their herds… the rustlers will have enough time to put maybe another fifty head or so into their bunch…only when they move them out they head directly north into Kansas. They get the jump on the herds that will be coming up later…and get a better price."

"The problem is," Corey said, "if we go snooping around up there, they're going to know we're onto them."

"Agreed. The problem is that if it is someone from around here…say, one of the ranch hands that wants to make a quick buck, he's going to get wise pretty soon. After all, Randall is now going to be posting guards… Harris has already been in here to report his losses."

"Think he might risk it and try to drive them out early?"

"I don't know…he would have to move them under the cloak of darkness, and that's not easy. Along with the fact that he's going to need help, moving a herd of two hundred head of cattle, or more, is more than a one man job."

"I don't like to think about it, Corey…but there is one more scenario."

"What's that?"

"That our culprit is one of the ranchers. He could take the rustled cattle, blend them in with his own herd and just send them in with the others and no one would know any better."

"In that case, we're back where we started."

"More or less. You've been around the area for some time, Corey, what is your impression of the ranchers around here?"

"I know some of them, but not all. Mostly they're upright citizens."

"Have you heard if any of them have been having financial problems?"

"There are always rumors. I know that old man Jenkins had some problems last year…but I haven't heard of anything recently."

"OK, Corey….this is Friday. Why don't you hang around the saloon tonight? See if you hear anything. Sometimes when a man drinks too much, he talks too much."

"Yes, Sir. Say, that will give me some time to get to know Sarah, the new saloon girl better."

"Corey…this is work….play on your own time."

"No reason a person can't accomplish both…got to go make my rounds," Corey said as he hurried out the door.

That evening, as the local ranch hands began to gather in the saloon, Corey had selected a table against the back wall where he could see everyone come in, but wouldn't be readily noticed. It was in the back corner, next to the stairs leading to the girls' sleeping quarters. What he couldn't see directly, he could watch in the larger mirror on the wall behind the bar. Sarah Riley hadn't been working at the saloon very long, only about a week. She had noticed Corey the first time he had come into the saloon, but hadn't had a chance to really meet him. That evening she had seen him sit down at the table and decided to join him for a few minutes. He had definitely noticed her, with her red hair, blue eyes, and a smile that would melt any man's heart. Any other night his full attention would have been on her, but that night he needed to keep his senses about him and concentrate on his job. "What's the matter, Deputy, don't you like my company?" She asked him as she stood beside his table.

"Oh, I'm sorry, Miss Sarah…I guess I'm just pre-occupied with other things tonight."

"Not another woman, I hope."

"Now how could I be interested in another woman when you're here?" He put his arm around her waist and pulled her down onto his lap. "I've just got a lot on my mind. I was hoping I could come here tonight and just forget about everything."

"What's the matter, Corey? Has the Marshal been onto you about something?"

"Nah…just the normal stuff. Thinks since I'm his deputy that I should do all the dirty work…you know, sweeping the office and sidewalk, filing old wanted posters, that kind of stuff."

"But isn't that the job of a deputy?"

"I thought a deputy was supposed to help tracking down the bad guys. So far, we haven't even found one bad guy. The only person we have locked up has been old Charlie…and that's just to let him sleep it off." One of the things that Corey had been thinking about before Sarah came up to him, was that if the locals thought that he might not be happy about his job, they might open up to him. He would just have to remember to mention his idea to the Marshal before someone else gave him the wrong impression.

"Hey, Sarah," Tom Lawson, the saloon owner's voice boomed out. He was about 40 years old and saloon keeping was all that he knew. He was also a big man, with black hair and eyes, and at over 200 pounds, there weren't many people that wanted to cross him…especially the girls that worked for him. "How about giving the rest of our clients some of your time?"

"All right, I'll be right there," she called out. "Sorry, Corey, got to go. I'll see you later, OK?"

"Sure…" Corey said as he watched her walk over to one of the other tables. "She sure is pretty," he thought to himself. "I'm definitely going to have to get to know her better. I wonder if she would want to go to the town dance with me Saturday night?"

For the next couple of hours Corey sat at his table watching the men come and go from the saloon. He couldn't put a definite finger on anything, but he did note a couple of hushed conversations at one of the tables. The men were not from one of the ranches close to Rio Madre but one of them did look somewhat familiar, Corey just couldn't remember where he had seen him. Another thing he noticed was that it seemed like every time someone wanted something from the bar, they always called out to Sarah to get it for them, even though there was another saloon girl at the next table. "Oh well," he thought, "she is the prettiest of the two…"

The next day Corey was already in the Marshal's office when Bill came in. "Morning, Marshal," Corey said looking up at him. He was again going through the stack of wanted posters.

"You're awful diligent this morning, Deputy, especially for someone who seems to think that life as a deputy is boring…"

"Oh, that," Corey said, getting to his feet and walking over to the Marshal's desk, where Bill had just sat down. "I was sitting at a table in the back of the saloon last night and was talking to Sarah, the new girl there. I mentioned that I wasn't happy with what I was doing…I guess I was hoping if some folks thought that, they might be a little more open."

"And…?" Bill said, a hit of a smile forming on his lips.

"Nothing really. I saw a man there that I don't know, but he looks familiar. That's why I was going through the posters again. I can't put a finger on where I've seen him before."

"Was he acting suspicious?"

"Just quiet. He was talking to some of the hands from the outlying ranches…very hush-hush. They kept looking around like they wanted to make sure nobody was listening to them."

"That's a good job, Corey. But for someone that spent the night in the saloon, you don't seem to be any the worse for wear."

"Maybe not me, but we'll see how that plant that's in the corner by the table where I was sitting fairs. I think it had at least three beers last night."

The Marshal couldn't help it and started chuckling. "You're going to be all right, Corey…good job."

"Thanks, Marshal." Corey said and went back to his desk and the stack of posters, old and new.

"Look, about your idea of letting some people think you're not happy…. don't play it up too hard, but also, don't deny it. It just might lead to someone saying something that they might not have otherwise…and believe me we can use all the breaks we can get right now."

"Sure thing, Marshall. Have you gotten any replies from those telegrams?"

"Just one….it seems like one of the ranchers near Cactus Lake mentioned something to their Sheriff, but like our ranchers…it's nothing they could put a finger on. But, Corey, I do know we have a problem, we just have to figure out how to catch them at it."

Deputy Corey Hansen

Chapter Four

Late that afternoon, Corey went to the saloon during his rounds. There were only a couple of customers in the place and Tom Lawson and the two saloon girls, Sarah Riley and Betty Walker were hovered over something in the back corner. Intrigued, Corey walked over to see what was going on. "Something wrong, Mr. Lawson," Corey asked.

"Just this plant we have back here. There seems to be something wrong with it."

Corey could see that the tall, stocky, cornstalk-like plant had started to lean to the side and the leaves were very listless…not standing straight out like they normally did.

"Well, it can't be because we don't look after it…I water it every day," Betty said looking at Tom, wondering if he was going to blame someone.

Tom looked at Corey, "If I didn't know better, I'd say it was drunk, the way it's listing to the side like that."

It was all Corey could do to keep a straight face. He knew that Tom had hit the nail on the head with that remark. "You know, I grew up on a farm and when one of Ma's plants didn't look too healthy, she would always put it in a new pot with fresh dirt. Maybe it just needs some fresh soil, you might also want to put it where it can get a little sunlight… might not be good for it to stay back here in a dark corner all the time."

"Yeah, maybe," Tom answered. "I'll go dig up some dirt out back and see if that will perk it up."

"Might want to get the dirt from around the livery stable…it's got good, natural fertilizing in it."

"Good thought, Corey." Tom turned and grabbed a nearby bucket that he used when mopping the floors and headed out the back door.

"Hey, Corey," Betty said as she came up and took him by the arm. "Why don't you sit and join us for a spell?"

Corey looked at her blonde hair and green eyes and for a moment was tempted. "Sorry, Betty, I'm supposed to be doing my rounds…you know how the marshal is," he said with a hint of displeasure.

"What's the matter, Corey?"

"Oh…same old stuff. Make the rounds, sweep the floors…see you all later." Corey turned and headed for the door.

"Come back and have a drink with me tonight?" Betty called out to him.

"Sure…why not?" Corey said over his shoulder as he walked out. He hoped that the word would get out soon that he might not be too happy with what he was doing. At least both of the saloon girls would think so, and that, in itself, should get the ball rolling. A few minutes later he was walking by the livery stable and noticed Tom using a shovel to fill up the bucket. Corey just shook his head and kept walking…next time he would have to find another way to ditch the drinks. As he continued his rounds he saw a couple of the hands from the Randall ranch ride into town and head for the general store. All-in-all that was not unusual, but they usually brought a buckboard if they were picking up supplies. Corey casually crossed the street and went into the store where he saw the men at the counter.

"Give us three boxes of .45 cartridges, 2 boxes of .30s, and better add a couple of boxes of shotgun shells too," Harry Ballard told Burt Norman, the storekeeper.

"Sounds like you're about to go into battle," Corey said as he came up behind them.

"Oh, hello, Deputy," Harry said as he turned and saw Corey. "We're starting to post guards around the herds at night, and we want to make sure every man has enough cartridges to hold his ground."

"Still losing stock?" Corey asked them.

"Another ten head were missing this morning. Just put this on the ranch's bill, Burt."

"I'll let the marshal know," Corey said as he looked around the store.

"Thanks, Deputy," Harry said as the two men left the building.

Corey watched out the window as the two men put the ammo in their saddle bags, untied their horses and walked across to the saloon. "Hey, Burt, any of the other ranchers beginning to stock up on weapons and ammunition?"

"A couple of them..same thing…saying they're losing cattle. I had to place a order to restock my shelves. Not that I am complaining about the business. Seems to me that you and the marshal ought to be doing something about it."

"We're working on it."

"Maybe you ought to work a little harder," Burt said as Corey walked out the door.

A few minutes later Corey entered the Marshal's Office walked directly to the stove and poured himself a cup of coffee. "You look like a man with something on his mind," the marshal said as he watched Corey go and sit down at his desk.

"You might say that. I just saw two of the hands from the Randall ranch in the general store buying enough ammunition for a small army."

"They lose some more cattle?"

"Yeah…another ten head, they said. They're going to be posting guards and wanted to make sure they were fully armed. We've got to do something, Marshal."

"I know…and we will. But we can't be in a half-dozen places at the same time. We've got to find out how they're getting their info about what herds are protected and which ones aren't. My bet is that the Randall ranch isn't going to be hit again for awhile."

"I'm still guessing that the saloon is the place where the info is being passed around. I just saw those two hands go over there, probably to get a drink before heading back to the ranch."

"Logical."

"You want me to hang around there again tonight?"

"Yes. But this time, go easy on the plant."

"Oh..."

"Yeah, I walked over there while you were finishing your rounds. Lawson was grumbling about having to replant the thing."

"I just made a little suggestion."

"Well, I suggest you keep on the same track you're on...we need more info on who's involved."

"Yes, Sir...Uh, Marshal, how far do I go if someone asks me about my job?"

"Try not to get in too deep. I just got you trained to be a decent deputy...I don't want to have to go through it again with someone else? Just ask them what they have in mind and see how far they will open up to you. Oh, Corey...try not to rake me over the coals too bad, OK?"

"It'll be tough, but I'll try," Corey said heading for the door and ducking as the marshal threw a wad of paper at him.

*****

That night, it was late when Corey finally got over to the saloon. Earlier, a couple of the local cowhands had bit too much and started a fight that he and the marshal had to break up. The two were now sleeping it off in adjoining jail cells. Corey sat down at one of the tables and ordered a beer. A little while later Sarah came over to his table. "What's the matter, Corey? You haven't downed much of that? Isn't our beer good enough for you anymore?"

"It's fine, Sarah...I just have to be back at the office in a little while...with our two 'guests' I have to stay there tonight to keep an eye on them."

"Maybe you should fine a new line of work," Sarah said as she sat down at the table.

"I've been thinking about it. I just need to make sure it's going to be a steady job."

"Didn't you have that at the livery stable?"

"Yeah…it was steady, but the pay wasn't any good. This 'deputy' job is paying better, but not by a whole lot."

"Maybe Rio Madre is not the place for someone like you. Ever thought about heading to one of the big towns…Abilene, maybe?

"Got to have a stake first. Hard to take off and go when you don't have enough cash." He looked up at the clock on the wall. "Sorry, Sarah…time to go…Marshal wants to go 'home' tonight." He stood up, paid for his beer and walked out of the saloon.

Chapter Five

That night, after the saloon closed, Sarah went to her room upstairs. When she opened the door she saw a cowboy stretched out on her bed. "I was wondering if I would see you tonight, Pecos," she told him.

"Saw you cozying up to that deputy. Anything I should be worried 'bout?"

"Come on, Pecos…you know you're the only man for me. Besides…I'm just doing my job…finding out how much the law knows about stuff." She took off her dress and put on a robe as Pecos came up behind her and put his arms around her.

"And…." He said as he turned her around to face him.

"They know someone's rustling the stock around here, but I don't think they have any clues to who's doing it," she told him as she put her arms around his neck and raised her face to kiss him. They separated and she continued. "I have found out that the deputy is not happy with his job. He's just staying here until he can get a stake so he can pull out."

"Think he might be persuaded to come over to our side?" He pulled open her robe and pushed down the straps on her camisole as he nibbled her neck and shoulder. "If we can get him on our side, he could feed the Marshal bad info and keep him off our trail."

"Want me to see if I can get him in a situation where you and the boys can 'talk' to him?" She said as Pecos finally removed the rest of her clothes and they fell onto the bed.

"Let's talk about it later…right now I have other things in mind," Pecos said as he kissed her again and let his hands roam over her supple body.

*****

About seven o'clock the next morning, Corey was sitting at his desk when the Marshal came in. "Everything quiet?" The marshal asked as he hung his hat on the peg behind his desk.

"Haven't heard a peep out of them," Corey said motioning toward the cell area. "I checked about twenty minutes ago and they were still sleeping it off."

"Let's roust them out and send them on their way."

A few minutes later the two cowhands, looking none the worse for wear, had been given their guns and belongings and sent along their way to explain why they weren't in the bunkhouse that morning.

"Did you find out anything last night?" The marshal asked as they went back to their desks.

"Not much…the new saloon girl seems to be quite interested in why I'm not happy with my job. She suggested I might want to try to find something else. Could be just a coincidence, but I got to thinking that she came to town about the same time as the rustling started."

"Might be something to think about. If she's just here to scout for information, maybe we can do the same to her."

"There's a dance Saturday night…I think I'll invite her."

"Be careful, Corey. If she is involved in this, there might be someone out there that might take offense at someone else dating his girl."

"I'll be careful. Besides, they've been keeping such a low profile I don't think they'll start anything at a public gathering like a dance." Corey headed for the door to the office then turned back to the marshal. "You know, Marshal…we're getting nowhere just waiting to see what happens…why don't we push the issue a little."

"What do you have in mind?"

"Do you think we could get a couple of the ranches to start their branding a little early...say next week? Might make the thieves hurry up their end...and when you're rushed...sometimes you screw up."

"Yeah...and Saturday night while everyone is supposedly at the dance, would be a good time to make a move to get any unbranded stock they can before the roundup."

"Exactly."

"What about your 'date'?"

"Well, it was a nice thought while it lasted."

The marshal thought for a moment, "No...go. It will look suspicious if both of us are not there. I'm going to take a ride out to the Randall and Harris ranches and see if we can get them to cooperate. If they will, I'll ride over to Salt Flats and see if the sheriff there will supply us with the manpower to cover both herds. Catch these rustlers in the act. I'll send a message to Cactus Lake from there to see if their sheriff wants to get in on it. The less people from around here that know about it, the better."

"Right, Marshal. I'll hold down the fort here."

"I'm sure you will," Bill said as he got to his feet and then followed Corey out the door.

While Marshal Bill Raines headed out of town, his deputy headed for the saloon. He went inside and saw that they had placed the newly repotted plant in the front corner of the room, near the large window. It was looking much healthier than it had the day before. "That looks like it's feeling better," Corey said to Jake Styles, the recently hired bartender who was in the process of drying a tray full of freshly washed glasses. Jake was in his late thirties and had black, curly hair and brown eyes. He was quite good looking and had already caught the eye of saloon girl, Betty Walker, who was leaning on the bar talking with him when Corey came in.

The two looked at Corey and saw him point to the plant. "Yeah...it does look better," Styles said. "I think it likes the sunlight."

"Most plants do," Corey said. "My ma used to say that 'just because they're plants doesn't mean they don't have things they like'."

"Guess she's right about that," Jake said.

"Is Sarah around?" Corey asked the two.

"Not right now…said she had a few errands to run. She's not in trouble with the law, is she?" Betty asked him.

"No…no. Just wanted to ask her if she wanted to go to the dance Saturday night?"

"Now, Deputy…you can't tell me that a good looking kid like you can't get a date with a regular girl," Jake teased him.

"Excuse me," Betty said, looking at Jake as she winked at Corey, "are you insinuating that I'm not as good as those 'regular' girls out there in town?"

Jake knew when he was stepping on thin ice. "I didn't say that at all, Betty. You're as fine a young lady as any…I mean…Corey, help me here."

"Sorry, Jake…you're going to have to get yourself out of this one. I've got to make my rounds. Don't want the marshal getting on my case… see you." Corey made a hasty retreat as Jake began to stack the whiskey glasses behind the bar and try to figure out exactly how to explain himself to Betty.

As Corey walked around town, he kept his eye out for any new faces in town. As he went by the mercantile, he spotted the same familiar face that he had seen in the saloon a couple of nights before. This time the man was getting off his horse in front of the hotel. Corey watched as the man untied his saddlebags and went inside. He waited for a couple of minutes and then followed the man inside. He saw Wade Barker, the hotel clerk, putting an envelope in one of the cubby holes behind the counter. Wade was sixty years old and had gray hair. He had been a long time employee at the hotel and had gotten to know just about everyone in town. "Hi, Wade," Corey said as he walked in.

"Hi, Deputy, how's it going?"

"It's going. Got a question…that man that just came in here. Did he register or did he come to see someone?"

"He registered. Said he would be here for a couple of days…just passing through and wanted to rest up before he continued on his way."

"What's his name?"

"Is this official business, Corey?"

"Yeah, Wade…can I see the register?"

"Sure, help yourself."

"Joe Brooks. I don't recognize the name...but there's something about him that is sure familiar. I saw him in the saloon a couple of nights ago... wonder why he's just now checking into the hotel."

"Can't help you there, Deputy."

"Look, Wade...would you keep an eye out to see if he gets any visitors. Get a name if you can, but don't be too nosey...don't want to start something if it's all innocent...know what I mean?"

"I understand, Corey," Wade said, "I'll keep it as nonchalant as I can."

"Thanks, Wade. See you later."

"See you, Corey."

As Corey continued his rounds, he saw Sarah coming out of the dressmaker's shop. He crossed the street and approached her. "Hello, Miss Sarah," he said as he tipped his hat.

"Good afternoon, Deputy. Is the something I could do for you?"

"Well, you would make me very proud if you would be my date for the town dance on Saturday night?"

"Well, Deputy, that is very kind of you to ask, but I'm afraid that I have already promised to go with someone else."

"Don't suppose I could get you to change your mind?" Corey asked as he smiled at her.

"I'm sorry, but I did promise him."

"Do you mind if I ask who your escort will be?"

"I don't think you know him. Now if you will excuse me, I do have some things to do before I have to be back at work." She turned and walked away toward the mercantile.

Corey just shook his head and went toward the office. Before he sat down at his desk he went to the filing cabinet and pulled out a stack of old wanted posters. "I know that face...where have I seen it?" He said to himself as he started looking at the posters. Another thing Corey didn't know that while he was talking with Sarah on the street, the stranger was watching them from the window in his hotel room.

"Corey Hansen...a deputy. Who would have guessed? I thought you were still up at Silver Creek Mining Camp. You've really grown up since I left there, although, it has been over five years. Guess it's a good thing I'm no longer going by Dave Bailey...wouldn't want you starting to ask questions, would we? I'd better get word to the boss and let him know Hansen's here. He's familiar with the Pecos Ridge and that could be trouble."

Chapter Six

It was late when Marshal Raines finally returned to his office. When he went inside he found Corey sitting at his desk with a foot-high stack of wanted posters next to him. "Corey, that's all you've been doing…how many times can you look through those posters?"

"I know I've seen him before, Marshal."

"Who?"

"That guy from the saloon the other night. He checked into the hotel today. Told Wade that he was just passing through. If that's the case, why didn't he check in two days ago? Marshal, there's something not right about him?"

"What's his name?"

"Joe Brooks, at least that's the name he used to sign the hotel register."

"Look, Corey, it's late, and I'm tired. Let's continue this in the morning. I'll send a telegram to the Territorial Marshal and see if he's got anything on this guy."

"Sure, Marshal, goodnight," Corey said as he headed toward the door.

The next morning, Corey was in the livery stable grooming his horse when Brooks came in to get his horse. "Morning, Deputy," Brooks said as he threw the saddle on his horse.

"Morning," Corey responded, continuing to brush his palomino's mane. They say that a cowboy's best friend is his horse, and Corey felt that way about Sunny. He had raised Sunny from a colt and, yes, he had been his best friend for the last five years. He wanted to ask Brooks if they knew each other, but decided that wouldn't be a good idea, just yet. He watched as Brooks got on his horse and rode out of town, making a mental note that he was heading north. He was tempted to follow the man, but figured he'd better check with the marshal first. An hour later Corey was in the office when Bill came in. "Morning, Marshal."

"Morning, Corey. Just got an answer from the Territorial Marshal. Seems like Brooks is pretty clean…spent a couple of nights in a cell for drunk and disorderly, but that's about it.

"I saw him at the livery stable about an hour ago, he rode out heading north."

"Lot of people go north, Corey."

"I know…I just can't shake the feeling that there's something about him…I just wish I could put my finger on it."

"Listen, Corey, don't get obsessed with this. Push it too far and you could find that you're the one that's going to come out on the wrong end of things…especially if he's just what he says he is…a stranger riding through."

"OK, Marshal…I'll let it go…for now. Oh, by the way, Sarah turned me down for the dance Saturday…said she already had a date. Think Peggy Harris might go with me?"

"Might…but you're not going to know unless you ask her."

"You know, Marshal…I think I'll ride out to the Harris ranch and see if they lost any more cattle last night."

"You just do that, Corey…actually, why don't you check the Randall place too. Make sure that they're not going overboard with their 'protection' out there."

"Will do, Marshal. Be back this afternoon."

"You'd better," the Marshal called after him. "You still got to sweep out the office."

*****

Later that morning, Corey rode up to the front yard of the Harris Ranch. He saw Peggy at the side of the house, hanging freshly washed sheets on a clothes line to dry. Corey smiled and walked over to her. "Morning, Miss Peggy," he said, tipping his hat.

"Good morning, Deputy."

"Why don't you call me Corey?"

"All right…good morning, Corey. What can I do for you?"

"Well, first, and foremost, I was wondering…if someone hasn't already asked you…if you'd go to the dance in town with me Saturday night?"

"Actually, no one has asked me…and…" she thought for a moment, then smiled at him, "I'd love to go to the dance with you."

"That's wonderful!" Corey exclaimed. "I'll pick you up around 5:00 o'clock if that's OK?"

"That will be fine," she said smiling at him. "Now, you said asking me to the dance was first, was there something else you wanted to ask?"

"What…oh, yes. Do you know if your father has lost any more cattle in the last couple of days?"

"I haven't heard him say…but, here he comes, why don't you ask him?"

Corey turned to see Ken Harris riding up. "Good morning, Mr. Harris," Corey said.

"'Morning, Deputy. What brings you out this way?"

"Well, I wanted to ask your daughter to the dance in town Saturday and she has accepted….if that's all right with you, Sir?"

"That's fine with me, Son," he said dismounting his horse. "Was there something else?"

"Yes, the Marshal and I were wondering if you had lost any more cattle in the last couple of days."

"I think there's five more head missing. I've got the hands making daily tallies now, so I think we're pretty accurate on the head counts. Does the Marshal have any leads?"

"Nothing definite, but we do have a couple of ideas. I think he's going to be coming out to see you himself to fill you in on what he has in mind."

"That sounds real fine, Deputy. Tell him, I'll be around any time he wants to talk."

"I'll do that, Sir," Corey said as he turned to Peggy. "I'll see you Saturday evening, Miss Peggy."

"I'll be ready, Corey," she said as she smiled at him then turned to her father as Corey rode away. "He's really nice, Father."

"I noticed that…" Ken said as Peggy turned back to the basket and picked up another sheet to hang up to dry as he led his horse toward the barn.

A little while later Corey had just ridden onto the Randall property when he saw Bob Randall riding toward him. Corey pulled his horse to a stop. "'Morning, Mr. Randall," Corey said as the rancher stopped next to him.

"'Morning, Deputy. What are you doing out this way?"

"The Marshal was wondering if you lost any more cattle last night. I saw a couple of your hands in the mercantile buying a lot of ammunition."

"No…as far as I know, last night was quiet. I expect it will be from now on. Yes, I did have Harry go into town and stock up. I can't expect my men to protect my property if they're not prepared. Marshal have a problem with that?"

"Oh, no," Corey quickly said. "He just wants to make sure that someone doesn't start firing indiscriminately and shoot an innocent person."

"My men know what they're doing. Especially the new hands."

"I'm sure they do, Sir…excuse me, but did you say new hands?"

"That's right…I hired a few 'experienced' men to handle things if these rustlers decided to try to hit me again."

"Are you sure hired guns are the answer?"

"Well, the law doesn't seem to be able to come up with an answer. I'm just protecting what's mine, Deputy."

"I'll let the Marshal know…by the way, he did say he would be out to talk with you in a day or so," Corey said.

"He'll be welcome anytime."

Corey tipped his hat to Randall and took a last look around the area, turned his horse and headed back toward town. As Corey reached the edge of the Randall property he was tempted to ride toward Silver Creek for a spell and see if he could spot anything strange. He started to turn his horse northward, but stopped when he remembered what the marshal had said about tipping their hand too soon, so he turned Sunny around and headed back toward town.

While Corey was at the Randall Ranch, Brooks arrived at a small cabin deep in one of the canyons inside the Pecos Ridge. He went inside and saw Jack "Red" Jackson sitting at a table playing cards with two of his men. The men were Ralph Taylor and the Pecos Kid. It was easy to see how Red had gotten his nickname. He was a big man, with red hair, brown eyes and was wearing a black hat, shirt and pants. "Howdy, Red," Brooks said as he walked inside.

"What are you doing here? Aren't you supposed to be keeping an eye on what's happening in town?"

"Yeah…that's what I have been doing. Got something interesting to report, too."

"What's that," Red asked as he played his next hand in the game. "Your turn, Pecos."

"We might have a problem with the deputy in Rio Madre," Brooks said as he sat down in one of the empty chairs at the table.

"How so?"

"I recognized him. Name's Corey Hansen. Grew up in the Silver Creek Mining Camp area where I did. He knows the lay of the land around here and that could be a problem."

"Sarah mentioned him," Pecos piped in. "Said he might not be too happy with his job. Claims he was looking for a little more 'action', I think."

"Think he might be interested in switching sides?" Taylor asked as he played his hand.

"Don't know." Pecos replied. "Want me to see if Sarah can find out anything else?"

"You may want to be careful, Red," Brooks said, "I grew up in the same mining camp, but left several years ago. He was just a kid then, but seemed to be a straight arrow. I don't think he recognized me, but I'm not sure. Saw him at the livery stable this morning and he didn't seem like he knew me, but…."."

"People change, Joe. Pecos, have Sarah to do a little more snooping, find out if he's as unhappy as he claims. Joe, you're better try to steer clear of the deputy, that is, until we find out if he can be lured to our side. If he can, he could be invaluable with getting the herd out of here and up to Kansas early. Ok, Boys, time to show your cards," he watched as Pecos and Taylor laid their cards on the table. He laid his cards down and smiled as he picked up the money in the 'pot'.

"Oh, one more thing, Boss," Brooks said, "the ranchers are realizing that their losses are not just strays wandering off. Randall had a couple of hands in town buying cartridges…lots of them. I heard he is starting to post guards on his herds."

"Let's lay off the ranches around Rio Madre for a few days," Red told the others. "We'll head up to Cactus Lake tomorrow night…haven't 'visited' them for awhile." The others nodded in agreement as Brooks headed for the door and back to town.

Late that afternoon Corey returned to the office. He entered to find the Marshal looking at a territorial map that was spread out on his desk. Marshal Raines looked up, "Hi, Corey, find out anything interesting?"

"Saw Randall. He admitted to arming his men, he also said he had hired some 'experienced' help."

"That's one thing we don't need…hired guns! This is getting closer and closer to a range war, Corey, and we're going to be caught right in the middle."

"Don't I know it. Are you still going to talk to the ranchers about setting up a trap for Saturday night?"

"Yes, I am. I'm going to ride out there tomorrow. Oh, speaking of Saturday night…how did things go with Peggy?"

"I'm picking her up at 5:00."

Marshal Raines smiled at him, "Congratulations, she's a sweet girl."

"It's just a dance, Marshal, not an engagement."

"You've got to start somewhere."

Corey put his leg up on the corner of the desk and leaned over, looking at the map. "Do you want me to hang around the saloon again to see if I learn anything?"

"Why not?"

"I'll see if I can get Sarah to open up a little. I don't know why, but I get a feeling she knows more than she's letting on."

"Logical..." the Marshal said, then sat back and looked up at Corey. "Corey, be careful. I've just got a bad feeling about things." Corey nodded and headed out the door. He took Sunny over to the livery stable and bedded him down for the evening, then went to get some supper before heading for the saloon. He made a mental note to find some other place to dump his unwanted beer. The plant was obviously not an option anymore.

*****

Corey had taken a chair at a table near the poker game. He realized that the dealer was new to the saloon, and obviously knew what he was doing. When Sarah brought him his beer he handed her the money and asked, "He's new here, isn't he?"

"Yeah...Mr. Lawson hired him today. Seems to be a good dealer, I guess we'll just have to see if he makes any money for the saloon."

"Everyone is out for their cut, I guess," Corey said. "Can't seem to have a friendly game between the customers any more."

"What's the matter, Deputy? You see to be more and more cynical lately."

"I don't know," Corey said, "guess I'm just tired of this town."

"Anything I can do?" Sarah said as she sat down and snuggled closer to him.

"Not unless you know where I can get a stake big enough to get me out of here," Corey said in all seriousness.

"Not off hand, but if I hear of anything, I'll let you know."

"Hey, Sarah...take this over to that table!" Jake called out to her.

"I'd swear," Sarah whispered to Corey, "you'd think I was the only girl working here." She got up and headed to the bar giving a disapproving look to Betty who was sitting between two of the players in the card game.

"You know, Jake, I'm not the only one working here," she said to him as she picked up the tray of drinks.

"Yeah, but Betty's doing what she's supposed to, you're just playing up to the deputy."

"What's that supposed to mean?" She asked him.

"Take it any way you want," Jake said as she walked away in a huff.

A short time later, Corey had been trying listen to what was going on in the card game when suddenly one of the men stood up, knocking his chair backwards. "I know when I'm being cheated!" He yelled angrily. "Barkeep…if you want to keep your decent customers coming in you'd better get rid of this tinhorn…and now!" Roy Scott was 38 years old and had been in many a card came and he was mad.

Corey got to his feet but stood back, waiting to see if the situation would calm down. "Come on, Mister," Dirk Rhodes, the gambler, said, trying to placate the man. "Why don't you sit back down and play another hand. Maybe your luck will change."

"Luck has nothing to do with it," Scott shouted, "I was watching and I saw you deal from the bottom of the deck."

By this time, Tom Lawson had heard the shouts, and come out of his office and into the bar area. "What's going on here?" By this time, the men around the card table were on their feet and beginning to back away from what could evolve into a risky situation.

"What's the meaning of hiring a card cheat for a dealer, Lawson? You're not going to get many men in here while he's here. He was dealing from the bottom of the deck, I saw him!"

"I will not be branded a cheat!" Rhodes said as he jumped to his feet. "I run a clean game!"

"Clean game? I don't think so," Scott challenged him. "Lawson, you better git rid of this card shark before I pass the word that the hands need to go somewhere, anywhere else for their games and drinks. I'll see you put out of business!"

"You're drunk, Scott," Lawson told him.

"Yeah, I've had a couple…but my head is clear enough to know a cheat when I see one…."

"I've had enough of you," Rhodes said as his hand started to go for his gun, but Corey had slipped up behind him and grabbed his arm, preventing him from drawing. He just hoped that Lawson would try to restrain Scott, but, that was not to be.

"Why, you!!!" Scott said as he leaped across the table to grab Rhodes and take him to the floor. The men that had been in the game started to grab for the money still on the table, pushing and shoving each other to grab as much as they could. The table collapsed, taking them with it and they got up, swinging at each other. It didn't take long before it seemed like the entire room was suddenly one big brawl. Corey was trying to pull Scott and Rhodes apart, but was knocked to the floor by one the men from the game that had gotten knocked into him. Betty and Sarah had decided that discretion was the better part of valor and ran behind the bar. As one of the fighters was thrown back against the bar, Betty grabbed an empty bottle and, reaching across, broke the bottle on his head. The man went down for the count, so to speak. Corey had gotten back on his feet and again tried to get between the two gamblers but instead, Scott sent him reeling back with a wayward fist to Corey's jaw. Lawson was trying to break up some of the other fights but, he too, was not having much success. The only thing being accomplished was the damage to most of the chairs and tables.

Meanwhile, Marshal Raines had heard about the commotion at the saloon and burst through the doors. Quickly observing the situation, he took out his gun and fired a shot into the ceiling. "ENOUGH, GENTLEMEN!!!" He shouted. That seemed to calm most of the fighters except for Scott and Rhodes who were still going at it. Corey had gotten to his feet, again, and managed to get his arms around Scott while Lawson was able to finally get Rhodes under control. Both fighters were now exhausted and finally able to be restrained. "Now, will someone tell me just what is going on?" Marshal Raines asked as he walked up to the two men being restrained.

"He's a cheat, Marshal," Scott said, still angry.

"Do you have any proof?"

"I saw him deal from the bottom of the deck!"

"Liar! "Rhodes retorted. "I deal a clean game."

"Deputy," Raines said to Corey, "were you here when this started?"

"Yes, Sir. It was pretty much like they said. Scott accused the dealer of cheating. They shouted at each other for a couple of minutes then Rhodes started to go for his gun, and the rest, as they say, is history."

"Lawson, does this man work for you?" Raines said nodding his head toward the dealer.

"Yeah, I hired him today. He professed to be experienced, and clean."

"Did any of you other guys see anything to make you believe he was cheating?"

"I didn't actually see him doing anything, but he suddenly seemed to be winning all the pots, at least the big ones."

"OK…I think the best thing is to let them both cool off in one of my cells 'til morning. Deputy, will you do the honors?"

"My pleasure," Corey said as he rubbed his jaw then herded the two off to the office.

Marshal Raines turned to Lawson. "I don't know if your new employee was cheating or not, but this is the first time we've had this kind of disturbance in some time."

"I agree, Marshal," Lawson said as he started trying to upright some of the undamaged chairs and tables. "I'll send him packing in the morning, soon as you release him."

"Sounds like a good idea…the next time you want to hire a professional gambler…you might want to ask for references." He took a last look-around. "Oh, you might want to get him over to the Doc's." He pointed to the man still on the floor in front of the bar. Betty put her hands on the bar and pulled herself up and just looked over the bar at the floor, dropped back down and shrugged her shoulders.

"I'll do that, Marshal," Lawson said, shaking his head at the mess to be cleaned up. "Thanks for your help. You two," he pointed to a couple of the men still standing around…"take him over to Doc's."

"Just doing my job," Raines said as he headed out and back toward his office.

Chapter Seven

The next morning the Marshal sent their two 'guests' on their way and turned to Corey. "I'm going to ride out to see Harris and Randall. See if we can set up a little 'surprise' for the rustlers on Saturday."

"Good luck," Corey said as the Marshal walked out of the office, got on his horse and rode out of town. Corey looked around for a couple of minutes then crossed over the street and went into the mercantile.

"Morning, Burt," he said as he walked into the building.

"Hey, Deputy, what can I do for you?"

"I'm taking Peggy Harris to the dance Saturday and I need to get some new cologne…got any suggestions?"

"Sure…just got this in from back east. Supposed to be the popular stuff nowadays. I'd go gentle with it 'though…seems to have quite the kick to it."

Corey opened the small bottle and took a whiff, and almost choked. "A kick is right. OK…I'll take it." He walked over to one of the tables and picked up a new white shirt in his size. "I'll take this too. Haven't really had a reason for dress-up clothes…at least for awhile."

"Well, if you're going to take Miss Harris to the dance, I'd say that's a very good reason."

Corey smiled, "Couldn't agree more." He paid for his purchases and took them over to his room at the boarding house, then decided to take a 'tour' around town. Everything seemed to be quiet so he stopped by the saloon to see what was happening there after the events of the previous night.

"Hello, Deputy," Jake said, as he was wiping down the bar.

"Hi, Jake, things been quiet this morning?"

"Yeah…haven't seen any of the guys from last night, except that dealer. He came by this morning. Tom gave him his walking papers and I think he rode out of town…and, oh yeah, he wasn't happy about it."

"I can imagine," Corey said as he looked around. "Looks like things have gotten straightened up."

"Yeah, we had most of the cleanup done last night. I think it looked a lot worse than it was."

"That's always good." Corey turned as he heard someone walk up behind him and saw Sarah standing there. "Good morning, Miss Sarah."

"Hi, Deputy, what can we do for you this morning?"

"Nothing…just making my rounds and thought I would see if things were back to normal around here."

"Well," she said, "if there's anything I can do, you just let me know." She smiled at him and casually brushed his arm as she went to sit down at one of the tables.

Corey looked back at Jake who just shook his head. "You know, Jake, I don't think I'll ever understand women."

"No man ever has, Deputy; and if anyone says different, he's lying."

Corey chuckled, looked back at Sarah and left the building. He looked up and down the street and, not seeing anything unusual, he headed over to the café for a late breakfast. Sally Roberts looked up when the door opened and smiled when she saw Corey coming in. "Hello, Corey, you're running late this morning." Sally was thirty years old and had green eyes, and long black hair that she usually wore pulled up into a loose bun on the back of her head. She wasn't what most men would call beautiful, but she 'sure was pretty'.

"Hello, Miss Sally. Yes, I had a few errands to run this morning. How 'bout some bacon, eggs and coffee?"

"Toast or biscuits?"

"Biscuits, Ma'am."

Sally turned around and started to work on Corey's breakfast while he looked over a copy of the Rio Madre newspaper that was lying on the counter. "How's the job going, Corey? You like working for the Marshal."

"Doin' fine, Miss Sally. Gets a little boring sometimes. Seems like the only excitement we get is when some of the cowhands get drunk and try to bust up the saloon."

"I heard about what happened last night."

"Whole town probably knows by now," Corey said as she poured him a cup of coffee.

"Looks like you had a part in it," she said smiling at him, and pointing to the bruise on his jaw.

He gingerly touched his face. "Yeah…I tried to break it up, but it seemed like they wanted to break me up first."

"Well, you just be careful…the young ladies in this town can't afford to lose an eligible young man like yourself."

"Uh..yes, Ma'am," Corey said as he blushed and suddenly got very interested in an article in the paper.

Sally couldn't help smiling at him, and then began plating his meal. She turned and sat the plate down in front of him. That'll be twenty cents, Corey. You want me to put it on a tab until the end of the month?"

"No…I'll take care of it now," Corey said as he pulled the change out of his pocket and handed it to her.

"I thank you, Kind Sir," Sally said as she rang up the sale in the register. "You going to the dance on Saturday?"

"Yes, Ma'am," he said happily, "I'm taking Peggy Harris."

"She's a nice young girl. Will make some young man a great wife someday..."

Corey concentrated on eating his breakfast and the newspaper, trying not to hear what Sally was saying. Sally just chuckled to herself and went to clean the skillet that had been used for Corey's breakfast.

*****

Marshal Raines rode up to the Harris ranch house and dismounted. He tied his horse to the hitching post and walked over and knocked on the door. A few seconds later the door opened and he saw Peggy standing there. "Morning, Miss Peggy, is your father home?"

"Yes, he is Marshal, won't you come in?" She stepped back and motioned for him to come inside. "If you'll have a seat, I'll get him."

Marshal Raines went over to the plush sofa and sat down. He looked around the room to see the sparse, but elegant décor. A sofa, couple of chairs and small tables and a woven rug furnished the room. He noticed a family portrait on the small table by the sofa, picked it up and was looking at it when Ken Harris walked into the room. He put the picture back on the table and stood up. "That's a nice family portrait, Mr. Harris."

"Thank you, Marshal. It was taken only a few months before Mary died. We still miss her…a lot."

"I know how you feel. Lost my wife a few years ago…don't think you ever really get over it."

'You're right. Please, sit back down. What can I do for you this morning?"

They both took seats on the sofa. "Well," the Marshal said, "I had this idea, that with the dance Saturday night, most of the people are probably going to be in town. Might leave the herds a little sparse on protection and that's something that would play right into the rustlers hands."

"You're right. I had thought about that. Was going to keep a few of the hands here and try to keep a watch. At least Peggy will have some fun."

The Marshal smiled, "I know…Corey said he had asked her."

"He's a nice young man, Marshal, you're lucky to have found him."

"Agreed…although I think he found me. Anyway, what I had in mind to do was to keep the 'guards' out of sight and see if we could lure the rustlers to come in and make another try, only this time we would be ready for them."

"Sounds like it might work. How are you going to cover all the ranches around here? I was thinking about trying to bring in some help from some of the areas up north. Most of the action has been around here lately. Randall has built up his own little army to protect his herds, but

I don't know how many he is going to keep away from the dance. I'm heading over there when I leave here."

"If I know Randall, he's not going to let any of his men have any kind of fun until this whole situation is cleared up."

"You're probably right, but I do have to keep him advised of what we're doing."

"I guess so. OK, Marshal, I'll go along with whatever you have in mind."

"Thanks, Ken. Look, could you keep our plan to yourself. I don't want too many people wise to what we're doing. Right now we don't know who we can trust."

"You don't think the culprits could be working for any of the ranchers, do you?"

"They're getting information somehow. We just have to figure out how. I've got my suspicions, but I'm not going to jump to conclusions. When we bring these guys in, I want a case that will stick."

"All right, Marshal, I'll back you. Just let me know what you want me to do."

"I'll have Corey bring you the final scoop when he comes to pick up Peggy on Saturday. Basically, we'll just have hidden guards posted on the most vulnerable areas of your herds. Just make sure that at least a couple of your hands are visible at the dance, with instructions to make sure that they say the others will be joining them soon."

"I do know that a couple of them have steady girls in town…they will be the best ones to be 'visible'. They will be expected to be there."

"Makes sense to me. I will see you on Saturday night."

"See you. Good luck with Randall."

Marshal Raines just smiled and nodded and then Ken walked him to the door and watched as the Marshal mounted and rode away toward the Randall ranch. Later, the Marshal rode up to the Randall ranch and saw Bob Randall coming out of the barn leading his horse. When he saw the Marsh he headed toward him. "Howdy, Marshal, what can I do for you today?"

"Just wanted to talk to you about something," Marshal Raines said and then proceeded to fill him in on his plans for that Saturday.

"As you already know, I have guards on my herds. Haven't had a problem since we started posting them."

"That's good to know, Randall, but what I would like to do is set a little trap and maybe catch some of these culprits in the act. If they think everyone is at the town dance they might get brazen and hit again."

"Tell you what, Marshal, I will tell my men to stay out of sight, but they will be doing what they're paid to do…and that doesn't include having a good old time at some dance."

"Maybe if you would just have a couple of them at the dance, it might give the impression that…"

"All right, Marshall, I'll have my sons at your dance…will that make you happy."

"I think that will do…you might want them to make a comment or two about some of the other hands are supposed to show up. Oh and one more thing, let's keep this plan between us, OK? No use in letting more people know what we're doing than have to."

"I can do that."

"Thanks, Randall. Give my regards to your wife."

Randall nodded his head. "Sure will, Marshal."

The Marshal mounted his horse and headed over to Salt Flats to talk with the Sheriff there about supplying some men to help with staking out the herds around Rio Madre. "I'd like to help you, Marshal," Sheriff Price told him, "but I got word a few minutes ago that one of the ranchers east of here thought he was missing about ten head."

"Thanks, Sheriff. I was just taking a chance that you might have some men available. There's a dance in Rio Madre on Saturday night and I figured it would be the opportune time for the rustlers to hit our herds when the men would 'supposedly' be at the dance."

"I see, Marshal…you're gambling that they will hit while everyone is otherwise occupied."

"That's what I'm hoping."

*****

It was almost supper time when Marshal Raines got back to Rio Madre. Corey was sweeping out the cells when he walked in. "Howdy, Marshal, how did it go?"

"All right, I think. Harris went along with it just fine, but Randall took a little 'convincing'."

"That figures," Corey said as he brushed the dirt into a dust pan and then dumped it outside. "It seems like he thinks it's his way or no way."

"Agreed. At least he consented to have a least some representation from his ranch at the dance. Said he would send his two sons."

"That will be a lot of help," Corey said a little sarcastically. "Those two 'boys' of his are almost as high on their horses as he is. They only thing they'll do is to start trouble."

"And you will be there to stop it." He grinned at Corey, "I guess we will just have to wait and see. Hopefully, if the rustlers think the town is the focal point for everyone Saturday night, they will be tempted to hit at least one of the herds. Randall seemed to think he could cover his end of things. I talked with Sheriff Price and he said he would try to get us some help, but they just got hit again up there, so I'm not sure. I don't know if their ranchers will want to let some men come help us or not."

"I don't know, Marshal, it just seems like they know the herds that are vulnerable before we do."

"Someone is keeping tabs on things, that's for sure."

"Why don't we feed them a little more 'gossip' to think about?"

"What do you have in mind?"

"The same thing I've already started, but let's take it further. If we don't get anywhere Saturday night, we need to get someone into their midst that's feeding info back here."

"And you think that should be you?"

"Why not?" Corey said, sitting down on the edge of the Marshal's desk. "I'd be willing to bet they have been told that I'm not real happy here. I've already let it out that I'm just waiting to get a stake so I can pull out."

"I know you were hoping that someone would let something slip when they were talking to you, Corey, but to go undercover…that's dangerous. If they even think you're not what you say you are…" Bill leaned forward, "they'll kill you. And I don't want that to happen…under any circumstances."

Corey smiled, appreciating what Bill was saying to him. "Thanks, Marshal. And just between us, I don't want that to happen either…but we have to do something more. We have to get someone on the inside."

"How do you plan to accomplish this?"

"If we don't come up with anything Saturday, then Sunday, we can stage a blow-up between us, accusations, that type of thing and you can fire me…I'll hang around for a day or so and see if anyone takes the bait."

"How do you plan on keeping me advised of what you're up to?"

"I haven't exactly figured that out yet, but I'll think of something."

"I don't like it, Corey. But let's see what happens Saturday and then we take it from there."

Chapter Eight

Saturday morning Marshal Raines was in his office when Paul McCain came hurrying in as fast as his 70 year old legs would carry him. He had been the town telegrapher for years and was finally admitting that it was time he might need to slow down a little, as he was breathing hard by the time he got to the Marshal's office. "Telegram came in for you, Marshal. Said to deliver fast so here it is."

"Thanks, Paul." Bill said to him as he pulled out a two-bit piece and handed it to him. "And don't mention this to anyone…OK?"

"Sure, Marshal…and thanks." Paul said as he turned and left the office.

Bill opened the folded piece of paper and read, *"Lightning Rock, Stop. Sunset, Stop. Hank, Stop."* Bill smiled, knowing that he would have some help that night. He had already decided that he would take the chance that if the rustlers hit, they would likely pick one of the bigger ranches… that meant the Harris or Randall ranches. He knew how Randall felt about any 'help', so he would take the added help to cover the Harris herds. He leaned back in his chair as Corey came into the office. "Morning, Corey. Everything set for tonight?"

"Yes, Sir. I'm going to pick Peggy up around 5:30, by the time I take her to dinner, we should get to the dance about the time it starts. I'll keep an eye out to see if there's any strangers show up."

"Also, make a note of who doesn't show up," Bill told him. "We know that the ranchers are only going to have a small representation there, what I want to know is if there is someone obviously missing that should be there."

"You're not thinking that someone here in town may be involved?"

"We can't count anyone out…anyone."

"I'll keep my eyes open, Sir."

"Just make sure you give Peggy some of your attention, I wouldn't want her mad at me because you weren't being attentive." He smiled at Corey, who suddenly became flustered.

"That is something I don't think I'll have a problem doing."

Bill started laughing and got up from his chair and headed for the door. "Think I'll take a tour around town, hold down the fort."

"Yes, Sir."

Bill turned back for a second, "I'll probably stop at the café, want me to bring you anything?"

"No, thanks, Marshal. I've had breakfast already. Tell Miss Sally I said, 'Hi'."

"I'll do that."

"Too bad you have to be out at the ranches tonight…you could have taken her to the dance."

Bill just gave Corey a funny look and left. After he had made his rounds, he did stop by the café. "Morning, Miss Sally," he said as he walked in.

"Why, hello, Marshal," Sally said as she got up from a table. Things had finally quieted down for awhile and she had decided to take a break. "What can I get for you?"

"Steak and eggs?"

"Coming right up," she said as she went behind the counter to start cooking. Bill took a seat at the end of the counter and watched as she started preparing his meal. Remembering what Corey had said, he started thinking that it was a shame he wasn't going to be in town. She was a mighty fine looking woman. He seemed to remember someone saying that her husband had been killed a couple of years ago, so it was time she stopped being alone. Maybe sometime soon he would try to get her out of the café and take her to dinner at the hotel. "Here you go, Marshal," she said a few minutes later as she sat the plate in front of him.

"That looks mighty good, Miss Sally," Bill said as he dug into the meal. And yes, it was as good as it looked. "You goin' to the dance, tonight?"

"I don't know. Haven't decided yet. I know it's been a while since Josh died, but I just can't get myself to go out and pretend to have fun, if you know what I mean?"

"I do know. Lost my wife a few years ago. Took a long time to even think about anything, or anyone, else."

"You goin' tonight?"

"No…have other things that need to be done. I'm leaving the fun part to Corey, he's young enough to handle it. By the way, he said to say 'hi'."

"He's a fine young man, Marshal. He did say he was taking Peggy Harris to the dance, they ought to make a real nice couple."

"Yep, I was thinking the same thing."

Shortly after noontime, Corey was sitting in a chair outside the office when he saw Joe Brooks come out of the hotel carrying a saddlebag, and go over to the mercantile. He decided that he needed to pick up a couple more things for that evening, so he headed over there. When he walked in, he saw Brooks at the counter, waiting to pay for rope, hardtack, carrots, and tobacco. Nothing that unusual, but he still couldn't shake the feeling he knew him from somewhere.

"Hi, Burt," he said as he walked up to the counter. "Got any boot polish?"

"Sure, Deputy," Burt said as he reached behind him and picked up a small tin can. "Black, right?"

"Yep, got to make sure my boots are real shiny before I go pick up Miss Harris tonight."

"You're a lucky young man, Deputy. She's a beauty."

"You don't have to tell me twice." He looked at Brooks' purchases. Hardtack, carrots and tobacco…odd combination," Corey said as he waited for Burt to put ring up his purchase.

"Hardtack and tobacco for me, carrots for my horse."

"Lucky horse," Corey said as he paid for his purchase, tipped his hat to Brooks, and left.

"Seems like a nice young man," Brooks said to Burt as he put his purchases in his saddlebag.

"Yep. Real nice. Hope those two young people get together."

"Little young to be a deputy, isn't he?"

"Well…I guess the marshal saw something in him."

"Guess you're right. Thanks, again." Brooks tipped his hat to Burt and left.

Corey went back to the office and got a shoe polish cloth and sat in the chair in front of the office, watching the townsfolk going about their business as he shined his boots. He didn't notice anything unusual. The town seemed to be busier than normal, but he guessed that was to be expected with the festivities that evening. He did see several young ladies come out of the dressmaker's shop carrying packages that he assumed were their dresses for that evening. He was glad that Mrs. Evans had the extra work. He knew she had been having a hard time making ends meet since her husband was killed in a saloon brawl a few months before. He was putting the final touches on his boots when the Marshal came walking up the sidewalk. "Come inside, Corey," he said as he went into the office. Corey quickly put on his boots, picked up his boot shining supplies and followed him.

"What's up, Marshal?"

"I got word from Sheriff Price this morning, he's bringing a couple of men with him for the stake-out tonight. We're going to cover the Harris place, Randall seems convinced he can take care of his own."

"Figures," Corey said, putting his things in a desk drawer. "Just wondering, you said that Price indicated that some of the ranches around him had been hit recently. Think our guys have moved their operation up there since it is known that we have a problem?"

"Possible. All we can do is to be prepared here. Makes sense that they would hit where they think the herds will be less protected. It's a gamble either way."

"I guess so. I just hope this doesn't blow up in our faces."

"Everything you do in life is a gamble, Corey."

*****

Corey pulled the buggy to a stop in front of the Harris ranch house. He was really looking sharp in his black jacket and pants and a white shirt. And yes, his boots were shined to perfection. He walked to the door and knocked. A few seconds later the door opened and Steve Harris stood there, and began to look Corey over from top to bottom. At twenty-one years old, Steve was over six feet tall, and muscular from working on the ranch since he was a small boy. Now, he had taken it on himself to have final approval on any of his sister's suitors. He nodded his head in approval and stepped back, motioning Corey to enter. "Have a seat, Deputy, my sister will be down in a few minutes. I'll let her know you're here."

"Thanks, Steve," Corey said as he took off his hat, walked over and sat down on the sofa. A couple of minutes later Peggy came down the steps dressed in a pale blue cotton dress with long sleeves and small ruffles around the slightly scooped neckline and skirt hemline. She was carrying a white draw-string purse that she could hang from her wrist, and her hair was drawn up into a pony-tail style with ringlets of hair hanging down. Corey took a deep breath as he looked at her with admiration. "Miss Peggy, you sure do look beautiful."

"Why, thank you, Corey," Peggy said, slightly blushing as she grabbed a shawl from the back of a chair and put it around her shoulders.

"Oh, come on, Sis. You know you've been up there all afternoon getting yourself ready," Steve said, not able to keep from teasing her just a little.

"Steve Harris, you behave yourself," she gave him a look that told him to back off immediately.

"Sorry," Steve said as he glanced at Corey and winked. "You make sure you take good care of her tonight…and don't keep her out too late."

"Oh, for goodness sake," she said, exasperated. "Come on, Corey, let's get out of here before I do something very unladylike and let him have it."

"You could never be unladylike, Miss Peggy," Corey said as he offered her his arm and they left the house.

"Come now, Corey, I think it's time you just called me 'Peggy'." Steve followed them out the door and watched as Corey helped her into the buggy and drove away.

"Make sure you have her home early!" Steve called after them, smiling as he pictured the way that Peggy would sometimes roll her eyes at him. But, he did have to admit to himself that she was beautiful; all the more reason to keep an eye on any suitors.

On the ride into town, the two young people talked about what they had been doing and who they expected to see at the dance. "I don't think a lot of our hands will get to go," she said. "Papa is making them stay back to guard the herds tonight. I think he is afraid something might happen."

"Anything's possible," Corey said, "I'm just lucky that the Marshal let me have the night off."

"Personally, I'm very happy he did."

A short time later they arrived at the Rio Madre Town Hall and Corey helped Peggy out of the buggy. She waited while he hitched the horse to the rail and they proceeded inside. The center of the large meeting area had been cleared of the chairs which had been placed against the walls, leaving the center of the room as a dance floor. A refreshment table was at one end of the room, while a bandstand had been set up at the other end, and the musicians were just taking their places and checking their instruments.

"Would you like something to drink?" Corey asked Peggy. "Might be a good idea before someone takes the opportunity to try to 'enhance' the flavor…"

"I know what you mean," Peggy replied. "I'd love some." Corey proceeded to escort her to the refreshment table and, using the ladle provided, filled a couple of cups. He handed one to Peggy and they went to sit in a couple of the chairs along the wall. They had only sat there for a moment when Mrs. Molly Mason approached them. She was the landlady at the boarding house where Corey lived. She had been widowed some years earlier and had opened her home to boarders as a means of making an income. She was 65 years old, and now had gray hair, but, in spite of being a large woman, she got around amazing well.

"Hello, Corey," she said as she approached them and Corey stood to greet her.

"Howdy, Mrs. Mason. I think you know Peggy Harris," he said as he motioned to Peggy.

"Yes, of course. How are you Miss Harris?"

"I'm fine, Mrs. Mason. You're looking well."

"I'm doing fine…how is your family?"

"They're doing fine, thank you."

"That's good to hear. Is your father coming tonight? Might just try to finagle a dance with that handsome man."

"No, Ma'am, I'm sorry. He isn't coming. Said he didn't want to put a damper on my evening by being here. Was afraid he would end up trying to play chaperone."

"Corey is a real gentleman, Miss Harris. I don't think your father has anything to worry about." She looked at Corey and smiled as the band finally started playing the first dance…and a slow dance at that.

"Uh, thank you, Mrs. Mason. Peggy…would you like to dance?"

"I'd love to, Corey…Mrs. Mason, if you would excuse us?"

"Of course," she said as she watched the two young people join other couples as they moved onto the dance floor.

"That was quick thinking," Corey said.

"What?"

"About why your father isn't here."

"I do have my moments."

He smiled at her. "To tell the truth, I'm glad he didn't come. I might not have been comfortable holding you close like this if he was here." He pulled her a little closer to him as he guided her across the floor.

"You won't hear me complain."

Within the hour the hall had become crowded with dancers as well as those who only wanted to socialize. A few of the young men that had come alone had asked Peggy to dance and she had accepted a couple of times. Although Corey wasn't happy, it did give him a chance to observe the crowd and see if he could see if anyone was notably missing. At one point he saw Sarah there with her 'friend'. Corey took a deep breath as he realized that she was with the Pecos Kid. Although there were no wanted posters on him in the territory, he did have a reputation for being involved in some not-so-savory activities. He didn't have a lot of time to dwell on it as Peggy was escorted back to him. "Thank you for the dance, Jess," she said then turned to Corey.

"Did you miss me?" She asked coyly.

"Every second," Corey told her smiling. "Still game, or do you want something to drink first?"

"Let's go," she said as she took his arm and they headed back to the dance floor. As they danced Corey maneuvered Peggy closed to Sarah and Pecos to see if he could pick up on any of the conversation, but there was too much noise. He did seem to feel that as they got close the couple deliberately moved away from them. Peggy seemed to realized that Corey's attention was not completely on her and reached up to turn his head to look down at her. "What's the matter, Corey?"

"What…oh, sorry, Peggy. I guess my mind wandered for a moment…I promise, it won't happen again." He gathered her closer and they moved around the floor. For the rest of the evening, they danced and socialized with their fellow revelers. As far as Corey could tell everyone that should be there, was there. He did make a mental note that Brooks was not in attendance. And for someone that had been popping up all over town the past few days…oh well, maybe he just didn't like to dance. About 10:00 they got ready to leave. They had a little over an hour's drive back to the ranch and Corey didn't want her brother coming to look for them. He figured that if everything went smooth that evening, hopefully, there would be many more. Peggy Harris was a beautiful, smart young woman, and he definitely wanted to see more of her. He pulled the buggy to a stop in front of the ranch house and hurried around to help her get down, then walked her to the door.

"Thank you, Corey, it was a wonderful evening."

"I'm glad you enjoyed yourself. If it's all right with you, I would like to come calling again?"

"I would like that."

Corey decided to press his luck and slowly bent down to give her a gentle kiss, when the door opened and Steve was standing there. "Oh, hi, Sis. Home already?"

"As if you weren't standing there listening," she said, irritated. "Thanks again, Corey. I had a wonderful time." She raised up on her tiptoes and gently kissed Corey on the cheek before she went inside. Corey stood there for a second, until Steve shut the door in his face.

"Yes, I would definitely like to call on you again," he thought as he turned and walked back to the buggy and drove away.

Inside the ranch house, Peggy turned to her brother. "Steve Harris, how dare you embarrass me like that?!"

"What did I do? I was just going to step outside for some fresh air."

"Of course you were! If you ever do that to me again….well, I don't know what I'll do to you…but it won't be pleasant, I assure you!!" With that she turned in a huff and headed upstairs.

"I just get no appreciation around here," Steve thought to himself and headed upstairs to his own room.

Chapter Nine

By the time it had gotten dark that evening, Marshal Raines, Sheriff Price and the deputies and distributed themselves throughout the different Harris ranch herds. The main objective they had decided to was to try to identify who the culprits were. If they could get a positive ID they would be able, hopefully, to identify the rest. The deputies and the hands from the Harris ranch were spread throughout the area around the herds. Although they were diligent, they saw no activity. Either the rustlers were hitting somewhere else, or they had taken the night off. Either way, by 2:00am they realized that it had been a wasted night.

The next morning Corey arrived at the office to find the Bill already there. "Good morning, Marshal, I'm surprised to see you here this early. Did you have any activity last night?"

"None at the Harris Ranch. I don't know about the Randall place yet."

"I'm surprised they passed up the opportunity," Corey said as he sat down at his desk.

"The question is, did they know what we were setting up?"

"If they did, they had to have gotten word from someone on one of the ranches."

"Sheriff Price said that they had been hitting some of the ranches up there recently. If they knew he was here…?"

"I'm beginning to think they have eyes and ears everywhere."

"They're sure getting info from somewhere."

"I don't think we have a choice. WE have to get someone on the inside."

"And you think that someone should be you."

"Why not? All we have to do is let everyone think I'm ready to jump ship here, so to speak. I've already made it known I'm just waiting to get money for a stake so I can get out of here. We just need to take the next step."

"There's only one problem with your scenario…you're too nice. No one would believe that you're capable of going that far."

"No one knows what they're capable of until they're pushed. So, let's push."

"Whatever we do, Corey, it will have to be public…and there won't be any turning back. If they even get a hint of what you're trying to do, they'll kill you…no questions asked."

"Hey…I know you've got my back."

"Here in town, yes. If they take you to their hideout…you'll be on your own. I don't like it."

"All we have to do is make contact. Once we know who is in on it, we can bring them in and force them to spill the beans on the rest."

"Huh, uh. That paints a big red target on your back. The only real option is to carry it through until we find the head guy. Bring him down and the others fall in place."

"How do you want to do this? We have to make them think that we've had a major falling out."

Bill thought for a moment, he didn't like it, but he also knew he didn't have much of a choice. "Let's not go too fast. We need to let it play out over the next couple of days to make it believable. You've already planted the seed, let's go with it. Seeing as it's Sunday, tomorrow afternoon you will do your regular tour, then go over to the saloon? I'll come looking for you. There will be more people around to witness our little play."

"I'll tell you that I'm doing my job and you challenge me. We can let it escalate and I'll storm out."

"OK, Corey. I don't like it, but I don't see we have much choice. I'll see you in the saloon in an hour."

The next day, Corey went into the office at the normal time and he and Bill again went through what they were going to do. Corey got up, left the office and walked down the street. He continued to make his usual rounds, stopping at the usual places, including the mercantile. "Morning, Burt," Corey said as he walked into the store.

"Hello, Corey, what can I do for you today?"

"Just checking to see if there was anything happening. Marshal's office has been kind of slow the last few days."

"Not enough excitement for you?"

"Excitement? Boredom is more like it," Corey said as he looked around the store. "Oh, yeah, I do need a box of .44 shells. I was doing some target practice the other day and I'm getting low."

"Sure, Corey. Here you go." Burt reached under the counter and pulled out a box of ammunition. "That'll be fifty cents."

Corey paid him and left the store. As he went back to the office he had to pass by the boarding house so he went in to take the box of shells up to his room. Mrs. Mason was coming down the stairs and saw him come through the door. "Hello, Corey. I thought you were over at the Marshal's office."

"I was, Ma'am. Needed to get some more cartridges so I thought I would bring the box back here instead of carrying it around all day."

"You do have a desk at the office, don't you."

"Oh, yes, Ma'am, but sometimes I just like to keep my supplies separate from the office supplies, if you know what I mean?"

"What's wrong, Son? You sound troubled."

"Maybe. Just restless, I guess."

"Did you and Miss Harris have a good time at the dance?"

"Oh, yes, Ma'am," Corey's eyes did light up at that.

"You two make a fine young couple. You just make sure you hang onto her."

"I'll try, I will really try. Now, if you will excuse me, I'd better put these away and get back before the Marshal comes looking."

"Well, you tell him, I said to be nice to you."

"I will, Ma'am, but I don't know if it will do much good these days." He turned and went up the stairs to his room as Mrs. Mason watched him, puzzled at his reactions.

A short time later Corey made his way to the saloon and had just ordered a beer. "Little early for you to start drinking, isn't it?" Jake asked him.

"Maybe," Corey said as he took a sip of the drink then walked over and sat down at a table.

"Hi, Corey," Sarah said as she sat down at the table beside him. "Saw you at the dance Saturday, looks like you got a date after all."

"Yes. Miss Harris is a nice girl," he took another sip of the beer.

"Anything wrong?" she asked him.

"Anything…everything. Who knows?"

"That doesn't sound like the Corey we all know and love?"

"Not everybody loves me."

"What is that supposed to mean?"

About that time Bill walked into the saloon and saw Corey sitting with Sarah. He took a deep breath and walked over to the table. "I thought you were making your rounds. Can't keep an eye on the town from a chair in the saloon."

"I made my rounds," Corey said, impatiently. "I just needed to sit for a spell."

"You could have done that at your desk while you do your paperwork."

"Paperwork! Sweeping the floors! Taking out the trash! Is that all that you ever think about?"

"It's part of your job. Now I suggest you get to it!"

Corey roughly sat the beer mug on the table, spilling a lot of it, got to his feet turned to leave. "Anything else you want me to do? Marshal?"

"Not right at the moment!" With that Corey stormed out of the saloon and headed back to the office. A few minutes later Bill walked in. They both looked at each other and smiled. Bill glanced out the window to see if anyone was within hearing range and decided they were safe for the time being. "Well, that should be the talk of the town in no time."

"Not that it's my favorite thing to do, but I think I'll go sweep off the sidewalk and make sure everyone that's looking knows I'm not happy about it."

"Good idea." He watched as Corey grabbed the broom from the back room and went outside. "I just hope we know what we're doing," he said to himself. "If anything happens to that kid…" He let the thought drop…not even wanting to consider the possibility.

As Corey was sweeping the sidewalk he was mumbling to himself, but he was also looking around to see if anyone was watching him. He didn't see anyone right away, but he did get a strange feeling that someone was watching, he just couldn't see them. A few minutes later, he finished what he was doing and went back into the office. Late that afternoon, Corey went to the café to get something to eat for dinner.

"Hello, Corey," Sally said as he came in and sat down at the counter. "What can I get for you?"

"I don't know…surprise me," he said, grumpily.

"Anything wrong?"

"Yeah…everything. I just wish I had the dough to get out of this town."

"I thought you liked it here," Sally said as she began dishing up a bowl of beef stew.

"I used to. I'm getting nowhere. What have I done? Cleaned out the livery stable….then Deputy Marshal…that's a laugh. I spend more time sweeping the place out that I do at any real work. And oh, yeah….file wanted posters. Real exciting. The only excitement this town has is in the saloon when someone starts a brawl."

Sally put the bowl down in front of him. "I wish I could help you, Corey, but I really don't know what I could do."

He gave her a slight grin. "Thanks, Miss Sally. I know you would. Look, if you hear of anyone needing a good hand, short term, would you point them my way? I just need some quick cash to get out of this place."

"Sure, Corey. Look…I'm sure things will get better, you just have to hang in."

Corey nodded and dug into the stew. When he finished, he paid for his meal and headed back to the office. When he walked inside he found the

Marshal intently studying what looked like a telegram. "Something sure must be interesting," he said.

"Yeah…a telegram from Sheriff Price. Seems our second guess was right on. While we were set up here to catch the rustlers, they were making a big run on the herds around Salt Flats."

"You know the Sheriff is going to go all out up there now, it may force them back down here."

"Maybe, or they'll decide to take what they've got and head out."

"That's going to be obvious, isn't it?"

"They would have to move out at night. They might be able to clear the area by morning, although it's a long shot." The Marshal sat back in his chair.

"They would have to have quite a herd by now…what do you guess two-three hundred head?" Corey got up and looked out the window, thinking.

"Sounds about right."

"They're going to need drovers. I figure since they've only been taking a few head at a time, there's probably not more than three or four of them."

"Makes sense."

"Let's hope that they think I might be a prospect. I let Miss Sally know that if anyone said anything about needing a good hand, to have them to contact me."

"Be careful…if you start getting invites from some of the legitimate ranchers and you turn them down, it might tip your hand."

"I did tell her that I was looking for quick cash. We'll just have to wait and see if anyone takes the bait."

"Meanwhile, we need to plan our next 'confrontation'."

That evening Corey again spent a lot of time in the saloon. He sat in the back, sipping a beer. At one point Betty came over and stood beside him. "What's wrong, Corey? You don't seem like yourself these past few days."

"I guess I'm just getting fed up with Rio Madre, Miss Betty."

"That's a shame. I wish there was something I could do to help."

"Not unless you can tell me where to get a job and make some quick cash. I need a stake before I can get out of here."

"Sarah mentioned the other day that you were looking for something different. If I hear of anything, I'll let you know."

"Thanks, Miss Betty." She left as Corey again started watching the patrons. He saw Sarah go and sit down beside Joe Brooks. For someone that was just 'passing through', Brooks seemed to have planted himself for a while. He still couldn't shake the feeling he knew him. As he sat there, Corey started thinking about that and decided that he needed to find out…something. Leaving his unfinished drink, he got up and walked out of the saloon. He walked down the street and went into the hotel. The night clerk was not at the desk, so Corey went up the steps. He had seen Brooks' room number on the register the morning they had asked Wade about him. When he reached room number eight he gently tried the knob, and not unexpectedly, it was locked. He reached into his pocket and pulled out his knife. Upon occasion, he had needed to pick the lock on the storage compartment at the livery stable when Abe wasn't there. He tried the same technique and a few seconds later the door opened. He went inside and quietly shut the door. He began pulling out the drawers in the chest and only found the expected changes of clothing and underwear. He opened the closet door and found a valise inside. He opened the catch but found it appeared to be empty. He started to close the valise when he spotted something that seemed to be stuck in the lining. Pulling the paper out, he realized it was a faded photograph. Two familiar faces were looking back at him and he suddenly realized where he had known Brooks before…the mining camp. The photograph was of Ben and Ellie Bailey who had a small claim there. He remembered they had a son that would be about Brooks' age now. It didn't explain why he was going by another name, but at least now Corey had a small piece of the puzzle. Through the open window, he heard a bunch of men coming down the street from the direction of the saloon. Deciding he shouldn't push his luck any further, he put the photo back and quickly left the room, making sure that he turned the latch to relock the door. He went down the back stairs to make sure he wouldn't run into anyone coming up.

He walked down the alley behind the hotel and finally went up another alley to the street and headed for the Marshal's office. Bill was still there when Corey came inside, seemingly looking back to see if he was being watched. "Something wrong?" He asked Corey.

"Not that I can put my finger on, but I do have some information. That guy, Brooks, I know where I've seen him before."

"Oh?" Bill said, sitting back in his chair.

"I did a little snooping in his hotel room…"

"You did what?!"

"I didn't get caught…but I did find out that he's really Dave Bailey from the mining camp."

"And that is a problem, because…?"

"Because, if he's not up to something, why did he change his name?"

"People do have a reason sometimes."

"Yeah…usually when they're running from the law."

"Not always."

"No, not always…come on…I thought you were on my side."

"I am on your side. I just want to make sure that when we finally decide to arrest him, it's because there's a legitimate reason."

"Legitimate!"

"Calm down, Corey. We'll get to the bottom of it. First, let's find out if he's a connection to the rustlers."

"Yeah…you're right….but, my guess is that he is connected. I wouldn't be surprised if he isn't the one that's posted here to keep an eye on us."

"How much did you know about him back at the camp?"

"Not a whole lot," Corey said as he sat down. "He was several years older than me, but I do remember hearing that he was a handful for his parents. Kept getting into trouble and stuff…little things, nothing major. Finally picked up one day and left, must have been around seventeen at the time. I don't know if they ever heard from him again."

"Right now, we keep an eye on him." Bill looked at Corey. "Don't let him know that you know who he is. It's going to be dangerous enough for you to go undercover, especially now."

Corey nodded in agreement. "So, how do we get me fired?"

Bill looked at him and grinned. "Well, it will have to be memorable."

"I guess we can follow on with what we have been doing….or what I have supposedly not been doing. Only this time…I retaliate."

"Why do I get the idea I'm going to come away from this with a sore jaw?"

"Sorry, I don't think there's any other way."

"I know. Ok…when do you want to do this? How about this evening… the saloon?"

"OK."

"About sunset I'll go over to the telegraph office and ask McCain if there's been an answer to the telegram you 'supposedly' sent out. Of course, he'll say he hasn't seen you."

"Shirking my duty again…."

"Exactly. You'll tell me where to go, I'll tell you you're fired, you take a punch and then throw your badge on the floor and walk out."

"That will definitely get their attention."

"I hope so…by the way…do you have enough cash to get you through for a while? I won't be able to get you paid after tonight."

"Oh, yeah…I hadn't thought of that. Let's just hope this doesn't drag out too long."

"Corey, we'll have to be able to keep in contact without drawing attention. We need someone to act as an intermediary. Someone we can trust."

"How about Miss Sally? I can leave a note with her and you can pick it up when you go there to eat."

"She's a smart lady…won't take her long to figure out what we're doing."

"I'm willing to risk it."

"OK…we'll do it tonight."

Chapter Ten

That evening Corey had taken his 'regular' seat in the back of the saloon. He had been there for about an hour when Marshal Raines came through the door. He spotted Corey at the table and, taking a deep breath, headed in his direction. "You might as well put a bed back here. You spend more time here than doing what you're supposed to do."

"Now, Marshal, I have done all my 'chores' for the day. There's nothing wrong with taking a little time for a drink."

"You're supposed to be making final rounds for the night. Not to mention the fact that you never sent that telegram I told you to send."

"I guess I forgot about that telegram, and I'll make those rounds…soon as I'm finished here."

"You are finished…now!" Bill had progressively raised his voice and gotten the attention he had wanted. "Now get out there and do your job!!"

"That's it!!!" Corey shouted. "Get off my back, MARSHAL!"

"I'll get off your back when you start doing the job you were hired to do. You've become a lazy good-for-nothing…." Bill didn't get any further as Corey suddenly hit him, knocking him to the floor. He got to his feet as Corey started walking away from him. "You're fired, Hansen!"

"I QUIT!!!" Corey shouted as he took off his badge and threw it at the Marshal and stomped out of the saloon. All talking had stopped and nobody moved as Bill picked up the badge and walked out the door, not saying anything to anyone.

After the little show they and put on, Corey went back to the boarding house. As he walked in the door, Molly was coming from the dining room and she could see how upset he was. "What's wrong, Corey?"

"Awww...the Marshal...I don't know what's gotten into him. Totally unreasonable."

"Do you want me to talk to him for you?"

"Thanks, Mrs. Mason, but it won't do any good now. He fired me, or I quit, or however you want to look at it." He had taken off his hat when he came in and now slapped it against his leg before putting it back on. He walked over to the banister and leaned against it as he looked at her.

"I'm sorry, Corey. What are you going to do now?"

"Find another job I guess. I just want to make some quick cash for a stake to get me out of this town. Go somewhere else where there's at least some kind of adventure. This place might as well be a ghost town."

"Well don't you worry, you'll find something. You're a good boy, someone will hire you."

"Thanks...I hope so. Besides, I going to need to pay my room rent in a couple of weeks." He smiled at her. "Look, I'm going to go get some shuteye. I'll see you in the morning."

"Good night, Corey. And like I said, don't worry, something will come up."

"Good night, Mrs. Mason," he said as he started up the stairs to his room. When he got to the landing, he looked down and saw her standing there watching him. He tipped his hat to her and went to his room.

Once he was out of sight, Molly turned and went back to the kitchen and poured herself some coffee. "I wonder..." was all she said as she sat down at the table and took a sip from the cup.

The next morning Bill was sitting on a chair in front of the office and was watching as Brooks came out of the hotel and headed toward the livery stable. He got up and walked down the street to where he could see the livery stable and then leaned back against the wall, and waited. A few minutes later, Brooks led his horse out of the livery stable, mounted and rode north, out of town. With the information that Corey had found, he had been thinking and was beginning to come to the same conclusions that Corey had. There was something not right about Brooks.

He walked over to the telegraph office and sent a message to the territorial marshal's office asking if there was anything outstanding on Joe Brooks, or Dave Bailey, or whatever his name was. "Paul," he said to the operator, "I'm going to take a chance that I can trust you to not say anything, to anyone, about any telegrams I send out over the next few weeks."

"Don't worry, Marshal, you can trust me. I won't even keep the original copy with the regular stuff."

"I believe you. Let me know as soon as an answer comes in for this."

"You got it, Marshal," he said and started to send the message as Bill left. When he was finished, Paul pulled a small box out from under the counter and placed the original message in the box then put it back and laid an old rag over it. He then took a sheet of the message paper, thought for a moment, and wrote a dummy message and placed it on the spindle holding the sent messages. The dummy message read, "*Territorial Marshal…stop…send any info man called Scott Rogers…stop.*" "That should keep 'em wondering if anyone starts snooping," Paul said as he smiled and let out a little giggle then turned back to straighten up the counter.

Bill went back to his office and sat down at his desk, then looked over at Corey's desk. He already missed him and just hoped that it wouldn't be too long until someone approached Corey. This waiting was going to be hell. "Oh, well," he said to himself, "I can't just sit here all day. Guess I'll go get something to eat and make my rounds."

Meanwhile, Corey had slept in that morning, trying to make up for a restless night, and then went down to have a late breakfast in the dining room. Molly always seemed to leave some sweetbreads and coffee out for her boarders. She was just coming out of the kitchen with a fresh pot of coffee when Corey walked in. "Good morning, Corey, how are you feeling this morning?" She asked him, concerned.

"I'm all right, Mrs. Mason, thank you. Think I'll just have some of that coffee and take a ride somewhere…anywhere that I won't run into the Marshal."

"Are you sure you can't talk to him…try to work things out?"

"My fist to his jaw last night pretty much cancels out any thought of a reconciliation."

"Oh, I didn't know."

"It's all right, I'm sure everyone will know soon. Look, if you hear of anyone needing help for a short run, would you let me know?"

"I sure will, Corey. Now, you take care of yourself, you hear?"

"I will. Thanks, Mrs. Mason." Corey finished up his sweetbread and coffee and left the house.

A few hours later, Joe Brooks pulled up outside the cabin, dismounted and went inside. "What are you doing here, Brooks?" Jackson asked as Joe sat down at the table.

"Just a little bit of information."

"It better be good if you risked coming out here again."

"It is. Seems like Marshal Raines is on his own. The deputy quit last night…or was fired, however you want to look at it."

"How do you know?"

"I was there…saw the whole thing come down in the saloon. Marshal called him out for 'dereliction of duty' and ended up with the deputy slugging him. Needless to say…they're not friends anymore."

"Think he might be interested in falling in with us?" Pecos asked as he got up off the bunk where he had been laying. "Might be. If he knows what the Marshal's plans are we could use him."

"I don't know," Jackson said. "You did say that Sarah said he was looking for some quick cash to get out of the area?"

"Yeah…has been grumbling about it for some time from what I understand."

"I've heard the gossip, too." Brooks said as he helped himself to a drink from the whiskey bottle in the middle of the table.

"Let's wait a couple of days…make sure that he's ready to join us. Joe… keep a close eye on him. Watch who he talks to, where he goes…we have to make sure that this isn't a setup."

"If you had seen that right cross he put to the Marshal's chin last night, you'd know it was real."

Jackson smiled and poured himself a drink. "OK…I'll get in touch with the boss and find out if we're ready to pull out. There's at least 300 head in that box canyon just waiting to go to market." He looked at another of his men. "Chambers…all those brands been changed?"

"Yes, Sir…" Johnny replied. He was the youngest of the band at twenty years old with dirty blond hair and green eyes, and was very eager to please his boss. "They're ready to go."

"OK, men…soon as the boss gives the orders, we'll pull out under the cover of darkness and use it to get as far away as possible before daylight. We'll lay off the northern ranches and hit the Harris Ranch again tonight. See if you can get about 20 head tonight and we'll test Randall's 'defenses' tomorrow night…just to keep them guessing."

"Right, Red," Pecos said as he headed for the door. "If it's OK, I think I'll go into town tonight and see if Sarah can give us any more info on what went down between Raines and the deputy. He might be more tempted to open up to her now."

"OK, Pecos. Brooks, why don't you nose around some of the other 'establishments'. See if there's anyone willing to talk about the Marshal and what he might be up to now that he doesn't have any help. I don't have to tell you two to not be seen together….?"

"Don't worry, I'll give Joe an hour's start before I head into town," Pecos said as he waited for Brooks to leave then closed the door behind him.

Corey had ridden back into town and was back at his 'favorite' spot in the saloon. Sarah soon walked over and sat down next to him. "Hi, Corey, how are you doing?"

"Fine, just fine," he said sarcastically and a little sharper than he had planned on. "No job…little money…what do you think?"

"Hey, you don't have to snap at me, I didn't fire you."

"I'm sorry, Miss Sarah, I didn't mean to take it out on you."

"That's OK. Anything I can do to help?"

"Yeah…tell me how to find some quick cash so I can get out of this town."

"I'll keep my ear out for something. No chance you can patch things up with the Marshal?"

"Are you kidding? I wouldn't go back there for all the tea in China… wherever that is."

She couldn't help but snicker at him. "Come on, Corey…where's all that youthful eagerness I used to see?"

"It must have left town. I just wish the rest of me had been with it."

"Look…things will get better, you'll see."

"I hope so," Corey said as he put his near-empty glass down and got to his feet. "I guess I'd better go. 'Bout time for the Marshal to make his rounds and I don't want to be here when he does." He started to leave then turned back to her. "Thanks, Miss Sarah."

"What for?"

"Listening to me, and not judging me."

"Anytime, Corey….anytime."

He walked out of the saloon and headed for the café. He looked in the window before he went inside and saw Bill sitting at the counter. He decided that it probably wouldn't be a good idea to be seen with him right then, so he turned and headed back to the boarding house, picking up a copy of the newspaper on the way. When he got to his room, he laid down on the bed and began to read. The headline was about the rustling that 'seemed to have gotten out of hand', and how the local law enforcement had not been able to do anything about it. "We're trying," he said to himself. "Just give us a little more time." He put the paper on the bed beside him and closed his eyes. He hadn't slept very well the night before and decided to try to get a little rest while he could.

Late that afternoon Bill was in his office when Paul came in with the answer to his telegram. "Here you go, Marshal," he said, then waited to see if there was going to be a reply. Bill scanned through the message and then looked at Paul. "Thanks, Paul. That will be it for now. I'll probably have a couple more to go out tomorrow. Here…" He handed him a tip and Paul nodded his head, turned to leave, then turned back.

"Oh, by the way, Marshal, I made a dummy message and put it on the spindle in the office, just in case somebody decided to pry."

"Good idea. Thanks…just try not to get too 'creative'." He smiled at him.

"No problem, Marshal…I got you covered."

"I know you do, Paul, I know you do." He watched as Paul left then looked back at the response to his inquiry and read, "*No warrants Joe*

Brooks or Dave Bailey. Minor offenses Bailey…fines only." He leaned back in his chair, thinking. He knew something was not right about the guy. Whatever it was, they were going to have to catch him red-handed. Right now, he couldn't help but wonder if Corey had been contacted yet. "Oh, well, I guess he'll contact me when he can."

Corey was walking down the street when he saw Mr. Harris and Peggy come out of the mercantile. He couldn't help it, he had to walk over and say hello. "Afternoon, Mr. Harris, Peggy," he said as he tipped his hat to her.

"Hello, Corey," Peggy said then looked at her father.

"Peggy, I've got to check in with the Marshal, I'll be back in a few minutes."

"OK, Father," she said, then turned to Corey. "I wanted to thank you again for a nice evening, Corey."

"Thanks, Peggy, it was my pleasure. Look, I don't know if you've heard the rumors yet, but the Marshal and I had a 'difference of opinion' and I'm not his deputy any more. I can't go into the details, just try to keep an open mind about anything you hear."

"All right. You're not in any trouble are you?"

"No…I just don't want you to get the wrong idea about me. I really do like you."

"I like you too, Corey."

He couldn't help it as a big smile lit up his face. "There's going to be a lot going on so I might not be around for a while. I promise I will explain things later. Until then, just don't believe anything anyone says." He looked over and saw her father coming back from the office. "Look, I'd better go. Remember what I said." He walked away as her father got to her.

"We'd better go, Peggy," her father said as he took her arm and guided her toward the buggy.

"Is anything wrong, Father?"

"I think it would be a good idea if you don't see Corey again."

"But, Father…"

"No, Peggy…I'm not going to argue with you about this." He looked at her stricken face and softened. "Look, Honey, I just don't want you to see him right now, OK?"

"I don't understand."

"I know you don't, but evidently he has a few things going on right now that I don't want you involved in."

"What things?"

"Peggy, that's enough. If things change, then he will be welcome at our place again, but not now."

She thought about what Corey had just told her and decided that she would play along…for now. "OK, Father. Whatever you say, but I'm not happy about it!"

"That's my girl, now let's get home, it's almost dinner time." He helped her into the buggy and they headed out of town, not knowing that Corey had been standing in the shadows of a nearby alley and had heard most of the conversation. He stepped out onto the street and watched as the buggy turned a corner and went out of sight.

"I'm sorry, Peggy," he said to himself. "I will make it up to you, somehow." He turned and headed up the street to the café.

He went inside and sat down at the counter as Sally came in from the kitchen. "Hello, Corey," she said when she saw him. "What can I get you?"

"Just some coffee, thank you."

"The marshal told me a little about what happened…are you OK?"

"Yeah…I'm fine."

"Look…don't let it get to you. You'll find something else."

"I know." He thought for a moment as she was pouring his coffee. Evidently the marshal had not said anything to her about their plan, so he just had to play along. Later, he had decided that if they wanted to contact him, he would have to make himself 'available' so he just walked around town for a while then ended up at the saloon. He took his customary seat in the back and just sat there nursing a drink when Betty walked over to him.

"Hi, Corey."

"Hello, Miss Betty."

"Jake just found this on the bar. It's addressed to you." She handed him an envelope with just '*Hansen*' written on it.

"No idea who left it?"

"Sorry."

"OK…thanks." Corey looked at the envelope for a second then opened it. Inside he found a note that read, '*Looking to get even with the Marshal? Be at Red Rock at dawn.*' Well, that didn't take long," he thought to himself. He hung around for a little bit longer then went back to the boarding house. If he had to head out before dawn, he would need the rest. He certainly didn't want to start this out tired. He was going to need all his senses to keep himself alive over the next few days. The next morning he got up and wrote a quick note saying, 'Red Rock. Dawn. Keep you posted. Corey.' He put it in an envelope with the Marshal's name on it and slipped it under the back door of the café on his way to the livery stable. He knew that Sally always came in the back and didn't open the front door until she was ready to open. He just hoped she would see the envelope and pass it on. He got to Red Rock, which was actually a clay deposit a few miles north of town, just before dawn. He got off his horse and tied the reins to some scrub brush that was in the middle of a grassy area. Might as well let his horse graze while he waited…and waited. An hour later he had decided that he was on a wild goose chase, got to his feet and headed toward his horse. He hesitated when he saw a rider approaching. He didn't recognize the rider, but, that didn't really surprise him. He waited as Ray Stewart pulled to a stop and got down from his horse.

"'Morning, Hansen. Hear you had a little trouble with the Marshal."

"You might say that," Corey said as his heart beat a little faster.

"Want to get even?"

"What do you have in mind?"

"Know that rustling problem he's been trying to get a handle on?"

"Of course."

"You know, if he doesn't catch the guys, he's going to be the one in trouble. Agreed?"

"I guess you could say that."

"Interested in being a part of it?"

"Maybe. What's in it for me?"

"A cut of the take when we sell the herd."

"And what makes you think you're going to get the herd through without being spotted?"

"We have a plan?"

"It better be a good one." Corey shook his head, signifying that he was skeptical. Inside, the butterflies in his stomach were on parade. He told himself that he had better calm down, so he took a deep breath and slowly let it out.

"The boss thinks so."

"I don't suppose you're going to tell me who that is?" Well, he thought… he had to try.

"Not a chance. At least not yet. You in?"

"What if I said I want to think about it?"

"Then you're dead…right now." Stewart pulled his gun.

"Then, I guess I'm in."

"Good. Now go back to town like a good boy, and we'll be contacting you. And, by the way, we have people there that will be watching you until you're needed."

"Can I ask how long until this goes down? I have rent to pay on the first of the month. Can't have that old bat throwing what little I have out onto the street."

"Don't worry. You'll be covered for it. Just keep your mouth shut."

"Then I'm not complaining…I'll be waiting to hear from you."

"Ok, Hansen, get going, I'll be waiting here until you're out of the area."

"Whatever you say," Corey responded as he headed for his horse, mounted, and rode back toward town.

It was mid-morning when Corey got back to town and he was definitely hungry. He pulled up in front of the café and went inside. "Morning, Miss Sally," he said as he sat down at the counter.

"Hello, Corey. Things going better today?"

"Maybe. How about some coffee, toast, bacon and eggs?"

"Coming right up." She turned to start making his breakfast as he looked around then pulled a piece of paper from his pocket and wrote 'I'm in.' on it, folded it and wrote the Marshal's name on the outside. When she brought him his plate he handed her a dollar bill with the note folded inside it.

"Thanks, Corey, I'll get you your change." She walked over to the register and rang up the sale. She saw the note with Bill's name on it and carefully hid it under the register drawer, then pulled out the change and handed it to Corey. "You know, I could run a tab for you until you get a new job."

"No, thanks…I'm OK for a few days…if I don't find something by then, I might just go ahead and pack up my stuff and head out."

"I hope you stay, Corey. It's kind of nice having you around." She looked at him and smiled.

Corey blushed. "Thanks." He finished his meal, then took his horse over to the stable and settled him into a stall. He was walking back toward the boarding house when he saw Ken Harris ride into town and pull his horse to a stop outside the Marshal's office. He could see that Harris did not look happy. "Uh-oh," Corey said as he stepped into an alley across the street and down from the office. "They must have hit him again."

Inside the office, Bill and Ken were going over what happened the night before. "Look, Marshal," Ken said, "this has got to stop. We have to find out who is behind this and stop it."

"We will, Mr. Harris. We will."

"And just when will that be? When all the ranchers around here don't have any cattle left!?"

"We just need a few more days."

"Really, Marshal. And what do you think you can accomplish in a 'few more days' when you don't even seem to be out hunting for clues?"

Bill thought about the envelope that Sally had given him earlier than morning. "I can't explain everything right now. You'll just have to trust me that things are being done."

"I think the ranchers around here are beginning to lose their 'trust' that 'anything' is being done." Ken got up from his chair and began walking around the room. "I've heard rumors that some people are thinking you're on the take…"

At that statement Bill came out of his chair as he slammed his hands down on his desk. "That is a bunch of crap, Harris and you know it!"

"Do I? I used to think you were pretty competent, Marshal, but lately, I'm beginning to wonder." Ken was getting frustrated and his voice showed it.

Bill saw caught sight of someone slowly walking by the office. Not knowing who it might be, or if they had stopped just out of sight, he decided to play the situation for what it was worth. "Look, Harris…I'll do my job. I'll find the rustlers…but I'll do it faster if you and the other ranchers would stop trying to tell me how to go about it!" He really didn't want to antagonize Harris, but he didn't see what else he could do. "Now, if you don't mind, I do have rounds to make."

"Oh, sure…you make your 'rounds' and protect your precious little town. It's obvious you don't care what happens outside the city limits. It just might be time to call for a 'town' meeting, and have the local ranchers there. Maybe you'll find yourself in the same boat with your deputy…out of a job." With that, Harris angrily opened the door and left the office.

Bill shook his head and looked around the office before he walked outside. A half-block, or so, down the street he could see Brooks walking away from the area. Was it him that walked by? Bill didn't know, but as he looked around he spotted Corey coming out of the alley down the street. He could pretty much figure that Corey had been watching the office and would know if Brooks had been listening. Now, if he could just figure out how he and Corey could communicate. He made his rounds and went into the café to get an early supper. "Hello, Miss Sally," he said as he went in the door.

"Hi, Marshal. What can I do for you?"

"Just some coffee and a ham sandwich? How's that?"

"Coming right up." She poured him a cup of coffee and then prepared his sandwich. "That'll be 35 cents." He gave her the change and when she went to ring it up in the register, she carefully took out the slip of paper that Corey had left earlier. She then went to top-off Bill's coffee and slipped the paper under the saucer, making sure he saw what she was doing. "Anything else, Marshal?"

"No thanks, Sally," Bill said as he used a napkin to wipe his mouth and slip the paper into his shirt pocket. He finished his sandwich and after leaving Sally a tip, headed back to his office. When he got inside, he checked to make sure no one was watching and went back to his desk and picked up the newspaper. He used it to hide the note that he took out of his pocket. He read what Corey had written and smiled. Things just might be looking up.

Chapter Eleven

That evening Corey was again at the saloon in what was now his favorite spot. Instead of his usual light colored shirt and pants, this evening he was dressed totally in black. He wanted to try to blend with the dark corner where he watched as Brooks come in and sat down at a table, then joined into the card game. Sarah went over to the table to see if he wanted anything to drink and put her arm around Pecos who was also in the game. Obviously they were a 'couple' and it set Corey to wondering if there was more to this than he first thought. After all, it was to Sarah that he had first voiced his 'displeasure' with his job and the marshal. He watched as she leaned down and whispered something to Pecos who looked at Brooks. A few minutes later she walked over to Corey's table. "Hi Corey, can I get you another drink?"

"No, thanks…I'm just going to finish this one and hit the sack, I think."

"OK. Let me know if you change your mind."

"I'll do that," Corey said and watched her go to one of the other tables and check the patrons there before she went back to the card game and again stood beside Pecos. He waited for a few more minutes, finished his drink, got up and left the building. After deciding to walk around town for a little while before returning to the boarding house, he looked around before crossing the street, but didn't see anyone that seemed to be watching him. Everything seemed to be quiet and peaceful, but he couldn't shake the feeling that something just wasn't quite right and it didn't have anything to do with the rustlers. He was walking by the Wells Fargo office and thought he heard something move inside. Slowing his pace he looked through the window and saw a shadow near where he knew there was a safe. Since he was no longer a deputy, he didn't know whether there was a valuable shipment there overnight or not. Trying to interfere would definitely blow his cover. Running over to the Marshal's Office wouldn't help his situation either. He would have to find a discreet way to notify Bill and fast. Looking down the street he saw Sally come out of the café and head for her house located on the edge of town. He cut down and alley and ran up behind the buildings and came up another alley ahead of where Sally was walking. He lowly called out to her as she got even with him. "Miss Sally," he said.

Startled, she jumped, then looked into the dark alley. "Corey?"

"Don't ask questions," he told her softly. "Just head over to the Marshal's Office and tell him to check out the Wells Fargo office."

"Corey?"

"Just do it, please."

"OK…" she said and changed direction, crossed the street and seeing a light on in the office she tried the door. When she realized it was locked, she softly knocked.

Bill was at his desk trying to concentrate on some paperwork when he heard the knock at the door. He pulled his gun and carefully unlocked, then opened the door. "Sally, what are you doing here?" He stepped aside and let her come in.

"To tell the truth, I'm not sure."

"Excuse me?"

"Marshal, I was just heading home when Corey called to me from an alley and told me that I needed to tell you to check the Wells Fargo office."

"Corey?" Then realizing what had happened, Bill went in to action. "Sally, stay here. Lock the door when I leave."

"But…"

"Just do what I say…stay here until I get back." Bill hurried down the street and carefully looked through the window of the express office. He could see a shadow moving around and carefully checked the door knob and saw that it was locked. He hurried around the corner and into the alley. When he got to the back door he carefully turned the knob, pushed it open then quietly stepped inside. Bill took a quick look around and then went toward the front of the building. Hearing footsteps, he quickly stepped behind a packing crate and waited as a man went by him, headed for the back door. Bill stepped out from his hiding place. "Hold it right there," he said as the man froze in his tracks. "Slowly take out your gun and toss it into the corner." The man did as he was told.

"Who are you?" The man said. "Look…I'd be willing to split the take…"

"Good try…" Bill said. "The problem is I'm the marshal in this town and we are going to take a little walk over to my jail."

"Come on, Marshal…sure you don't want…" The man didn't get a chance to continue as Bill pushed him toward the back door. They went out of the building, across the street, and down the sidewalk to the jail. Sally had been watching out the window and saw them coming. She opened the door for them and stepped back, putting it between herself and the thief. Bill took the keys from the hook beside the door to the cells and pushed the man forward and into the first cell. Locking it, Bill went back to the front office as Sally closed the door and stood there watching him.

"Can I go now? It is getting late?" She crossed her arms in front of her as she leaned back against the door.

Bill couldn't help smiling at her. "Yes, you may, Miss Sally. And thank you for your help."

"Is there a reason that you wanted me to stay here and wait for you?"

"I just didn't want you to run into that guy back there."

"Oh," she said coyly. "And I thought it was because you just wanted me to be here when you got back."

Bill did a double-take as he started looking at the bag the man had been carrying. He saw the smile forming on her face and started to smile back at her. "Well, that is not a bad thing to think about. Maybe I will have to reconsider things a bit." He walked over to her. "Sally, thanks for what you did. He was robbing the express office."

"Don't thank me, thank…" She stopped as Bill put a finger to her lips.

"It doesn't matter how you knew." He nodded his head toward the cells and she suddenly understood what he meant and it confirmed her suspicions as to what was going on.

She took a deep breath, then, "Well, Marshal, I do have to get home. Please let me know if I can be of assistance to you again. Anything to keep our lawman happy." It wasn't often she got the chance to tease someone and this time she wanted to make the best of it....especially when it was Bill Raines. She turned, opened the door and left as Bill locked the door behind her and returned to his desk. He sat there and thought about things for a few moments, remembering a comment Corey had made about him taking Sally to the dance. Maybe, after this whole situation was over with, he would ask her out...dinner, a dance, or something.

The next morning Corey came down the stairs from his room and went into the dining room to see if Mrs. Mason had put out anything for breakfast yet. Most of the time she would set out a buffet of some kind: toast, coffee, eggs, etc., for her boarders. This morning he found a selection of biscuits, hotcakes, syrup, jellies and jams along with a large pot of coffee. He fixed himself a plate of hotcakes with butter and syrup, and got a cup of coffee. He sat down at the table and had just started to eat when Molly came in from the kitchen. "Oh, good morning, Corey. I thought I heard someone come in here."

"Good morning, Mrs. Mason."

"I hope everything is good with you this morning."

"It might be looking up. I just don't know yet. I guess I'm getting a little antsy waiting for something to happen."

"You'll be OK, Corey. I have faith in you."

"Thank you, Mrs. Mason, that means a lot to me."

She put a motherly hand on his shoulder. "You're a good boy. You'll be fine."

He smiled and went back to his breakfast as she continued into the front room. When he finished eating he headed out and went down the street toward the livery stable. He saddled Sunny and headed out of town. He wanted to go to the Harris Ranch and try to explain things to Peggy, but he knew that wasn't possible. Still, a little while later he found himself on the outskirts of the ranch. He stopped near a small stream so he could give Sunny some water and let him graze a little. After replacing Sunny's bridle with a halter and tie rope, he sat down on the ground and leaned back against a tree. There was a lot on his mind that morning, most of it wondering if he would be able to pull off this little masquerade. The sound of the running water and the soft breeze lulled Corey into a doze. "Hello, Corey." He sat upright, startled until he realized that Peggy was standing there beside him.

"Uh, hello, Peggy," he said as he scrambled to his feet.

"What are you doing out here?"

"I, uh, I just had a lot of thinking to do and I thought I would bring Sunny out here and let him graze a little. Better for him than what he gets at the livery stable, I guess."

"He's a beautiful horse, Corey."

"Thank you. I've had him since he was colt. Don't know what I would do without him," he said as he walked over and grabbed the tie rope and led Sunny over to Peggy. "Say hi to the pretty lady, Sunny." The horse bobbed his head toward Peggy and softly nickered.

"He's well trained, too."

"Just knows a pretty woman when he sees one," Corey said smiling at his horse, then at Peggy.

She couldn't help blushing a little, then turned to stroke the head of her horse, a beautiful sorrel, with a deep chest and lean appearance. "What's going on, Corey? I know something's up, but nobody will tell me anything."

Corey had to do some quick thinking. He wished he could explain everything but knew that was not possible. "Nothing really. The marshal and I just had a difference of opinion and now I'm looking for another job."

"Do you want me to talk to my father?"

"No, Peggy. I get the idea he doesn't want me around either."

"But…"

Not even thinking about it, he stopped her with a quick kiss. "Things will work out, Peggy. We just need to have faith and a little patience."

"I hope so, Corey. I really like you."

"I like you too, Peggy…a lot. Look, you'd better head back to your house. I don't think it would be a good idea for one of the ranch hands to see us and report back to your father."

"I guess you're right. Can I see you again? Maybe meet here again tomorrow?"

"Peggy…right now it's not a good idea. Just give me some time to work some things out and I'll call on you the proper way."

"All right, Corey…take care of yourself. I don't want anything to happen to you."

"Don't you worry your pretty little head," he said as he smiled at her and gently tapped her on the nose with his fingertip. "I can take care of myself."

"I'll see you soon," Peggy said as she quickly kissed him then stepped over to Sunny and pulled his head down and spoke into his ear. "Take care of him," she whispered, then mounted her horse, turned and rode away.

"What was that about?" Corey asked Sunny. "Conspiring against me?" Sunny just nodded his head up and down and went back to grazing. "You're supposed to be on my side," Corey said as he patted the palomino's neck, then let him graze for a little while longer before he put the bridle back on him and headed back to town.

*****

Late that afternoon Bill received a telegram from the territorial marshal regarding his new 'tenant' in the cell. He found out that Jed Ingram was wanted in New Mexico for the robbery and murder of an agent at the express office in Taos. New Mexico was filing for extradition and were sending their own marshals to take him back for prosecution. Since the money here was recovered, and no one had been injured, Bill was instructed to turn the prisoner over to the New Mexico marshals, who would be there in about three days. He got to his feet and walked back to the cell to give Ingram the news. "Well, Ingram, it looks like the New Mexico authorities are more interested in you than we are."

"Yeah…well, they'll have to get me back there first." Ingram was a wiry man, with black hair and a thin mustache. He may not have looked like much, but Bill got the idea that he was a lot more dangerous than he was letting on.

"I don't think that will be a problem. They're already on the way to pick you up. I'll just make sure you're 'comfortable' 'til they get here." He heard a knock at the door and went to open it, learning a long time ago that when he was there alone with a prisoner in the cell, the door stayed locked. When he unlocked the door he saw Sally standing there with a covered tray.

"Hello, Marshal, thought I would bring over your prisoner's supper while there was a lull at the café. I've only got a couple of customers, and they're already eating their dinner."

"Thank you, Sally. If you'll just place the tray on the desk I'll take it back there."

"Sure. How are things going?"

"They've been better."

"I understand. Well, I'd better get back. Take care, Marshal. I'll send someone to pick up the tray in an hour or so."

"Thanks, again."

"Anytime, Marshal, anytime," she said as she went out the door after he unlocked it, then relocked it behind her. Bill then poured some coffee into a cup, did a quick inventory of what was on the tray, picked it up and walked back to the cells. He ordered Ingram back against the wall as he bent down and slid the tray through a small opening in the bars at the floor that was just big enough to accommodate a small tray.

"I'll be back to get the tray in a few minutes," he told Ingram.

When Sally got back to the café she found Corey sitting at the counter reading the newspaper. "Hello, Corey. What can I get for you?"

"How about some of your famous stew?"

"Well, I don't know how famous it is, but I think I can find a dish for you."

"Thanks. Heard there was some action in town last night."

"If you want to call it that. Marshal caught some guy trying to rob the express office. He has him locked up right now."

"You might know things would start happening around this town after I got booted out of my job." He smiled conspiratorially out the side of his mouth as she sat a bowl of stew in front of him.

"Maybe they were afraid of you and waited until you were not on the job anymore," she said, following along with the banter as she glanced over at the other diners.

"That has to be it." He winked at her. "Maybe that's why the marshal got rid of me…he was jealous."

Sally just shook her head and went over to the two diners who were some of her regular customers. "Anything else I can get for you gentlemen?"

"No thanks, Sally. The meal was excellent, as always," one of the men said to her.

"Why, thank you, Mel. It's always nice to serve customers that really appreciate good food," she said as she handed them the bill for the meal.

"That I do, Sally…that I do," he said as he patted his stomach then handed her the money.

"Just keep the change," he told her.

"Thanks, Mel. Let me know if you decide you need something else." She went back to the counter and started cleaning the area. "Will there be anything else, Corey?"

"No thanks, Miss Sally. And yes, if that stew isn't famous it should be." He handed her the money for his meal, and wiping his face with a napkin, got up and left the café.

A little while later when Bill went back to retrieve the dinner tray from the cell, he had Ingram push the tray back through the opening and step to the back of the cell. Bill checked the tray and sat it on a nearby chair. "OK, Ingram…hand it over."

"What are you talking about, Marshal?" He asked innocently.

"The butter knife…"

"I don't know what you're talking about."

"OK, Ingram…over there." He motioned to the far right front of the cell. "Put your arms through the bars, and hook one around the second bar in the other cell."

"Come on, Marshall…."

"NOW, Ingram." The prisoner did what he was told and Bill handcuffed his hands, then unlocked the door and entered the cell. Since the prisoner was secure and in a position that it would be difficult to try to kick at him he began to investigate the area. After a brief search he found the knife under the mattress on the bunk. He double checked to make sure that Ingram had not hidden anything else in the cell. "Nice try," he said as he left the cell, locked it, then pulled on the door to make sure it was secure. He then went over and unlocked the handcuffs. "Don't try it again, Ingram, I inventory every tray that goes in and out of here."

"We'll see, Marshall….we'll see."

"This is the last warning, try anything else, and you'll find yourself handcuffed to your bed at night. See that iron ring on the wall above the head of the bunk…well it's there for a purpose. Think about it." With that Bill picked up the tray, left the cell area and went back to the office as Ingram glared at him.

Chapter Twelve

Two days later, Corey had grabbed a quick breakfast at the boarding house, and then went to the livery stable to saddle Sunny. He found an envelope attached to his saddlebag. He opened the envelope and read the note inside. *'Red Rock at noon.'* He looked around to see if he could see anyone watching, but didn't see anything, or anyone, out of the ordinary. He knew he had to get a message to the marshal. He hoped that he wasn't putting Sally at risk, but he had no other choice. He turned the message over and quickly wrote a note on the back of it. *'This may be it…wish me luck.'* He put the note back into the envelope, scratched out his name and wrote 'Raines' on the outside. He folded the envelope as small as he could, and put it in his pocket, then led Sunny to the café.

"Morning, Miss Sally," he said as he went inside.

"Hello, Corey."

"Could you pack me a couple of sandwiches…I'm going for a long ride today and probably won't be back until late."

"Of course, Corey. You are a growing boy…and you do need your nourishment."

"I am not a boy," Corey corrected her.

"Of course you're not. Hang on just a minute…ham OK?"

"That's fine. And, can I get a couple of carrots and an apple for my horse?"

"I don't know about you. Sometimes I think that horse of yours eats better than you do."

"Maybe…but he doesn't get to eat that famous stew of yours…."

Sally just shook her head and handed him a bag with the sandwiches and treats for Sunny. He handed her the money along with the note. She went to the register, got his change, and placed the note under the drawer. "Here you go, Corey. Come back for dinner tonight and I'll see if I can't fix another batch of that 'famous' stew you like so much."

"I'll do that, Miss Sally. I'll definitely do that."

He left, put the bag of food in his saddlebag, mounted and rode out of town. He got to Red Rock shortly before noon and dismounted. Leading Sunny to a shady spot, he made himself comfortable, then gave Sunny the carrots. He sat there stroking his friend's head while waiting for any 'company' to arrive. He had finally decided to bring out one of the sandwiches and had eaten about half of it when he saw a figure riding up. Not wanting to appear too anxious, he kept eating and waited until the man dismounted and walked up to him. "Comfortable?" The man asked.

"Sure," Corey said, still munching on the sandwich. "Just sharing a little lunch with my friend here," he said as he extended his hand with the apple to Sunny, who took it and happily crunched into it.

"Well, when you've finished your 'lunch' the boss wants to meet you."

"I guess I'm done," Corey said as he gathered the wrapper from the sandwich, put it into the bag then put both into his saddlebag. The two men mounted their horses and rode north, away from Red Rock. A couple of hours later, after making what Corey figured out were some definite detours meant to confuse anyone that might be following them, they entered a canyon. A short time later, Stewart led Corey up a trail that seemed to lead up toward the ridge of the canyon. They rode through a wide crevasse in the rocks and found themselves in a clearing. A stream that seemed to come from somewhere high in the rocks was running alongside a cabin. The two men dismounted and tied their horses to the hitching rail and entered the cabin.

Inside the cabin, Corey saw two men sitting at a table playing cards. Red Jackson looked up from his hand and seemed to give Corey the once-over. "So, Hansen, I hear you're looking for some quick cash?"

"You might say that. Anything that will get me out of this area and somewhere that has a lot more 'opportunities' than this place."

"I guess you know what we want from you?"

"Yeah…he told me," Corey motioned to Stewart. "Move some cattle north and sell them ahead of the regular drives. In return, I get a cut of the take."

"That's a pretty loose interpretation of what we want. But, we need to insure all of our movements are kept under wraps. No word gets out to anyone."

"No problem here. Only people I really care to associate with these days are two women…one owns a café and the other…well, I guess I've pretty much cashed in my chips on that one. Her daddy doesn't seem to care for me anymore."

Red couldn't help but give him a half-way smile. "Women trouble…that can do you in faster than any lawman."

"So I've heard," Corey replied.

"What about the woman at the café?"

"What about her? Just the best goddamn cook in the territory. You really need to try her stew sometime. And those biscuits she bakes…."

"OK, I get the message. Sit down," Red motioned to a chair at the table and Corey sat down and leaned back.

"So, when do we do this? I'm going to need money soon," he looked around the cabin. "You know…food, boarding house, stable fees."

"Got anything in town you don't want left behind? Just saying we decide to head out now."

"Yeah. In fact there is. Some photos of my mother and a couple of pieces of her jewelry." He paused for a moment. "Not much really, but it's all I have left of her."

Red became very thoughtful as he studied his hand for a long moment before he laid his cards face down on the table then looked at his men, who also seemed to be in a thoughtful mood. He looked at Corey again. "I wish I had something from my mother…." He kind of shook his head as if to clear any thoughts, "Nevermind. OK, Kid. Go back to town, but only get what you really need. Don't want the folks to think you're not coming back, do we? Be back here at dawn. We got a lot to do."

"Sounds good," Corey said as he got up and started for the door.

"Oh, and Kid…" Red said and Corey turned back to him. "Remember… we got people in town…and they are watching you. So, don't get any fancy notions of trying to tip anyone off."

"Don't worry. If this will get me out of that town, no way am I doing anything to get in the way. Besides it will give me a chance at one more bowl of that stew. You should try it."

"Maybe…sometime. See you tomorrow morning…early. Ray, make sure he finds his way back to town."

Corey nodded his head and walked out of the cabin as Stewart followed him.

*****

That afternoon Corey rode back into town and took Sunny to his stall in the livery stable then went to the saloon. The ride had been hot and dry and he did need something to drink. He ordered a beer and went to sit at his favorite table in the back. A half-hour later, there had been no one show up other than the 'regulars' that came in about that time. While he was sitting there, he pulled a piece of paper out of his pocket and, trying to keep his glass in front of the paper, wrote a quick note to the marshal. He put the paper in his pocket, finished his beer and went outside. He walked around the town for a little while then went to the café. "Hello, Miss Sally," he said as he walked up to the counter and sat down.

"Hello, Corey. I made some more of that stew…want a bowl now?"

"You bet."

"Anything to drink?"

"Just water, thank you."

"Coming right up," she said smiling at him.

"I've been out riding all day…anything interesting happen?"

"No…same as usual."

“It figures…nothing happens around here.”

“Now, Corey, most people like it when the town is quiet. You get a town with something happening all the time and that’s when people have a tendency to get hurt.”

“True…but you also have to have a little ‘spice’ in your life, or it gets boring…real fast.”

“I don’t know about the spice in your life, but here’s your stew. See if there’s enough ‘spice’ in it.”

He scooped a large spoonful into his mouth. “Oh….absolutely divine. Sally, will you marry me?” He said after he swallowed.

She just laughed at him. “Oh, Corey…you know I’m much too old for you.”

“And what has that got to do with anything? You’ve got everything a man could want…beauty, nice personality, good cook,” he took her hand in his, and kissed it as he passed her the note. “Especially the good cook part of it.”

“Well, they do say the way to a man’s heart is through his stomach.” Laughing, she pulled her hand away from him and held it close to her chest with the other hand, and sighed as she secretly put the note into the top of her dress then leaned over and kissed Corey on the forehead. “I’ll be right back…I’ve got some bread in the oven and I don’t want it to burn.” She went into the kitchen and pulled out the note and hid it in a drawer until Bill came into the café again. As she opened the oven door, the aroma of the freshly baked bread made its way into the dining area. The noses of all the diners in attendance suddenly started sniffing, and taking in the wonderful fragrance. Taking the bread out of the loaf pans and sitting it out to cool, she went back to the dining area.

“Miss Sally,” one of the male diners about to finish his meal called out to her. “If you won’t marry Corey, how about me?” Which brought a laugh from the other diners, one of whom chimed in, “Or me.”

“Oh, you men…” she said laughing and blushing. “You’re all alike.”

“Hey,” the first man replied, “we just know a good woman when we see her, that’s all.”

“If you guys don’t stop, You’re going to give me the biggest head in this town.”

"No, we won't, Miss Sally," Corey said as he finished his meal and leaned onto the counter and looked at her. "You'll never be anything other than the warm, wonderful woman you are right now." He paid her for the stew and, tipping his hat to her, he left. She watched him leave and wondered what had triggered his current mood. Was he getting involved in something he shouldn't be?

"Only time will tell," she thought to herself.

Late that evening Bill went to the café for a late supper. "Hello, Marshal," Sally said when he walked in. "You're late this evening."

"I know. I was just finishing up the paperwork so I can transfer my prisoner to the New Mexico marshals tomorrow. It will be good to get rid of this guy. For some reason, he gives me a very unsettled feeling."

"Are you sure it's him that's doing it?"

"What else could it be?"

"I have no idea, Marshal. What can I get for you?"

"Somebody said you had made a pot of your stew…still got some left?"

"Of course."

"Great! I'll have a bowl of that and some of that fresh bread you baked."

"Coming right out," she said as she went back into the kitchen. A few minutes later she came back with his meal and put in on the counter in front of him with the note from Corey just sticking out enough that he could spot it. He picked up his napkin and stuck it into the collar of his shirt as he also tucked the note into his shirt pocket.

"I don't know how you do it, Miss Sally, but your food seems to taste better every time I come in here." He looked at her and smiled, making her slightly blush. Between Corey and him she had been doing a lot of that lately. Maybe there was something going on, after all it was springtime and just maybe Cupid had made a stop and started shooting some of his arrows in Rio Madre this year.

Bill went back to his office after eating his dinner and sat down at his desk. He began to shuffle through some of his papers using them to hide the note from Corey. As he began to read, he got a very uneasy feeling. *"I'm in. Herd in hidden canyon like you first guessed. Probably moving out tomorrow night. Not sure of route. Leader is Red Jackson. Also involved, Pecos Kid, Brooks and Ray Stewart...don't know who head honcho is yet. Will try to send more info if possible. Will try to ride drag and leave markers...if I can. All l know for now...Corey."* Corey was going to be out on the trail with a bunch of rustlers. Anything could happen, especially when they were near their destination. Over the years, Bill had heard too many stories about trail hands that had suddenly 'disappeared' right at the end of the drive, leaving their share of the take to be split between the other cowhands, or go right into the pocket of the rustlers' leader.

Chapter Thirteen

At dawn, Corey arrived at the cabin. He went inside and found the others waiting. "You ready to get to work?" Jackson asked him.

"More than ready…let's get to it."

"That's what I like…a man that's willing to work." Red looked around at the other men who suddenly decided that discretion was the better part of valor and headed out the door. He looked back at Corey and smiled. "Stick with Stewart, he'll show you where the herd is and what we need to do to get ready to pull out."

"You got it," Corey said as he followed the other men out.

A short time later the group rounded a bend and Corey could see the herd in a box canyon below them. He let out a low whistle and Stewart turned to look at him. "That's a nice haul," Corey said in supposed admiration.

"We've done pretty good. What we have to do now is to move them out of here and into another box canyon a little ways north. That's where we'll head out of tonight."

"Why two moves?"

"We want to try to get a definite head count and also make sure that we haven't missed any of the brands. If we move them in small groups we can do that."

"Makes sense," Corey said as he and Ray started down the hillside, following the others. A few minutes later Corey and Pecos had cut out a bunch of the herd and started moving them out as Ray started counting. Throughout the day the men continued to move the cattle from one canyon to another through a small gap in the mountain as they gathered a total head count. After the herd had been moved and settled in, the men were again at the cabin.

"That was good work today, Men," Red said as they finished their supper. "As you probably know by now, there's a storm moving in and I don't want to try to move this herd at night during a storm. We're going to give it one more night and hit the trail tomorrow night. Pecos, I want you and Corey to take shelter in that cave in the rocks above where we have the herd. You will be dry and fairly comfortable."

"Oh, come on, Red," Pecos said unhappily. "They ain't going anywhere."

"I'm giving the orders here, Pecos. The last thing we need is for the storm to spook them and cause them to break down the barriers and stampede out of there. Now, you'd both better get your stuff together and get up there before you end up in the worst of it and have to sit through the night in wet clothes. I checked out that cave a few days ago and there should be plenty of room for you and your horses."

"Come on, Pecos," Corey said, winking at him as they gathered up their stuff and headed out to the corral, saddled their horses and rode out.

"What was that all about, Red?" Ray asked. "Two of them aren't going to be able to stop a stampede."

"Maybe not," Red replied, "but I'm still not too sure about Hansen. I just feel like it will be better to have him up there than down here."

When they finally arrived at the cave, Corey began to bed down the horses in the back of the cave, while Pecos began gathering wood for a fire. He had thought about trying to hide a message in the cabin while everyone was asleep, but that didn't seem to be in the cards any more. He was going to have to find some other way to leave Bill a clue. Pecos had just finished bringing in another armload of wood and branches when the storm began to hit and within a few minutes it was coming down in 'buckets' and bolts of lightning began to light up the sky, followed by a thunderous booms. "Looks like I just made it," Pecos said as he spread out his bedroll. "I still don't know why Red sent us up here. If those critters do stampede there's not going to be a lot the two of us can do about it."

"At least we're dry," Corey said as he also spread out his bedroll and laid down by the fire facing the front of the cave.

"Yeah," said Pecos, "but it's not as dry and warm as that cabin is right now."

"I wouldn't be too sure about that," Corey said with a chuckle. "I noticed a couple of small holes in the roof…I'd bet they are already beginning to find the need to set out a few buckets, so to speak."

"Really? I hadn't noticed."

"That's one thing I learned growing up back in the mining camp. The first thing you do is check out the building you're in as soon as you walk in. I spotted those holes this morning, along with a few rotten boards in the roof that will probably start giving way to the water after a few minutes of this type of storm."

"How come you didn't say anything?"

"I already had my eye on a nice dry spot over in the corner far away from the bad areas and had planned on deciding to 'turn in early'. My guess is we're going to be a lot more comfortable here than they will be in that cabin tonight. By the way, I saw you with Sarah at the dance. We talked sometimes at the saloon. She's a nice girl, not to mention very pretty. I did ask her to the dance, but she told me she already had plans. You're a lucky guy."

"Thanks, she is pretty special…at least to me. Seems you did all right with your date."

"Yes, Peggy is pretty special too. I guess we're both kind of lucky." He laid down on his bedroll and put his hat over his face. "Night, Pecos."

"Night, Corey," Pecos said as he chuckled, thinking about the cabin and settled himself back for a good night's sleep.

The next morning, after a night of trying to stay dry in a leaky cabin, Red and the others met up with Corey and Pecos at the herd. "'Morning, boys," Red said as he rode up to Corey and Pecos, who were sitting on their horses at the temporary gates.

"Morning, Red," Pecos said. "How was your night?" He tried to keep a straight face, but couldn't help busting out into a big grin as he winked at Corey.

"Eventful," Red replied. "And yours?"

"Nice and comfy…we slept like babies."

Red let out a loud "Humpf," as he looked out at the herd. "They seem to have come through OK."

"Yep," Corey said. "We heard them getting a little restless one time, but they settled down pretty quick."

"OK…today we just hang out here or at what's left of the cabin." Corey and Pecos just looked at each other as Red continued. "Tonight, as soon as it gets dark we'll head out. There will be a full moon so we should be able to find our way without too much trouble. I want to take it nice and slow, with as little noise as possible. With any kind of luck, we'll be several miles from here by sunrise."

"What then, Boss?" Stewart asked.

"Then we carry on like any normal cattle drive. We'll get a few hours sleep and head out mid-morning. We won't have a full moon forever, so we'll have to chance traveling in the daylight."

"Joe, have you got the trail maps we'll need?"

"Sure thing, Boss. I've been through the maps at the land office. Told the manager I was thinking about buying some land north of town. He didn't pay much attention to what I was doing, so I had access to most every map he had. Was able to make some pretty good maps of my own."

"They'd better be accurate," Red said as he studied Brooks.

"They are. I know the location of all of the water holes and mileage between them."

"OK, Men," Red said, looking at everyone. "Get whatever rest you can… we've got a long, hard trek ahead of us. If we don't run into any obstacles, we should be in Wichita in about three weeks."

*****

Back in Rio Madre, Bill had had a restless night. The storm, along with worrying about Corey, had kept him from getting much sleep. He had tried to think of anything that he might have missed that would give him a lead as to where Corey and the others were, other than a hidden canyon in the Pecos Mountains. He began his morning rounds and decided to make a few stops along the way. Finally, he stopped at the hotel to see if he could get a status on Brooks, or Bailey, or whatever the guy's name was. "Morning, Wade," he said as he went into the hotel.

"Morning, Marshall. What can I do for you?"

"Just curious…I haven't seen one of your customers, Brooks, for a couple of days. He still here?"

"Let me see," Wade looked at his book and at the key slot for the room. "His key's here, but I haven't seen him since he went out yesterday morning. He's paid up until the end of the week, so I don't know if he's gone or not."

"Can I see his room?"

"Sure, Marshall. I guess that's all right, but I'll have to go with you. You do understand?"

"Of course, Wade…no problem. I just want to see if he's cleared his things out or not."

A couple of minutes later Wade unlocked the door to the room and they went inside. They found a few things still there, but it looked as if the majority of his things were gone. "Looks like he left just enough to make one think he might be coming back."

Bill went back to his office and sat down at his desk. His prisoner had finally been picked up by the New Mexico marshals early that morning. Better late than never he guessed. The only thing he had left to do right now was to think about Corey and what he had had let him get himself into. It wasn't that he didn't think Corey could handle himself, it was just that he, himself, had no control over the situation. If Corey got into trouble, he wouldn't be able to help him. "Oh, what the hell," he said to himself as he left the office, mounted his horse and headed out of town. Yes, he knew it was a gamble, but he wanted to see if there was any sign that the herd had moved out. A couple of hours later, Bill was in the vicinity of the mountains. There didn't seem to be any activity in the area other than a few jack rabbits that hopped away as soon as he got close to them. He continued north and hoped he would find some kind of sign left by Corey. Realizing that he should have come out here when he first came to town, and scoped out the area, he pulled his horse to a stop and just sat there. Knowing that there were canyons in these mountains, and actually mapping them out were two different things. Maybe he WAS getting too old for this job. He had studied that set of maps that he had in his office for hours over the past couple of weeks, but they really hadn't shown him what he needed to know. Whatever was hidden in those mountains wanted to stay that way. He couldn't help but feel that he was being watched and knew that he couldn't make any mistakes now…it might cost Corey his life. He rode around the area for a while longer, but, not finding anything, he headed back to town.

Hiding under an outcropping high in the rocks, Johnny Chambers, along with Ray, had been watching Bill. "Want to make a bet that I can pick him off from here?" Johnny asked as he raised his rifle to take aim, but Ray put a cautioning hand on his shoulder.

"Hold on, Johnny, we can't take a chance on having someone coming out here to look for him before we get the herd out of here."

"Aw, who's going to be looking…he doesn't have a deputy anymore."

"No…but he does have friends; and if he doesn't make it back to town, someone will come looking. I promise…you'll have your chance at him. Just give it a little time." The two rustlers settled back against the mountain wall and relaxed as they watched Bill turn his horse and head back toward Rio Madre.

Meanwhile, Corey had been on his own, watching the herd. He had always loved to whittle and now he had come up with an idea. He started whittling small arrows from some of the small branches that were near the 'corral'. As he finished each one, he dropped it into his saddlebag. He had also started to create a small figurine of a horse from a piece of a larger branch, just in case someone came up and asked what he was doing. As he worked on the horse, he thought of Peggy and the horse she had been riding that morning and subconsciously had begun replicating her horse into this figure. Now, he just hoped that he would have the chance to give it to her. When, and if, they reached Wichita, he would find some paint to finish his project. He just wished he had some now that he could use on the arrows…at least they might be a little more noticeable when he dropped them on the ground behind the herd as they headed out of the area. He looked around the area and realized that there were clay deposits in these mountains…red clay. With small amount of the clay, and a little water, he might be able to dye those arrows. He slowly pointed Sunny in the direction of some the red clay. Looking around to see if he was being watched, he dismounted, pulled a piece of hide out of his saddlebag, picked up some of the clay and wrapped it up in the hide. He then used the butt of his gun and, striking the hide several times, he broke the clay into fine, almost sand-like pieces and put them into a leather pouch he kept in his saddlebag. If anyone asked, he figured he would just tell them he was going to use it to dye the horse figure he had been carving for Peggy. He wasn't sure if they would find any more deposits along the way and might as well get a supply while he could.

Using the piece of hide, he put a small amount of the clay onto the hide and added a spoonful of water. He rubbed the mixture together and dipped three of the arrows into it. He smiled as he realized he had guessed right and the arrows were now a dull red instead of white. It didn't take them but a few seconds to dry in the heat of the afternoon sun. He then carefully dropped them back into his saddlebag.

*****

When Bill got back to his office he pulled out the regional maps he had and started reviewing them again. If he was going to catch the guys in the act he would have to come up with a plan to catch up to them while they were on the trail, but still in the general vicinity. How he was going to find them, at least right now, he had no idea. As he reviewed the maps he realized he would have to start thinking like a rustler instead of a lawman. "If I had a herd I needed to move from the Pecos Mountains to Wichita, which way would I go?" He asked himself. As he studied the maps, with a pencil, he lightly drew a straight line from the mountains to Wichita. He knew the closest river was the Red River but it ran east to west, he would need to find where they would be able to find water. Waterholes? Yes, there would be some available, but none were noted on his maps. He sat back in his chair and thought for several minutes. As he sat there he saw Ken Harris ride by his office. "Oh, what the heck," he said as he got up and left the office. When he got outside he saw Ken coming out of the mercantile. "Mr. Harris…" he called out to him.

Ken heard him and waited as he approached. "Marshal…what can I do for you?"

"Do you have a few minutes? I would like to talk with you in my office."

"Sure…I don't know why not."

The two went into Bill's office and Ken could see the maps laid out all over the office. "Looks like you've been busy."

"You might say that," Bill said to him. "I was wondering if you could point out the route your herds usually take to go to the market in Wichita."

"OK…" Ken started pointing out the usual route that his men would take.

"What about waterholes?"

"If we're lucky, there are several along the way." He pointed to different areas on the map as Bill marked the locations. "Sounds as if you're onto something," Ken said as he watched how Bill was studying the maps.

"Maybe…I've got a feeling that whoever these rustlers are, they're going to be heading out soon."

"Any particular reason?"

"Well, for one, nobody has come in complaining about losing any stock."

"There's got to be more to it than that."

"OK, Mr. Harris…I'm going to trust you with something. But what I'm going to tell you can't go out of this office….and I mean to anyone."

"You've got my word, Marshal."

"I've got a source on the inside that has been trying to feed me status reports. I've got an idea of the general location where they're holed up, but going in there to get them would be foolhardy. I've got to wait until they're on the move."

"Is this 'source' reliable?"

"Unquestionably."

Ken thought for a few seconds and started putting two and two together. "Oh, God…that business between you and Corey…it was a setup to try and get him on the inside," he said almost whispering. "And the things I had started think about that kid. Peggy tried to tell me I was wrong about him….but...I owe him a big apology."

"Save that until we get him out of this. If they get any kind of a notion that he's not for real…he's dead."

"I know. Don't worry, Marshal, I won't breathe a word of it to anyone."

"Good…look, Mr. Harris…"

"Come on, Marshall…I think it's time you called me 'Ken', don't you?"

Bill smiled and let out his breath, "All right, Ken…I know I can't do this on my own and I'm going to need help when it comes down to making my play."

"You can definitely count on me."

"I'll let you know when I'm ready to make my move…just be as ready as you can be. It may be sooner than you think."

"How many of my men will you need?"

"Everyone available at the time. Like I said it's going to have to be a surprise…to everyone. I haven't been able to contact Corey for a couple of days, so I'm just going to have to go with my gut feeling. Just be ready when you see me coming."

"Don't you worry, Marshal…Bill…I wouldn't want anything to happen to Corey. Peggy would never forgive me." He smiled then turned and left the office.

Bill got to his feet and went to the stove to get a cup of coffee. As he took a sip, he remembered that first pot of coffee that Corey had made and smiled. He just hoped that they would be able to laugh about that again…sometime. "Stop it, Bill," he said to himself. "He will be fine… just keep thinking positive…"

*****

The rustlers had managed to get some rest during the day and after dark they began to move the herd out of the canyon. Red and Ray were near the front of the herd on either side, as the others spread out behind them. Corey was bringing up the rear. Much to his delight, since he was the new kid, he had been selected to ride drag, making sure that no stragglers were left behind. It was a dusty job, but it gave Corey the opportunity he had hoped for. A couple of hours into the ride he leaned over as if to pet Sunny on his shoulder, but actually he dropped one of the arrows onto the ground. He tried to drop it straight down…hoping it was going to point in the right direction. They continued on through the night and a slow, steady pace. Just as the sun was beginning to make its appearance, they approached the first water hole. They settled the herd down for a few hours, giving the men and animals some needed rest before they got ready to move out again. By now they were a little over fifteen miles from the canyon. "We made good time last night, men," Red said as they started to break camp late that morning. "I want to make at least another fifteen miles today, more if possible. I know it will be pushing it, but I want to get as far away from that canyon as I can before we start to breathe easy. I want to keep on the move until right before dark. We'll camp tonight and head out again before dawn." He heard some grumbling from some of the men but they all pulled together and were able to break camp and get back on the trail within a few minutes. For the rest of the day they actually made good time covering almost seventeen miles by sundown. The steers had cooperated and they hadn't had to slow down to chase after the occasional mavericks that would try to break away from the herd. They made camp that night alongside a small river where they could water the stock and replenish their own water supply.

Chapter Fourteen

At dawn the next morning, Bill was thinking about Corey's last message. With the storm that hit, they would probably have been delayed…now…they must be on the trail by now. If he was going to find them he had to move now. He grabbed some hardtack and jerky out of his desk, went to the stable, saddled his horse and headed out. A couple of hours later he rode up to the Harris Ranch. Ken was leaning on the corral watching some of his men work with some new horses and turned when he heard someone riding up. When he saw the look on Bill's face he knew it was time. "All of you men…come here," he said calling out to them. As they gathered around him he explained. "OK, Men, I want you to get your horses and gear together we're going to join the marshal in a little 'operation'. Sam, have the cook put together provisions for us for at least three days." Ken went into the house and explained to Peggy that they were going with the Marshal to look for the rustlers. A short time later the men had their horses and a pack horse saddled, and were waiting for instructions.

"I know you are probably wondering what is going on," Bill said to them. "We're going to try to catch some rustlers…now hold up your right hands." The men responded and Bill continued, "By the authority invested in me by the town of Rio Madre, I deputize all of you until this 'operation' as Mr. Harris coined it, is finished. Now let's go." The seven men all mounted their horses and headed toward the Pecos Mountains.

As they approached the mountain range, Bill turned to Ken. "From what you showed me on the maps, you usually go further east. Have you ever taken your herds through this particular area?"

"Only once," Ken said. "We usually do take a route about twenty miles east of here, but there had been range fire that took away most of the grazing that we needed, so we came this way. There are not as many waterholes or grazing on this route either. That's why we prefer the other way."

Bill looked at him for a few seconds. "Let's head north and see if we can pick up their trail." Ken nodded and they rode on. Three hours and several miles later, they had not yet picked up any sign of the rustled herd. After the storm that had passed through a couple of days ago, Bill had hoped that the trail would be easy to follow, but the ground was hard. "There has to be something…some kind of sign…" Bill thought. They rode on for a few miles and began to see signs that a herd might have been through there within the past couple of days. "This has to be them," Ken said as he studied the hard ground. "I know none of the ranchers are running any of their cattle through here."

The group headed out again after a short break for lunch and to rest the horses. A little while later Bill brought the group to a stop when thought he saw something on the ground. He got off his horse and picked up a small reddish piece of wood roughly shaped like an arrow. Showing it to Ken, he began to smile. "Corey. It has to be him. I used to see him whittling on pieces of wood when things were slow. He's showing us the way." Bill mounted his horse and they began following the trail in earnest.

For the rest of the day the posse followed the trail of the cattle that led to the first waterhole. They could see where the men had camped. "I don't know if we're gaining ground on them or not," Bill said to Ken.

"They must have been travelling all night to have gotten this far," Ken replied. "And we did spend a lot of time just trying to pick up the trail."

"I know."

"Don't worry, Bill. We'll catch up to them. Normally you can make good time for the first day or two, but then the animals and men start to get tired. They'll slow down and we'll catch them. Right now, there isn't a lot of grazing opportunities, so they're going to have to keep moving pretty fast until they can slow down and let the herd graze and gain back some of the weight they will lose the first few days. They're also going to stay on the trail as much as possible to put as many miles between us and them as they can. What they don't know, is that we're already on their trail. My guess is we'll catch up with them tomorrow. We just have to refrain from pushing ourselves too hard. Fatigue causes mistakes…and mistakes get you killed!"

"OK," Bill said, "let's camp here and we'll head out at dawn."

The next morning the posse broke camp and headed out at dawn. There were a few times that they thought they had lost the trail, but about mid-morning one of Ken's men spotted something on the ground. "Hey, Marshal," he said as he dismounted. "Is this another one of those arrows?"

"Yes, it is," Bill said as he took the arrow from him. "Good eye, Cal." He looked at Ken. "We're on the right trail. Let's go!

*****

The herd had reached another one of the waterholes on Joe's map and they had stopped for a needed rest. Red was looking over the map with Joe. "Where's the next waterhole, Joe?"

"That's the problem, Boss….there's quite a gap between this one and the next. I suggest we take a few extra hours here and let the herd drink as much as they can. My guess is that we won't hit the next waterhole until about noon the day after tomorrow….going at our current pace, that is."

"That pace is going to slow down with no water. We can't push them as hard." He looked at the herd, most of it was just standing around. "Ok… Joe, I did hear what you said, but there's still a couple of hours of daylight and they look like they've got their fill. Let's get on the move and then make camp at sunset." The men got on their horses and headed the herd out again.

At sundown, they made camp again and tried to get a good night's sleep. The next morning they were breaking camp just before dawn when Red called out for Pecos. "Pecos…I want you to backtrack a few miles…see if we have any 'shadows'."

"Come on, Boss….." He stopped as Red glared at him. "OK, OK…I'll go. I'll try to catch back up with you by noon."

"You do that," Red replied a little sarcastically and watched as Pecos mounted his horse and headed back the way they had come. He then turned to the rest of his men. "We won't be hitting any waterholes until late tomorrow, so keep the herd going at a steady pace, but don't push them the way we have been. That's why I sent Pecos back. If someone is following, they'll have a better chance of catching up and I want to be ready for them." The men finished packing up their stuff and went to saddle their horses.

Corey was more than a little apprehensive about Pecos going back to check the trail. About an hour before they made camp the night before, he had dropped his third arrow. He could only hope that Pecos would be looking ahead, and not at the ground, and didn't spot it. Nobody had asked him about his whittling, and of that he was glad. But if Pecos found the arrow, he would have a pretty good idea where it came from. And that wouldn't be good.

As Pecos retraced their trail, he was thinking about Sarah and how he was beginning to wish that he hadn't gotten involved with Red and his bunch. He could be with Sarah right now…they would probably be just waking up after a night of lovemaking. Instead, he was out here in the middle of nowhere looking for 'shadows' that might be following them. He rode for a couple hours and then decided to rest for awhile. He was near a ridgeline and headed his horse toward the top to see if he could get a good vantage point to wait, and watch, before he headed back to the herd. When he reached the top, he stopped got off his horse. There was some sweet grass there, so he let his horse graze while they both rested. After an hour or so, he was getting ready to head back when he spotted riders in the distance. He realized he had not brought a telescope with him, so he couldn't make out who they were, and he didn't want to wait around to find out. He mounted his horse and headed back to the herd. When he finally caught up with Red and the others, he made his report. "I caught sight of some riders. They're probably a couple of hours behind us. I came back here as fast as I could after I spotted them."

Red thought for a moment. "You don't have any idea who they were?"

"No. I didn't want to wait around until I could see them up close and then have them see me. I thought it would be best to get back here and let you know."

"There's not much we can do about it right now. I know I said to slow down the pace today, but we can't take a chance at them catching up to us yet."

"Ray!!" He called out and Ray rode over to them. "Do your maps note anywhere that we could set up an ambush of our own? Seems there are some riders headed this way. We don't know if they're after us or not, but I don't want to take any chances."

"There's a pass through the hills a few miles ahead. If we can get the herd through it, we might be able to set up a trap at the other end."

"Good thinking. Let's get these cattle moving. We have to get through that pass before those riders catch up to us…assuming they're following 'US'. OK, Men…." he called out, "…let's get these doggies moving." The men started hollering and pushing the herd forward and at a quicker pace.

Corey wasn't liking this one bit. He hadn't heard the conversation that Red, Ray and Pecos were having, but picking up this kind of pace had to mean that Pecos had spotted something. A few miles further on and the herd entered a narrow pass in the mountain range. Corey realized what it could mean. If there was someone following…especially if it was Marshal Raines and a posse, they would be sitting ducks. Corey took his regular position at the rear of the herd and tried to drop another arrow, pointing backwards this time. He just hoped they would see it. Luckily the men were more interested in keeping the herd moving and picking out a spot for an ambush than watching what Corey was doing.

The herd finally reached the end of the pass where it opened up onto a vast grassy plain. After a day of not much to eat, the herd was more interested in trying to graze than moving forward. That was probably just as well, Red was thinking. At least they wouldn't be straying away while his men set up an ambush, just in case it was a posse coming after them. As they were setting up their defenses, Red couldn't help but wonder, if it was a posse, how they knew they were here. Sure, 500 head of cattle is going to leave some kind of sign, but how did they know when they were leaving. There had to be a leak somewhere. Only three of the men had been in town right before they got ready to move out, Pecos, Brooks, and Hansen. He pretty much knew he could trust Pecos and Brooks, but Hansen…he just wasn't sure. He knew the marshal had been snooping around the area, and he also knew that he didn't find anything. If these men following them were not members of a posse, no harm. But if it came to the fact that it was a posse after them…he figured he knew who to blame…and he wouldn't let him get away with it.

A couple of hours later the posse neared the mountain pass and pulled their horses to a stop at the entrance to the pass. They could see that the tracks of the cattle led right into the pass. They could also see that anyone following them would be sitting ducks. "Ken, do you know the area well enough to know if there is another way around..."

"I think there's a route several miles east of here, around the base of the mountain, but it's going to take time. We'd catch up with them, just south of the Oklahoma border."

"Time for them to gain a lot of time on us," Bill said, leaning his forearm on the saddle horn. He began looking around and spotted something on the ground a few yards in front of them. Getting off his horse he walked over and found one of Corey's arrows, only this time it was pointing away from the canyon. He took it back to Ken. "Corey's left us a warning."

"They know we're following them," Ken agreed.

"And if they know…" Bill just let the thought hang there for a moment.

"Bill, I don't think we have a choice. We have to go around the long way. I would much rather take them on when we're on open range, than in tight quarters."

"You're right, Ken. OK, Men…let's ride." The group turned east and headed around the mountains.

Chapter Fifteen

A few hours later, Red and his men realized that the riders were not coming through the pass. He signaled for everyone to go back to the herd. "Sorry, Boss," Pecos said. "I guess it wasn't a posse after all."

"Don't be sorry. You did what you were supposed to do. Now let's get out of here…we've still got a lot of daylight left." The men went back to their horses, mounted and headed the herd northeast.

The delay had actually enabled the posse to make up some of the time they would have lost circumventing the mountain. It was almost dark when they again picked up the trail of the herd. Cal got down from his horse and to get a good look at the tracks. "They're pretty fresh, I'd say we're only a few miles behind them," he told his boss as he got back onto his horse.

"It's going to be dark soon," Bill said. "I would rather not get into a shootout in the dark. I say we get as close as we can and hit them as they're breaking camp in the morning." Ken and the others nodded in agreement and they continued their chase. An hour later, the posse hit signs that the herd was probably only a couple of miles ahead of them and decided to bed down for the night. "Ok, men. No campfire tonight. We're close enough that we don't want them spotting the light."

That night, Corey had been on the second watch as they kept an eye on the herd, and finally got back into bed about 2:00 am. He went to sleep quickly, considering how tired he was. Even growing up in a mining camp, he had no idea how strenuous it was to be a drover. He had been asleep for a little while when he began dreaming about Peggy. He didn't know why, but it seemed like he was riding toward her, but could never close the distance, no matter how hard he rode. She wasn't moving, but he just couldn't get to her. He suddenly woke up and found himself drenched in sweat. Realizing it was just a dream, he settled back down and soon fell into a restless sleep. Daylight came all too soon, for Corey. He felt as if he had not gotten any rest at all. He went about his business and then went to saddle Sunny. "Hi, Big Fellow," he said as he rubbed Sunny's muzzle and stroked the forelock. "Going to be another long day, I guess," Sunny bobbed his golden head up and down and nuzzled Corey's pockets for any treats. "Sorry, Pal. I don't have anything right now, but I promise, I'll get you a whole bushel of carrots when we reach the next town....OK?" Again, Sunny bobbed his head and softly nickered. Corey chuckled and proceeded to finish saddling his horse.

The men were just getting ready to mount their horses and head for the herd when they heard Bill call out, "EVERYBODY JUST STAY RIGHT WHERE YOU ARE!!!" For a split second the rustlers did just that. Red looked around and saw that Bill was wearing a badge. He realized that the men that had been following them was a posse, and now they had caught up with them. He looked over at Corey, who was standing beside Sunny a few feet away from him. He had his gun out and pointed at Red.

"So, Hansen...you weren't one of us after all. I didn't think so."

"Just button it," Bill said as he walked over to Pecos, who was the closest to him and took his gun from its holster. The rustlers were all looking at Red to see what to do as one of Ken's men went to get Red's gun. Red wasn't about to let that happen and swung around grabbing the man and throwing him to the side as he went for his own gun. As he did that his men all, except for Pecos, dove to the ground and tried to draw their guns, but Bill and the posse were ready and began to fire, trying to disarm instead of kill. When Corey saw what Red had done, he dove for him and the two men began rolling around on the ground struggling for the gun. Seconds later, Corey thought he had Red's gun hand under control, but Red shifted his weight and was able to bring his gun hand down and all anyone heard, was the muffled blast of Red's 45. He slowly got to his feet and feigning being hurt, tried to turn and fire at Bill. Ken realized what he was doing and fired his gun, dropping Red to the ground where he stayed, not moving. Within seconds, everything stopped. The rustlers had been contained and when Bill looked around he saw Corey lying on the ground. In shock, Bill ran to him and knelt down. He lifted Corey into his arms and saw the red stain spreading on his chest. "Corey….." he whispered.

"Sorry, Marshal…thought I could take him," Corey gasped. "There's someone else…giving orders…don't know who. See…that Peggy…gets Sunny…tell Peggy…she's special…" Corey relaxed back into Bill's arms as his eyes slowly closed.

"Oh, God, Corey…" Bill said as he sat on the ground holding Corey's lifeless body in his arms. He didn't even look up as Ken walked over and put his hand on Bill's shoulder.

"Bill…I'm sorry. Why don't you let me take care of him?"

"No," Bill said softly. "I let him go through with this…it's my responsibility. I'll take care of him." He gently laid Corey back on the ground and placed a blanket over him. The rest of the posse began gathering up the survivors of the shoot-out. The men in the posse had all survived with nothing more than a couple of flesh wounds, but Pecos and Johnny were the only rustlers that survived. The deceased rustlers were buried there, but Bill insisted that he was going to take Corey home and give him 'proper' burial with his friends surrounding him. After he had wrapped Corey in the blanket and placed him on Sunny, Ken came over to him. Look Bill, let's take the prisoners and Corey home and my men will bring the herd back. I'll take care of contacting the other ranchers and making arrangements to figure out which steers belong to who."

Bill just nodded as he got on his horse. "Marshal," Pecos said, "I'm sorry about Corey. I really liked him. He was a good man." Bill just nodded, took Sunny's reins, and turned his horse toward home. He knew it would be a long ride, even longer under the circumstances.

Thirty-six hours later Bill and Ken rode into Rio Madre with the prisoners and Corey. Ken took Pecos and Johnny to the jail while Bill led Sunny over the undertaker's office. Horace Tanner had been the undertaker in Rio Madre for several years and he never found his job easy, especially when the 'victim' was someone he knew. He was sixty years old and had grey hair and green eyes. He had been in his office when he saw Bill ride up and he got up to go out and meet him. When

Horace saw Sunny, he realized who Bill was bringing to him. "Oh no, not Corey," he said to himself as he walked over to Bill who had slowly gotten off his horse and was beginning to untie the ropes holding Corey onto the saddle.

9/25/14

"Marshal, let me take care of him now."

"No, he's my responsibility..."

"Marshal...please...let me do this. Go over to your office and I will let you know when I've finished. Just let me know what arrangements you want to make and I will take care of it." He knew how much Corey meant to Bill and would do anything for either of them. This was one funeral that he was going to make sure that everything was perfect. Sure, it wasn't one of his duties, but in this case, he was going to make sure it was. He watched as Bill turned and went back to his office. He pointed to a couple of the men standing nearby to help him get Corey inside. "Hank," he pointed to another man, "take Corey's horse over to the livery stable and tell Abe to give him the best grain he has." Hank took Sunny's reins and started to lead him away, but Sunny tried to stay where he was, and softly neighed as Corey was taken from him.

"It's all right, Fella," Hank said as he stroked the horse's neck. "We'll take good care of him." He was finally able to turn Sunny away and lead him toward the livery stable.

When Bill got back to his office Ken was waiting for him. "They're locked up tight in one of the cells," he told Bill.

"Thanks, Ken...for everything. You'd better get back to the ranch and let Peggy know what's happened. Tell her how sorry I am."

"We're all sorry, Bill. Corey was a good man."

"Oh, by the way, tell Peggy that he wanted her to have Sunny, his horse. He also said that she was 'special'."

"I'll tell her, Bill. I'll make arrangements to get Sunny after the funeral."

"That'll be tomorrow morning, about ten, I guess," Bill said. "There are some things I need to take care of this afternoon."

"Peggy and I will both be here."

"I know Corey would be pleased..." Bill's voice broke as he turned and sat down at his desk. Ken hesitated for a moment then left the office.

A few minutes later, Sally came into Bill's office. She stopped cold as she saw the way he was sitting there looking at Corey's deputy badge. "Stop it, Marshal. He wouldn't want you to do this to yourself. He knew what he was doing. He knew the dangers."

"I shouldn't have let him..."

"Do you really think you could have stopped him? The way I hear it, it was his idea to try to work his way into the gang."

"I'm the marshal, I didn't have to go along with it."

"Marshal...Bill, Corey loved his job...loved working with you. All you have to remember is that...nothing else. You were both just doing your jobs."

"And what did it get us...?"

"Well, from what I heard, you got the rustlers...two of them are in your jail."

"It wasn't worth Corey's life."

"Dammit, Bill. Corey thought it was worth it! And that's what counts... whether you like it or not. How do you think he would feel right now if he heard you talking like this? I happen to think he'd be pretty pissed off at you."

An hour later, after Sally left, Bill finally got up and went to the church to see Father Michael. "Hello, Father," he said as he entered the church and walked up to the priest who was just coming down the aisle, heading for the door.

"Hello, Marshal. I heard about what happened to your deputy and I was just on my way to see you to extend my condolences."

"Thank you, Father. As far as I know, Corey doesn't have any relatives near here and I want to make the arrangements for his service, tomorrow morning about ten a.m. if possible."

"Of course, Marshal. Would you like a church service or a graveside service?"

"I think a graveside service is what he would have wanted."

"Do you want him to rest here in our cemetery or do you have another site in mind?"

"I think here, Father. He was well-liked in Rio Madre and I think he would like to be where his friends could visit him."

"Would you like to go choose a location?"

"Of course, if you don't mind."

"Of course not…please follow me, Marshal." Bill let Father Michael proceed him as they left the church and walked to the adjacent cemetery."

As they looked around, Bill saw a spot beneath a large willow tree. He began walking toward the area. He stopped just beneath the outer branches. "Would this be OK, Father? I think Corey would like this."

"I agree with you, Marshal, this location would be perfect. I will make arrangements for everything to be ready for tomorrow morning."

"Thank you, Father," Bill said sadly, and slowly turned and left the cemetery as the priest watched him walk away.

Late that afternoon, Bill was at his desk trying to finally fill out the report on what had happened when Sarah knocked at the door. He got up to see who it was and then opened it. "Hello, Sarah."

"Hello, Marshal. Would it be all right if I went in and talked with Pecos?"

"Sure, I guess so." He looked at her closely.

"Don't worry, Marshal, I'm not concealing a gun, or anything. I just want to talk to him. I love him."

"All right, Sarah, but I will have to leave the door open, and he is in there with another prisoner."

"I understand…I just want to talk to him."

Bill opened the inner door to the cells and escorted her to the middle cell. "Pecos…you have a visitor."

Pecos had been lying on one of the cots and got to his feet when he saw Sarah. "Sarah…what are you doing here?"

"I had to come, Pecos. I had to make sure you were okay…especially after Corey…" her voice choked for a moment.

"I know, Sarah. I liked Corey too. We didn't know each other for very long, but I could tell he was a good kid…I truly wish things had turned out different."

"You're good, too, Pecos. I know you are."

"If I was so 'good', I wouldn't have let myself get in with that bunch."

"Why did you do it, Pecos?"

"They promised a quick pay-off at the end of the job. I was hoping to get enough to get you out of that saloon and maybe get us a small spread of our own somewhere."

"You mean…?"

"Yes, Sarah, I want to marry you, but now, all I've done is ended up in jail."

"Don't worry, Pecos, I will still be here waiting for you when you get out, and we will get that little 'spread' you want. I know we will."

"I love you, Sarah."

"I love you too, Pecos," she said as she leaned toward the cell bars and they kissed.

"I'm sorry, Miss Sarah," Bill said as he stood in the door. "Your time's up. But you can come visit him again tomorrow."

"Thank you, Marshal. Goodbye, Pecos, I'll come again tomorrow."

"Goodbye, Sarah…" he said as he watched her leave. "Thanks, Marshal," he called out to Bill, who nodded his head and then closed the door. Bill walked Sarah to the door and opened it for her.

"I'm real sorry about Corey, Marshal. I liked him a lot."

"Thank you, Miss Sarah," he said as she turned walked toward the saloon.

Chapter Sixteen

After a restless night, Bill dragged himself out of bed the next morning, dreading what was going to happen that day. He hadn't eaten anything the night before, even when Sally had brought him his supper and given him a lecture about not taking care of himself. But he couldn't eat… Maybe after the services this morning, but not yet, not now. He just hoped he could make it through everything. He heard a knock at the door and opened it to find Sally there with breakfast for his prisoners. "Good morning, Marshal."

"Right this way," he said motioning for her to come inside and watched as she sat the tray on the desk.

"I don't suppose you ate anything last night."

"I wasn't very hungry."

"You know, the least you could do is try, seeing all the trouble I went through to prepare it just right for you."

"I do apologize for my thoughtlessness. Now, if you will excuse me, I need to take this to my prisoners and get ready for a burial."

"Look, Bill, I am sorry about Corey. I really did like him, and I need to go get ready for the services too. I'll see you there."

Bill nodded as he opened the door and watched her head back to the café. He checked the tray then took it back to the prisoner area. "OK, gentlemen…step back…" he watched as they did as instructed and he passed the tray through the opening in the bars.

"Thanks, Marshal," Pecos said as he stepped forward, picked up the tray and placed it on the cot.

"I'll be back for the tray in a little while," Bill said as he closed the inner door and went back to his desk.

In the cell, Pecos and Johnny began to eat their breakfast. "You're sure gettin' chummy with that Marshal," Johnny said to Pecos.

"Look, Corey was a good kid…I liked him. Under different circumstances, I think we could have been good friends."

"Yeah…well all I know, is I'm gonna bust out of here the first chance I get. And if I can take care of that Marshal in the process…well, I'll like that even more."

"Come on, Johnny, right now we're not looking at a long stint in prison… we could get off with a year or two. Just don't make things worse than they already are."

Johnny lowered his voice, "Well…Red said that there was someone else involved in this, someone giving him orders. I'll bet whoever it is won't let us rot in no stinking prison."

"Why not? All he would do is give himself away. We just need to stay put and keep our mouths shut. You start spouting off and someone will stick a gun through that window up there and we won't have to worry about jail time." Johnny just glared at Pecos and took another bite of the biscuit he had been eating.

It was 9:30 a.m. when Bill headed to the undertaker's office to accompany the coffin to the cemetery. Horace met Bill at the door and stood back to let him have some time alone with Corey before the coffin was sealed. He had dressed Corey in the suit he had worn for the dance and had made sure that everything was 'just so'. He had visited Corey's room at the boarding house to get the suit and found a photo that had obviously been taken of Corey's mother. Knowing how much Corey had loved his mother, he had placed that photo in Corey's hand, as if he were holding it against his chest. A few minutes later he stepped back inside and told Bill that he would need a couple more minutes and then they would leave. Bill almost shivered as he felt a cold chill go through him. A chill that he figured he would probably have forever.

It was exactly 10:00 a.m. when the coffin bearing Corey's body arrived at the cemetery and was placed next to the grave. Many of the townsfolk were there, including Sally and Sarah, in fact the saloon had been closed for the morning and the entire staff was present. Also present, were Peggy, her father, and the ranch hands that had been with the posse. Abe was there as well, and he had brought Sunny, knowing that above all else, Corey would want him there too. Once everyone had solemnly greeted each other, Father Michael began his ceremony. He spoke about how Corey was loved by his friends and that although his death had been difficult for those around him, he had died doing what he believed in. When he was finished, he asked if anyone had anything to say. Bill wanted to, but at that moment, he didn't think he would be able to get through it, so he just shook his head. Father Michael then stepped back as Peggy walked over and placed a single red rose on the coffin and stepped back. The designated pall bearers gently lowered the coffin into the grave as those present began to return to their homes or businesses. Bill left the cemetery with the others and stopped beside Abe. He took Sunny's reins and led him over to Peggy. "Peggy," Bill said sadly, "Corey's last request was that he wanted you to have Sunny. He also said to tell you that you were very special to him."

"Thank you, Marshal," Peggy said as she choked back a sob and took Sunny's reins, then gently stroked his muzzle. "I will treasure him."

"I know you will." As they left, Bill walked back into the cemetery and stood, leaning against the willow tree as he watched the men slowly shovel the soil back into the grave, again feeling the chill. He stayed there until they had finished and left the area, not wanting to leave Corey behind.

"You know, I didn't realize how much the people around here liked me," Corey said to Bill as he appeared beside him. "I'm glad that Peggy agreed to take care of Sunny." Bill jumped away from the voice.

"Corey…how…what...you're dead!!!?"

"Yep…seems that I am."

"What are you doing here? Aren't you supposed to be in Heaven, or wherever it is that a person's spirit goes?"

"I guess I could be, but, I didn't want to go right now. Got some unfinished business."

"What do you mean 'unfinished business'?"

"Got to find out who was behind this whole thing."

Bill suddenly realized that he could see right through Corey. He had taken just about as much as he could at that point and slowly sat down on the ground and leaned up against the tree. "But we got them all."

"Nope…there was someone else giving Red the orders."

"And you know this?"

"I heard them talking. Now we just have to find out who that person is."

"We?"

"Sure…last I heard, I was still a deputy when I died…guess I still am. Unless you want to fire me again?"

"You know that was just a ploy….oh, what am I saying? I must have lost my mind, I'm sitting here talking to a…ghost?"

Corey sat down beside him. "Yep…I'm a ghost, and you're not losing your mind. Oh, by the way, you're the only one that can hear, or see me."

"I'm the only one…Oh, God."

"By the way, he said to say 'hello'. He likes you. And he said that I could stay as long as I needed so I could see this through to the end. And, so I could convince you that this was not your fault."

"So, you intend to haunt me for the rest of my life. I guess that's an appropriate punishment."

"I wouldn't exactly say that 'haunt' was the appropriate word, but I guess it will do for now. Only you're not the one I'm really going to haunt."

"And that would be the rustlers' boss."

"Yep…and maybe your prisoners. Who knows what they'll spill if they think they're not 'alone' in there."

"Look, Corey…you can't just…"

"Why not?"

"Because…I don't know…just because…it wouldn't be right."

"And what they did was right? Now, why don't we get back to the office and get started." Corey got to his feet and watched as Bill just sat there. "Uh, Marshal, I think we should go now."

9/29/14

Bill looked up at Corey and shakily got to his feet. "Oh, by the way, my clothes and stuff," Corey said as he started walking away, "why don't you give them to Father Michael so he can give them to someone who needs them. And the ring and locket of my mother's that's in my saddlebags…. just hang on to them for now. I'll let you know what to do with them later." Bill started following Corey back toward the office and watched as he slowly faded from sight. He finally got back to his office and went back to the cells to check on the prisoners. Both of them appeared to be asleep. The breakfast tray had been pushed through the opening in the bars. He checked the tray and found nothing missing so he took it back to his office, figuring he would take it back to Sally when he went to pick up the lunch for his prisoners. Bill couldn't help looking over at Corey's desk and realized that when Abe brought his saddlebags to him, he had placed them on the desk. He walked over and picked up the bags and took them to his desk. As he opened the bags and looked inside, he found the two remaining arrows that Corey had whittled to leave for markers. He carefully wrapped them in a handkerchief and placed them in his desk. He also found the small horse that Corey had been carving for Peggy. He wasn't quite sure what to do with it when he heard Corey's voice again. "I was making that for Peggy. Supposed to be her horse. Guess I won't get to finish it now."

Again, Bill jumped at the sound of his voice. "I guess I wasn't hallucinating after all."

"Nope…it's me." Corey went over and sat down at his desk and put his feet up.

"You planning on just sitting there and getting on my nerves?"

"Not really. Thought I might hang out back there while our visitors are having lunch. Just to see what they're thinking." Both of them looked around when they heard a knock at the door.

When Bill unlocked the door, he was surprised to find Mrs. Mason there. "Hello, Marshal," she said, "could I come in and talk with you for a few minutes?"

"Of course…" he stepped aside and let her enter, then pulled up a chair in front of his desk and held it for her as she sat down. "What can I do for you?"

"I was just wondering what to do with Corey's things. You know he was staying at my boarding house?"

"Yes, Ma'am. I was going to talk with you about that tomorrow. Would you mind packing his things for me? I just don't know if I could do that right now."

"Of course, Marshal. I'm so glad that you two were not mad at each other after all. I hear he was really trying to help you catch those bad men."

"Yes…he <u>died</u> helping me do that." Bill got up and walked over to Corey's desk and leaned back against the front of it as Corey just leaned back, smiling at him. Changing the subject back to why she was there, Bill continued, "when you're packing his things, if you would just put all of his clothes together and anything else, pack it separately, then have someone bring it over here. I will take it from there."

"I would be glad to, Marshal. Did you get all of those awful men? I mean, I don't like the idea of having men like that running loose around here."

"Don't you worry, Mrs. Mason, I don't think you will be in any danger. We got the whole bunch. The one's that survived are locked up tight in a cell, right back there," he said, pointing toward the door.

"Oh, that's a relief. Thank you, Marshal. I will get Corey's things packed up and sent over here this afternoon."

"Thank you again, Mrs. Mason. Oh, by the way, Corey always spoke highly of you. I know he would appreciate any help you could give right now."

"God bless you, Marshal," Molly said as she got to her feet and waited while Bill unlocked the door and then closed it behind her.

"The old bat," Corey said as Bill turned back around. "The only thing she wants is to get my stuff out of there so she can rent out the room again."

"Now, is that anyway to talk about a nice woman like that?"

"Hummpf," was all that Corey said. "Oh, she's nice enough, I guess. Just seemed like she was always thinking about money."

"Think about it, Corey, she doesn't have any way to support herself except for the rooms she rents out. She doesn't have a husband to do that for her anymore."

"Yeah…I guess you're right."

In the cells, Pecos and Johnny had picked up on the 'conversation', but they could only hear Bill's part of it. "Who is he talking to? I thought I heard him say 'Corey'?" Johnny asked raising up on one elbow as he laid on the cot.

"Beats me," said Pecos. "Maybe he's losing it." He continued lying there on his back with his hat across his eyes.

"That might just be what it takes to get us out of here."

"What?"

"Convince a judge he's crazy and they'll let us go."

"You're forgetting one small thing, Johnny…he wasn't the only one on that posse. I seem to remember at least 5 other men there."

"Yeah…I guess. All I know is, they're not going to keep me in here."

"Well…you do what you have to. I'm going to stay right here and pay my dues. It won't do Sarah any good if I get myself killed trying to break out of here."

"Ain't nobody going to get killed…except'n maybe that Marshal. I had him in my sights the other day, but Ray stopped me. I knew I shouldn't have listened to him."

"Yeah, well, you do what you want, just keep me out of it." He turned on his side away from Johnny and tried to take a nap.

A short time later, Bill picked up the tray and headed over to the cafe' to pick up lunch for his prisoners. "Keep an eye on the place," he said to Corey, then shook his head, not believing he had just given him an order like he used to.

"I've got it," Corey said, smiling.

Bill walked into the café as Sally was just putting a plate of food down in front of a customer. "Hello, Marshal," she said to him.

"Hello, Miss Sally. Thought I would bring this back and pick up lunch for my prisoners, that is, if you have it ready?"

"All I have to do is put it on a plate. Have it for you in a couple of minutes." She picked up the tray and went into the kitchen area to prepare the lunches. When she came back to the counter, Bill was just sitting there, staring at the morning newspaper with the headline, 'Rustler's Caught'. "Are you all right, Bill?"

He looked up at her. "I'm OK…beginning to think I'm going crazy, but I'm OK."

"Why? What happened?"

"Oh, never mind, you wouldn't believe me anyway."

"Want to try me?"

"I don't think so," he said as he picked up the tray and headed back to his office. Sally just looked at him, sadly, knowing just how badly he must have been hurting. When Bill got back to the office, he checked the tray and then took it back to the cells. He hesitated when he saw Corey lying on a cot in the one of the empty cells. Just shaking his head, Bill put the tray through the opening and went back into the office.

"How long are we going to put up with this?" Johnny softly asked Pecos as he began eating his lunch.

"I've told you…I'm going to take my medicine and when I get out I'm going to make a life with Sarah…if not here, then somewhere. I'm not going to let her work in that saloon forever."

Corey smiled at what he heard. He liked Pecos and Sarah…he hoped they would be able to make it. But, Johnny, that was another story. He knew he was hot-headed, but he was now getting an idea of how dangerous he could be.

"I don't care what you and that girl do, Pecos. I'm getting out of here and you can either go with me or stay here and rot."

"That Marshal is no push-over Johnny…the only place you'll go is boot hill."

"So you say. I say I'll get out of here…and soon."

Pecos just shook his head and went back to eating his lunch as Corey 'popped' back into the office. "Looks like Johnny is planning a little jailbreak."

Bill looked up at him. "Don't they always?"

"Just be careful, OK. I got the impression he can be very dangerous."

"I'll keep that in mind."

The rest of the day was rather uneventful. Several of the townsfolk, who had not been at the funeral, stopped by to extend their sympathies, much to Corey's surprise. He couldn't help but chuckle a couple of times. "Can you believe that?" He said to Bill. "Mr. Sawyer never even liked me."

"Maybe he's feeling a little guilty now. Give him a break."

Shortly before supper time, a couple of men brought over the first of Corey's belongings from the boarding house. "Here's the first load, Marshal," one of the men said. "There's one more box. I'll bring it over in a few minutes."

"Thanks, Luke."

"Sorry about Corey, Marshal…he was a good kid."

"Yes, yes he was." Bill watched as the two men left and headed back toward the boarding house.

"Marshal…" Corey said, "what happened to the gear that the rustlers had?"

"It's back there in one of the other cells until I decide what to do with it."

"I can't help but think about what Red said about someone else giving orders. I wonder if there would be a clue in his saddlebag."

"I took a quick look when Horace brought everything over yesterday afternoon, but I really didn't think too much about it, had other things on my mind," he looked at Corey. "I thought we had them all. But, you're right, maybe we should take a closer look…maybe even see if we get a rise out of either of those two back there when we start going through their buddies' gear." Bill got up and went back into the cell area with Corey following behind him. He retrieved the lunch tray and gave it a once-over for missing items, then sat it down on the floor and walked into the other cell and started looking at the saddlebags that were there. He threw a couple of them over his arm and picking up the tray, started to leave the area.

"What you doing with those?" Johnny asked as he went by.

"Oh, just seeing what I might find."

"That's private property you know."

"Either one of these belong to you?"

"No, you know that."

"OK, then, shut up!" With that Bill went into this office as Corey hung back for a few minutes.

"What's the matter with you, Johnny?" Pecos asked.

"What do you mean…those don't belong to him."

"They do now… confiscated goods."

"What? What are you talking about, Pecos?"

"Just that the owners were caught and killed during an illegal act, so their property now belongs to the law."

"And how do you know all of this?"

"Never you mind how, I just know…that's all."

In the office, Bill was starting to go through one of the saddlebags when Corey came over to him. "Anything interesting?" He asked Bill.

"Not really…you recognize any of this stuff?"

Corey looked at one of the shirts, but when he went to pick it up, his hand went right through it. "Looks like I haven't quite gotten the hang of this ghost thing yet."

"I think you're doing just fine," Bill said, actually smiling at him. "Learn anything while you were in there."

"Not much…except, I don't know, but there's a lot more to the Pecos Kid than we know."

"Oh?"

"Can't put my finger on it yet…so to speak, but there's a lot of good in him. I can feel it."

"Oh, great…an emotional ghost…spirit… or whatever you are," He smiled again at Corey. "Let's just say it's going to take a little getting used to having you around in 'this' fashion."

"I'll try not to 'bother' you too much."

Bill looked up as there was another knock at the door. When he opened it, he saw Luke standing there with another box. "I think this is all of it, Marshal."

"Thanks, Luke," Bill said as the man turned and walked out the door. He turned to Corey.

"We'll go through your things a little later and you can tell me what you want me to do with them."

"Like I said, the clothes you can give to Father Michael. The rest…I'll just have to think about it."

"No problem…take as long as you want."

A short time later, Bill had finished going through both of the saddlebags he had brought into the office when there was a knock at the door. He opened it to find Sally there, with a dinner tray.

"Thought I would go ahead and bring this over," she said as Bill hurriedly cleared a spot on his desk.

"Thank you, Miss Sally," he smiled at her. "The other tray is right there," he pointed to Corey's desk. Corey was sitting at his desk when Sally went to pick up the tray and suddenly gave a little shiver. Bill saw her reaction. "Anything wrong?"

"No, just a cold chill. Maybe I'm coming down with something."

"I doubt it," Bill said, "probably just a draft or something. My old bones are telling me it might storm soon. It looked like some clouds were rolling in the last time I was outside."

"Yes, I suppose," Sally said as she headed toward the door then turned back. "Bill, why don't you take care of feeding your prisoners, then take a break and come over to the café for some supper…I made one of those apple pies you like so much."

"Thanks, Sally…maybe I will."

She left the room as Corey got up and walked over to Bill. "Sounds to me like there are some fair skies coming…not cloudy ones."

"What? Oh, you young people. Is that all you think about?"

"She's a nice lady. You two would be perfect together." Corey looked up. "Even the man up there says so."

"Who?" Bill realized who Corey was referring to. "Sheeesh." He checked out the tray then went back to the cells.

"OK, you two…you know the drill." Pecos and Johnny stepped back as Bill slid the tray into the cell.

"Thanks, Marshal," Pecos said as he took a plate and coffee cup to his cot.

"I can't figure you out, Pecos. I just don't get you." Johnny said as he finally took the remaining plate and cup to his own cot. Pecos just shrugged his shoulders and began to eat.

An hour or so later, Bill collected the plates and tray from his prisoners and decided to take it back to the café and get something to eat for himself. He suddenly realized that he hadn't eaten in almost two days. As he went into the café, Sally was just taking an order from one of her customers as Bill sat the tray on the counter. For the first time in a long time, Bill looked around the establishment and saw just how much of Sally's personality was in the furnishings. From the tables to the right of the door, to the counter area, to the curtains on the windows, to a small newspaper stand by the front wall; they all added a definite softness in the décor, but not so much as to turn away any range toughened cowboy that might want a nice meal. Sally came back from the kitchen to take his order. "What can I get for you, Marshal?"

"How about a steak, some potatoes, and a cup of coffee, to go along with a piece of that apple pie you mentioned?"

"Now that sounds a lot better. I was beginning to worry about you."

"You don't have to worry that pretty little head of yours about me, I'm just fine," Bill said, then realized what he had said, and a slight blush came to his face.

"Why, thank you, Marshal." She went back to the kitchen with a little more spring in her step and even began humming as she plated his meal.

Chapter Seventeen

That evening Bill and Corey had started going through the boxes sent over by Mrs. Mason. Bill had set aside the two boxes that were obviously clothing and boots, and was looking through the other box, finding mostly personal items, including the normal shaving brush, razor, and soap. He noticed a frown on Corey's face. "What's wrong?"

"Have you examined my saddlebags yet?"

"Briefly. Just a minute." He walked over to Corey's desk and retrieved the bags. "What's wrong, is something missing?"

"I'm not sure. I had some of my mother's jewelry. A ring and locket that were both on a chain. Those are supposed to be in a pouch in the saddlebags, but there was also a ruby brooch that belonged to my mother. I thought I had left it in the room, just to make it look like I was coming back. Which I had definitely planned on doing." He gave Bill a slight smile. Bill looked in the saddlebags and pulled out a small drawstring pouch. "That should be the locket and ring," Corey said. Bill opened the pouch and the ring, locket and chain fell into his hand.

"No brooch."

"I didn't think I had taken it. It has to still be in the room….unless…"

"Unless Mrs. Mason suddenly got sticky fingers…is that what you're thinking? Where did you keep it?"

"In the top drawer of my dresser…wrapped in a white handkerchief."

"Let's look through the clothing, maybe it got put in there." After carefully going through the boxes of clothing, they still hadn't found the brooch.

"It's still at the boarding house, it has to be." Corey said, starting to get a little upset.

"OK, Corey," Bill said to him. "I'll ask her tomorrow if she saw it. I'll tell her that you had mentioned the brooch to me one time when you were talking about your mother. We'll see what her reaction is."

"Maybe I should pay her a personal visit."

"And do what?"

Corey thought for a moment. "See if I find anything."

"You just put your hand right through that shirt a little while ago…you're not going to be able to do much searching."

Corey looked as if he was really concentrating and then reached over carefully lifted the chain from the locket that Bill had placed on the desk. "I guess I just have to really want something. He told me that it would take a little time to adjust to life down here again. To gather the strength that I would need."

"He…?"

Corey just rolled his eyes and looked upward.

"Uh…yeah…"

"I'll see you later."

"Corey…just be careful, OK?"

"I'm already dead…what else can happen to me?"

Bill shook his head, "Just get out of here."

"Oh, Marshal," Corey hesitated for a few seconds. "Would you please put that locket and ring in your safe?"

"Sure, Corey. I won't let anything happen to them." He picked up the small pouch and placed the locket and ring back inside and pulled the drawstring tight, opened the safe and put the pouch inside, then locked it.

"Thanks," Corey said as he faded from Bill's sight.

Inside the cells, Johnny was pacing back and forth. "Will you just sit down?" Pecos said, beginning to get exasperated with Johnny.

"I don't get it…that Marshal has been talking to someone all day, and from what I can tell, there's nobody in there with him."

"Well…sometimes people talk to themselves when they're trying to figure out a problem. Helps to concentrate, I've heard."

"There's something not right around here…it's just not right!" Johnny finally stopped pacing and laid down on his cot again.

A short time later Corey appeared in his room at the boarding house. He looked around the area, trying to see if maybe the brooch had fallen on the floor while they were packing his things, but he didn't find a thing. The room had already been cleaned and made ready for the next boarder. He faded out and reappeared in what he knew to be Mrs. Mason's room. He carefully looked around the room, but didn't see the brooch anywhere. He figured she wouldn't just leave it out in the open, but, he had hoped. Corey tried to open the dresser drawer but realized he didn't have that much strength…yet. He would have to come back, so he decided to pop downstairs and see what was going on there. Nobody was going to see him, so what would it hurt? He was in the 'library' area and began looking around. He found a couple of envelopes and realized one of them was from Wichita. He wondered why she would be getting mail from Wichita, but then, there wasn't a whole lot he did know about her. After a few minutes, Mrs. Mason came into the room carrying a cup of coffee and sat down in the chair. Feeling a slight chill in the air, she pulled her light shawl closer around her shoulders. Corey wanted to play a couple of playful pranks on her, but decided otherwise. Wouldn't be nice to do that to an older woman, would it? As he thought about it, there were a couple of people in town that had hassled him over the years, maybe he would be able to 'get even' sometime soon. Maybe being a ghost wouldn't be so bad after all. Suddenly he felt a chill of his own and realized that he had just received an admonishment from 'upstairs'. "OK, OK….I'll behave," he said, looking upward. Shaking his head, he went outside and walked down the street. As he neared the saloon, he saw Sarah come out, and head toward the Marshal's Office. He decided to hang out in the jail cell again and see if Pecos or Johnny might drop any hints about their 'intentions'.

Bill heard a soft knock at the door, and when he opened it, he saw Sarah there, wearing a shawl and carrying a small drawstring bag. "Hello, Marshal," she said softly. "Would it be all right if I visit with Pecos for a few minutes."

"Sure…come on in," Bill said as he stepped aside. "I'll have to ask you to leave your bag on the desk."

"Of course, Marshal. Thank you for letting me see Pecos…I care for him, deeply."

"I can see that, Miss Sarah. I hope that, eventually, things will work out for you."

Sarah walked into the cell area and over to Pecos. "Hi, Pecos."

"Sarah…I told you before, you shouldn't be coming here."

"I have to…I just want to be near you."

"What did I ever do to deserve a girl like you?"

"Oh, this is disgusting," Johnny said from his cot as he rolled over and turned his back to them."

"Oh, Pecos, what are we going to do?"

"We don't have a choice, Sarah. I'll have to do my time, and when I'm done, I'll come back for you…I promise." He reached through the bars and brushed a stray lock of hair off her forehead. "I'll get you out of that saloon, and we'll have our own place…I don't know how, yet. But it will happen…I know it will."

"I hope so, Pecos…I can't wait until we're together…just the two of us."

"I know…I feel the same way."

"Oh, God, you're making me sick," Johnny said as he sat up. "Come on, Girl…do you really think he's going to do all those things he says?"

"Shut up, Johnny!" Pecos said sharply.

"Yeah, and what are you going to do about it?"

Corey suddenly popped back into the office area. "Marshal, you'd better get back there before those two go at each other."

"Which two?"

Corey rolled his eyes. "Pecos and Johnny."

Bill got to his feet and walked back to the cells just as Johnny shoved Pecos backward against the cell as Sarah cried out. "Marshal…stop them!"

"That's enough, both of you!"

"I'm sorry, Miss Sarah, but I think you should leave right now. You can come back in the morning and visit with Pecos again."

"OK, Marshal, thank you." She turned to Pecos and smiled, then walked out to the office area as Bill followed her, and let her out the front door. He then went back to the cell area.

"OK, you two, what's going on in here?"

"Just ribbing ol' Pecos, Marshal," Johnny said, laughing sarcastically.

"Maybe it's time I separated the two of you." He motioned to Johnny. "OK, you come over here."

"Why?"

Bill pulled out a set of handcuffs. "Because I'm going to cuff you to the bars while I move Pecos to the other cell."

"And what makes you think I'm going to cooperate?" Bill pulled his gun. "OK, OK…" he said as he walked over to the bars.

"Put your hands through here." Johnny did as he was told and Bill cuffed him in place then turned to Pecos. "Back away from the door, Pecos."

Pecos backed up as Bill unlocked the cell and stepped back, motioning for Pecos to step out. He opened the other cell door and Pecos went inside. "Put those saddlebags here by the door then back up." Pecos did as he was told and Bill picked up the bags, closed the door and locked it. "OK, you two. Any more trouble and you will be handcuffed to those bunks…understand?"

Both of them nodded as Bill picked up the saddlebags, went back into his office and put them on Corey's desk. "Those the other bags?" Corey asked as he materialized in the office.

"Yep…those two are in separate cells now. Seemed the safest thing to do if we want them in one piece and able to testify in court."

"Any idea when that will be?"

"No. I'll have to talk to the judge tomorrow morning and get him to assign them a lawyer. Then he can set a date for trial."

"I think that one was Red's," Corey said as he pointed at one of the bags. Bill opened the bag and pulled out the contents. He didn't find a lot in the first bag, just a couple of extra shirts and socks. The other bag had a spare gun, ammo and some papers. Bill lifted an eyebrow as he looked at Corey.

"Let's see what we have here." He started reading through the papers and realized they were the agreement from the buyer for the herd. From what he could tell, the buyer seemed legitimate. Just wanting to buy some cattle for his own ranch near Wichita. "Seems like this buyer was just looking to add onto his herd."

"Might have changed his mind if he realized that the brands had been 'altered'."

"I'll send a wire to the law in Wichita in the morning and see what I can find out about this guy. See if he is just a regular rancher looking to expand his herd." He paused for a moment as he found another slip of paper that read, *'Better move now. M'* "Could be orders for him to get the herd moving. 'M' could be anybody. Matt down at the shoemakers shop? I think Randall has one of his hands that has a name starting with 'M', Miller, Mitchell?"

"Could be, 'Mason'," Corey added.

"Oh, come on, Corey…you can't believe Molly Mason has anything to do with this?"

"Can't I? I don't know why, but I just have a feeling…something's not right with her. I usually tried to stay away from her, didn't always succeed. Although, we did have some nice conversations. She seemed genuinely upset that I had lost my job, but, that could have been because she was afraid I wouldn't pay my rent. Who knows?"

"Why don't you ask him?" Bill looked upward.

"He did tell me I would have to figure some things out on my own if I wanted to 'earn my wings'."

"Wings? You?" Bill tried rather unsuccessfully to keep from snickering. "If there's one thing you're not…it's an angel." He stopped short as they heard a loud crack of thunder and it began to rain.

"See…" Corey smiled, "never question his judgment."

Bill just shook his head, closed the saddlebags he had been searching and picked up the other set. "If we don't find anything here, I might have to go out to the cabin and see if I find anything there."

"Yeah, and who's going to 'look after the shop'?"

"Well, I guess I need to start looking for a new deputy."

"Uh…yeah," was all Corey could come up with for a response as he watched Bill open the remaining pair of saddlebags. They found nothing unusual, just spare clothes and ammo. "Red mentioned that they were ready for anything. Ammo-wise, I guess they were."

"I'm beginning to be glad that if we had caught up to you before they got out into the open it could have come out a lot different…" He paused for a moment, realizing what he had just said.

"Marshal, stop it! What happened to me was not your fault! I made the choice to try to jump Red."

"We should have made our move before the gang was up and moving around. It would have been a lot safer if we had gotten there while they were asleep."

"I don't think so. They had the mindset that they were not going to be taken down, no matter what. Nothing you could have done would have changed anything. It was meant to be."

"Maybe…I just keep thinking that I should have done something else…."

"Oh!" Corey said, exasperated. "What am I going to do with you? IT WAS NOT YOUR FAULT!!!"

"You don't have to yell at me."

"Well, it looks like somebody has to."

"Marshal!" They heard Johnny call out from the cell.

"What now?" Bill asked Corey as he headed for the door to the cell area. "What do you want, Chambers?"

"Who you talking to, out there?"

"What business is it of yours, anyway?"

"Lots…if we're being held here by a 'crazy' man."

"Crazy?"

"Yeah…as far as I can tell there's nobody out there and you've been talking to someone all day."

"Let's just say whoever I'm talking to is a much better conversationalist than you are." Bill turned and left the room.

Bill went back to his desk as Corey sat down on the edge of it. "Maybe we should keep these conversations at a lower tone."

"You mean 'me' don't you?"

"Well…" Corey smiled at him. "Look…maybe we should be careful. The last thing we need is to have the town 'wondering' about their Marshal."

"Let them wonder," Bill said as Corey just shook his head.

Chapter Eighteen

The next morning Bill was doing his morning rounds when he saw Ken Harris pull his buggy to a stop in front of the mercantile. "Good morning, Ken," he said as he approached the rig, then paused when he saw Peggy getting out. "Sorry, Miss Peggy, I didn't see you in there."

"No apology necessary, Marshal," she said as she stepped onto the sidewalk.

"Honey," Ken said to her, "why don't you go on in, I'll be there in a few minutes."

"How is she doing?" Bill asked him after she went inside.

"She's fairing pretty well, I guess. Apparently she cared a lot more for Corey than I originally thought. She's been spending a lot of time with his horse." He shook his head for a moment. "Sometimes I think they actually understand each other."

"I wouldn't be surprised. Some people do have a way of talking to animals. Maybe she has that gift."

"Could be."

"I have something in my office that she might want. Why don't you stop by before you head back to the ranch?"

"We'll do that, Bill. Thanks." They shook hands and Ken went into the mercantile as Bill headed back to his office.

When Bill got back in his office Corey was sitting as his desk. "Uh… Peggy and her father will be stopping by in a little while, I thought I would give her the horse figure you carved, if that's alright with you?"

"Sure…I just wish I had been able to finish detailing it."

"I'm sure she will appreciate it anyway."

A half-hour later there was a knock at the door and when Bill opened it, Ken and Peggy were standing there. "Please come in." He stepped back as the two entered the office. Peggy looked over at Corey's desk and she could almost feel him there, looking at her. "Peggy, one of the things that Corey liked to do to pass the time was to carve little figures. I found this in his saddlebags." He opened his desk drawer and pulled out the carved figure of the horse. "I guess he didn't have time to finish all of the detail work…" he paused for a moment and took a deep breath, "but I think he would have liked for you to have it."

Tears began to form in Peggy's eyes as she took the small figure from Bill and just held it close to her breast. "It almost looks like Firefly," she said, "that's my other horse, Marshal," Watching this, Corey couldn't help himself as he got up, walked over and, as best he could, placed his hand on her shoulder. She looked around, thinking that her father had touched her, but he was not really close to her. Suddenly, although there was a certain chill in the air, she also felt a comforting warmth envelop her. She looked up at Bill. "Thank you, Marshal. I will treasure this, always. I just hope Corey knows how much I cared…and still care about him."

"I'm sure he does," Bill said as he watched as Corey gently stroked her hair.

"I can almost feel him here with us right now," Peggy said, touching her hair as she looked at her father, then Bill.

"You know, Peggy," Bill said as he sat down on the edge of his desk. "I'd bet he is watching right now. And, I'd also bet that you're going to have a guardian angel looking down on you from now on."

"Do you really think so? Do you really think he knows when I'm talking to him?" She looked at her father. "Yes, Dad, I do find myself talking to Corey sometimes."

"It's all right, Honey," Ken said as he put his arm around her. "To tell the truth, I still talk to your mother, quite often."

She smiled at her father then turned to Bill. "Thank you, Marshal, for everything." She clutched the figure to her breast again, carefully put it into her reticule, then stepped over to Bill and kissed him on the cheek. She turned to her father and they left the office as Bill just sat there with a stunned expression on his face.

Corey just raised an eyebrow, smiled and went back to his desk.

*****

First thing the next morning Bill walked over to Judge Stanley Cramer's office in the court house. He knocked on the door and heard a voice say, "Come in." He opened the door and went inside and saw the Judge sitting at his desk. "Good morning, Marshal." The two shook hands and Judge Cramer motioned for Bill to sit in the chair in front of the desk. The office was austere, but functional. The only furniture in the room was the desk, a couple of chairs and a bookcase filled with books. "What can I do for you today, Marshal?"

"Well, Judge, I guess you have heard about the circumstances surrounding the two prisoners I have in my jail."

"Yes, Marshal, I have heard. It is my understanding that they were both 'caught in the act' so to speak with the rustled cattle."

"Yes, they were. The rest of the rustlers decided to try to shoot their way out, unsuccessfully."

"And your deputy?"

"He was working with them, but as an inside person, trying to feed me information on who they were and where the herd was being held."

"Then everything that happened between the two of you…"

"Was staged, Judge. Corey was working with me the whole time. It was because of the information that he got to me that I knew the general area that they were in and that they were about to try to move out."

"Was he killed in the shootout?"

"The leader of the gang went for his weapon and Corey jumped him. In the struggle, the gun went off and Corey took a bullet in his chest. He died a hero, Your Honor."

"I didn't know him very well, but I do know that I did like what I saw. When he quit his job as your deputy, I was disappointed. But I also somehow knew that there had to be more behind it. I'm glad he didn't go bad, as some people thought for a while."

"I know…it was part of the plan. He wanted to make the rustlers come to him…and it worked. Too well, I guess."

"About your prisoners…how do you want to proceed?"

"They will need a lawyer. I was hoping you could appoint someone to represent them. Nobody has stepped forward to take the job."

"Under the circumstances, I doubt that they would. I will appoint Cal Stafford to handle the case for them. He's a good attorney…a bit young perhaps, but very bright. We will leave it up to him to talk with them and decide whether they want to make a plea, or go to trial. I'll contact him and have him come over to your office this afternoon."

"Thanks, Your Honor." Bill stood up and the two shook hands then Bill left the judge's office and went back to the jail. He went back to the cells to pick up the breakfast tray. Bill had both of the men to push their plates and cups through the opening and step back before he bent down to pick up the dishes. He kept his eyes on both of them, especially Johnny. There was something about the young man's demeanor that had Bill think he was about to 'explode'. Each time he went back to the cell area, the young man seemed to be more agitated. "By the way, Boys," he said as he loaded the tray and started for the door, "your lawyer will be by this afternoon to speak with you."

"I don't want no stinking lawyer!" Johnny shouted. "If you think I'm going to trial…well…you got another think coming!!" Bill just shook his head and went back to his desk.

"He's going to be trouble," Corey said as he appeared at his desk.

"I know," Bill said softly. "I just hope that the lawyer will be able to talk some sense into them and this thing won't have to go to trial."

"My guess is, he won't let it get that far," Corey said as he nodded his head toward the cells.

"That's what I'm afraid of. There's been enough bloodshed already," Bill said, this time, not wanting to look in Corey's direction.

"Marshall….I've told you…."

"I know…I know." Bill picked up the tray again and headed out the door to take it back to the café.

"Say 'hi' to Sally for me." Corey couldn't help it, he started to laugh. "You know," he thought to himself, "I'm going to have to do something to get those two together. Maybe He'll have some suggestions." Corey looked upward then disappeared.

When Bill walked into the café Sally was just cleaning up after the breakfast customers had departed and she looked up when she heard the door open. "Good morning, Bill. I see your prisoners cleaned their plates again," she said with a slight giggle.

"With you cooking…how could they not?" Bill smiled at her.

"Now that's much better."

"What?" He asked as he sat the tray on the counter.

"Seeing you smile."

"I guess I have been kind of a grouch lately."

"Not really…just worried…and sad." Without thinking, she placed her hand over his. "Bill, you can't let what happened get to you."

"I know. It's just taking some getting used to, I guess."

"Now…I don't remember you having breakfast yet…what can I get for you?"

"I hadn't really thought about breakfast…been a busy morning. How about just some coffee and a couple of those sweet rolls you make, that is if there are any left?"

"I think I might be able to scrounge up a couple. I'll be right back." She went into the kitchen and came out a couple of minutes later with the sweet rolls and a pot of coffee. "Here you go."

"Thanks, Sally." He took a sip of coffee from the cup she had sat down for him. "How are things going here? You seem to be pretty busy lately."

"A little busy…but that's good. Makes paying the bills a lot easier."

He nodded. "By the way, can you put together a daily bill for what you send over to the jail and I'll get it to the judge and make sure you get reimbursed as soon as possible."

"Sure, I've been keeping a record. I'll get you the balance for the last couple of days and I'll bring you the tab for the preceding day when I bring breakfast over. How's that?"

"That's perfect." She reached into cash drawer and pulled out a slip of paper.

"This is the current total, through yesterday."

"I'll take this over to the judge this morning."

"Thanks, Bill."

He soon finished his breakfast and paid her, then decided to do a tour about town. It was something he had been neglecting to do over the past couple of days, at least not as much as he should have been. When he got in front of the boarding house, he decided to take a chance and see what Mrs. Mason had to say about the brooch. He went in the door and saw her sitting in the small front parlor room. "Good morning, Mrs. Mason."

"Oh, good morning, Marshal. Is there something I can do for you?"

"I was going through Corey's belongings last evening and I remembered a ruby brooch that he had talked about having. It had belonged to his mother. I didn't see it in the boxes and I wondered if you knew anything about it."

Caught off-guard for a second, Mrs. Mason, quickly gathered herself and said, "I, uh, I don't remember seeing anything like that when we packed his things. But, I will keep an eye out and check to see if it may have fallen behind some of the furniture in his room."

"I would appreciate that, Mrs. Mason. He once told me about some of his mother's jewelry and who to give it to if something happened to him."

"Oh, I'll definitely look for it, Marshal. If I find it, I'll bring it over immediately."

"Thank you, Mrs. Mason. I know he would appreciate it." With that, Bill tipped his hat to her and left the building. Outside, he paused for a moment and scratched his head. Maybe there was something to Corey's suspicions after all.

After he left, Molly sat down in the parlor and then turned and opened a small drawer in the table next to her. She pulled out a handkerchief and unwrapped it so she could see the object inside. "So beautiful," she thought to herself. "But I'll never be able to wear it now…at least not in this town. I can't even sell it here. What a waste." She wrapped it back up and put it back into the drawer. She felt a slight chill and pulled her shawl closer…not knowing that Corey's spirit was watching her from the doorway. He couldn't help himself. He went over to the table and, concentrating deeply, knocked a small book onto the floor. Molly jumped as it hit and looked around but couldn't see anything except for the pages in the book turning as if there was a breeze blowing them. "No…no… it can't be…" Her heart began to race as she quickly got up and ran up the steps to her room, closed and locked the door behind her. Corey just smiled and slowly faded from sight. A few minutes later, Corey was in the office when Bill came back.

Bill could tell that something was going on with him. "What's wrong with you?"

Corey just cocked his head to the side and looked at him. "Other than the obvious," Bill said shaking his own head.

"She has the brooch…it's in the drawer of a table in her parlor."

"You saw it."

"Yeah…she took it out and was looking at it right after you left."

"Well, I'm going to need a little more than the word of a ghost to go over there and accuse her of stealing it."

"You may not have to…she might be bringing it back. We'll have to see… especially if something else happens…." He smiled at Bill.

"What did you do?"

"Not much…a book just fell off that table and to the floor…"

"Corey…"

"Why not?! She's behind this whole matter, I know she is."

"Then we need some hard evidence."

"I was there the other day and saw some of her mail…the return address was from Wichita. That's where they were taking the herd."

"There could be a lot of reasons she could be getting mail from Wichita. Was there a name in the return address?"

"Not that I remember."

"Ok…let's pull out those papers we found in Red's saddlebags…see if they ring a bell with you on the address." He went to his safe and retrieved the paperwork he had found in the saddlebags. "I figured these would be safer here than the saddlebags."

Corey grinned at him then started looking at one of the envelopes. "This looks familiar…I just can't be sure if it is the same as the one at the boarding house. I'll be back in a few minutes." He disappeared and a few minutes later he was in the boarding house. He started looking around, but could not spot the papers anywhere. "I wonder where she would keep them," he said to himself. Pulling open drawers and searching through stuff was something he was not quite able to do…yet. He decided to see if there was anything in her room. He cautiously peeked through the door, but evidently she had gone out. He looked around and spotted some papers on top of her dresser. He went over to them, but realized it was just a list of things that she needed to do and some receipts from the mercantile. Next, he went back downstairs and over to a roll-top desk. He decided to try to open it, but his hand just passed right through it. He knew he wasn't going to find anything laying out in the open now, he went back to the office.

"Well?" Bill said as Corey materialized in front of him. It dawned on him that he was now becoming used to 'this' Corey. He wasn't surprised when Corey suddenly appeared in front of him anymore.

"Nothing. She must have put everything away. She has a large roll-top desk where she keeps her paperwork for the boarding house. I figure that's where everything is."

"It will take a search warrant from the judge to make her open it for us. And right now I don't think he's going to want to go along with it."

"What's it going to take?"

"We'll just have to wait and see what happens, I guess." Bill stopped as there was a knock at the door. He went to open it and saw Cal Stafford standing there. "Hello, Cal."

"Afternoon, Marshal. The judge told me that your prisoners were in need of some advice."

"I guess you could say that," Bill said as he stepped back and let Cal come inside. He was a young man. Had only been out of law school for about a year and was still getting his feet wet, under the tutelage of the judge.

With blond hair, and a slight build, one probably wouldn't think that he was old enough to be a lawyer, but he had found that he could use that to his advantage. He was good, and if his appearance made a foe doubt him, all the better. That's when he liked to swoop in and 'make the kill'.

"What can you tell me, Marshal?" He began looking around.

"Anything wrong?"

"No, I just thought I heard you talking to someone when I came up to the door."

Bill looked over at Corey who was at his desk again. "No, must have been talking to myself…have a habit of doing that sometimes. Helps me think things through a little better, I suppose."

"I have heard people say that," Cal said as he sat down in the chair in front of Bill's desk. "Now, what are these two guys charged with?"

"Rustling, for the most part. Accessory to murder, possibly."

"And how is that?"

"My deputy, Corey Hansen, was killed while trying to bring them in."

"So I hear. Did either of the two prisoners pull the trigger that killed Mr. Hansen?"

"No, he was struggling with the leader of the gang when the gun went off."

"Then, Marshal, the only charge that can be brought against these men is rustling. The murder charge is out of the question."

"I suppose you want to talk with them?"

"Yes, I would."

"OK, follow me." Bill opened the door to the cell area and allowed Cal to precede him into the room. "Gentlemen, this is Cal Stafford…your attorney. Mr. Stafford, I will be in my office if you need me."

"Thank you, Marshal," Cal said as he sat his briefcase on a chair, opened it, and pulled out a pad of paper. "Now, from what I understand, you were both caught in possession of a herd of cattle that did not belong to you. This was witnessed by the marshal and his posse. Now, to make things easier on everyone, a guilty plea would seem to be the way to go here. It would save a lot of time, and turning in a plea of guilty, might make things more favorable in the eyes of the judge and result in a shorter sentence."

"I ain't pleading guilty to nothing…and I ain't going to stand no trial… you'll see!" Johnny said as he grabbed onto the bars of the cell. "I'm getting out of here and ain't nobody going to stop me! And I don't want you for my lawyer…in fact, I don't want a lawyer. No lawyer is anything other than two-faced liar."

"What's your name, young man?"

"Johnny…Johnny Chambers, remember it…OK?"

"And yours?" He looked at Pecos.

"Most people call me the Pecos Kid."

"Care to give me your real name?"

"Not really," Pecos said hesitantly.

"OK…for now, but if we get to court it might be a different matter."

"I understand…and for what it's worth," Pecos said as he approached the bars of the cell. "I'm willing to cut a plea and get this over with."

"That's good thinking," Cal said as he made notes on his pad. "I'll talk to the judge and the marshal and see what arrangements can be made. You'll have to give them a statement, of course. Everything you know about the operation."

"I'll tell you what I can…but that's not much. I was approached by Red… he asked if I wanted to make some quick cash. When I said yes, he told me he was putting together a herd to drive to Wichita. That's about it."

"Did you know they were rustling the cattle?"

"Yeah…I figured as much. Once I was in, I knew."

"OK, Pecos. I'll see what I can do for you."

"Why don't you just shut up, Pecos?" Johnny said from his cell.

"If you had the attitude that Pecos has, it might go a lot easier on you." Cal told him as he got up to leave.

"That'll be the day," Johnny said as he went back and plopped down on the cot and covered his eyes with his hat. Pecos just looked at Cal and shrugged his shoulders.

Cal went back into the office and Bill motioned for him to sit down, which he did.

"Well?" Bill asked.

"Pecos is ready to plead guilty. He knew what he was getting into and now, he just wants to get everything over with. Chambers, on the other hand, said he has no intention of pleading anything. He's an angry young man, Marshal."

"I know. I've already had to separate him into a different cell. Pecos, on the other hand, well…I think there's a lot of good in that kid. He just needs a push in the right direction."

"Agreed. I'll talk to the judge and see how he wants to proceed. I'll do all I can for both of them."

"I know you will, Cal," Bill said as they both stood and he escorted Cal to the door. "Tell the judge I will come to see him in the morning to make all the arrangements for a trial."

"I will do that, Marshal. Thanks for your help."

Bill closed the door and walked back to his desk. "I hope that kid comes around and decides to cooperate," he said to Corey.

"I wouldn't count on it, Marshal. He's got a chip on his shoulder and he's just daring someone to try to knock it off."

A short time later, Bill walked over to the telegraph office, which also served as the local post office. "Afternoon, Paul," he said as he walked inside.

"Afternoon, Marshal, what can I do for you?"

"I need to ask you a couple of questions…I know they are out of line and you don't have to answer…"

"You know I'll tell you what I can, Marshal."

"I know, Cal. Now…the mail that comes in here. Do you remember how much has come in from Wichita in the past couple of weeks?"

"Gosh…I get a lot through here, Marshal…Wichita…yeah, I think I've seen something, but I couldn't rightly say I remember who it went to."

"If anything else comes in, or goes out, to Wichita…could you let me know? It could be real important. I'm not asking to read it or anything like that…just who it's going to. Oh, Paul, as usual…don't mention this to anyone."

"No problem, I won't say a word, and I'll let you know if I catch anything coming in or going out."

"Also, I want to send a telegram to the territorial marshal and see if he has anything on my two prisoners."

"Sure thing…just write it out and I'll send it right away." He handed Bill a message form and waited as Bill filled it out. "I'll let you know when I get the answer."

"Thanks, Paul," Bill said as he left.

It was getting close to suppertime, so Bill walked over to the café and went inside. "Hi, Sally" he said when he saw her behind the counter.

"Hi, Bill," she said. At the moment she had no customers and didn't see a reason to be so formal.

"How about a dish of your stew and then I might as well pick up supper for my 'guests'?"

"I think I can manage that. Be back in a minute. You want coffee?"

"Sure…"

"How are things going with you?" She asked as she sat the bowl of stew in front of him.

"Doin' all right, I guess. Looks like we're going to have to set a trial date…one of the prisoners has decided that he doesn't want to plead guilty to something he was caught at red-handed. I guess nothing in life is easy, is it?"

"Rarely is, Bill. I'll start putting the tray together for your 'guests'," she said with a smile, then headed back into the kitchen. When she came back with the tray, she couldn't help but see that Bill was almost staring at her.

"Anything wrong, Bill?"

"No…nothing…just…are you wearing your hair different today?"

She slightly blushed as she touched her hair. "Yes…I decided to let it hang down in the back today. I…uh…had been sensing a chill the past few days and thought it might be warmer this way."

"Well, it looks real nice. You should wear it that way more often."

"Thank you…maybe I will."

"Oh, by the way, I gave your tally to the bank," he said as he paid her for his meal. "You will probably get the reimbursement tomorrow."

"That would be great, Bill. Thanks." She tucked the current receipt under the silverware on the tray and Bill picked it up and headed back to the office.

Chapter Nineteen

Later that evening, Bill got ready to make a final check on his prisoners before he turned in for the evening. As in a lot of the jails, this one had a small room that the marshal could use as his living quarters. He did have a room elsewhere, but when there were prisoners there, he didn't have much of a choice, but to sleep at the office. That was always something he had felt a little guilty about when it came to Corey. Knowing what he had to pay for the boarding house, he knew that it hadn't left Corey a whole lot for other 'expenses'. "I think I'll pay Mrs. Mason another visit in the morning," he thought to himself. He hadn't exactly come up with a reason for the visit, but he was sure he would think of something. "Evening, Gentlemen," he said as he walked back to the cells.

"Marshal," Pecos said as he continued to lie on his cot. Johnny just rolled over turning his back to Bill and Pecos.

"Has he given you any more trouble?" Bill asked Pecos softly as he walked over to his cell.

Pecos just shook his head and stood up to talk to Bill. "Nah…just keeps griping about stuff."

"Well, we'll find out in the morning what the judge is going to do. Hopefully, this will come to a conclusion soon."

"I hope so…I just want to do my time and get back here so I can get Sarah out of that saloon."

"So that was what you wanted the 'quick cash' for?" Pecos just nodded. "Well, hang in there. Things will work out for you. I'm sure of it."

“Thanks.” Pecos went back to his cot, laid down and tried to go to sleep. Later that night, he didn’t know what time it was, but he was awakened by a noise. He sat up, but the only thing he could see was Johnny restlessly moving around on his cot. Still a little groggy, he laid back down and quickly went back to sleep.

The next morning Bill got up and went about his normal routine. He went to check out the cell area, but both of the prisoners seemed to still be asleep. When he got back to his desk, he saw Corey sitting at his desk, as if nothing was wrong. “Morning, Marshal. Sleep good last night.”

“Same as usual. What about you? Do ghosts sleep?”

“We have to rest…but, sleep…I don’t know if you would call it that. As it was, last night I was checking out the cabin. Didn’t find much…at least they didn’t leave anything lying around, not that I expected them to. Still…I know there’s something we’re missing. Something specific that will tell us who was behind this whole thing.”

Bill smiled. “Giving up on your theory about Molly Mason?”

“Not on your life. I know she’s the one…I’ve just got to find the proof.”

“We’ve got to find the proof…”

Corey smiled and nodded. “We’ll find it.”

A short time later, there was a knock at the door, and when Bill opened it, he saw Sally standing there with the breakfast tray. “Good morning, Sally.”

“Good morning, Bill. How are you this morning?”

“Just fine, Sally…you look nice today.” He said as he took the tray and couldn’t help admiring what appeared to be a new dress that she was wearing…at least he didn’t remember seeing it before.

“Thank you, Bill.” She looked around the office, of course not seeing Corey sitting there watching them with a big smile on his face. “It seems strange not seeing Corey in here. I miss him a lot…and I know it’s worse for you.”

“Sometimes,” Bill said as he glanced toward Corey and rolled his eyes. “I’m trying to get used to it, ‘though. I guess I’m going to have to start thinking about getting a new deputy, but I just haven’t been able to bring myself to do it.”

"You should, you know," she said. "You're going to wear yourself thin... especially when you have to watch the prisoners and keep tabs on everything else around town."

"I'll think about getting help...I promise. Now, I'd better get this back there," he nodded toward the cell area.

"OK, Bill, just remember what I said."

"I will...now...scoot," he said chuckling as she giggled, and then he locked the door behind her as she left. When he turned around he saw Corey laughing. "What's so darn funny?"

"You...you're actually falling for her."

"Awww...she's just a friend...a nice woman."

"Uh huh." Corey shook his head and started chuckling again. "Now don't get me wrong. I think you two make a great couple. And..." he couldn't help himself, "you're not getting any younger. Better be careful before you're too old to think about getting hitched again."

"Hitched!? Me? Not again. I think being dead must have addled your brain a little bit." Bill just threw up his hands, then grabbed the tray, did a quick inventory, and took it back to the cell area. "Morning, Gentlemen," he said as he sat the tray on the chair and began to separate the meals and slide them through the opening in the cells. "Eat up...I'll be back in a little while."

"Oh, I can't wait," Johnny said sarcastically. Bill just shook his head and went back into his office.

"Keep an eye on things here, Corey. I'm going to take a little stroll over to the telegraph office and see if there's been any response to a wire I sent out yesterday."

"Morning, Marshal," Paul said as Bill walked into the office. "I was just about to come see you. Finally got an answer to your inquiry. Just came in a couple of minutes ago."

"Well, I guess my timing is right on today." He took the piece of paper from Paul and read it. "Pretty much what I thought....thanks, Paul." He turned and left the telegraph office and walked over to the café.

"Hi, Sally," he said as he walked through the door. "Smelling the delicious aroma off that tray a little while ago, reminded me that I needed to get myself something to eat."

"What can I fix for you?"

"I don't know…surprise me."

"Oooooh…living dangerously, I see." She smiled and went back to the kitchen. A few minutes later she came back with his plate.

"Interesting," he said as he eyed what was on his plate.

"It's called an omelet. I've been reading about them…seems to be the rage in the big cities, so I thought I would try putting it on the menu here. Let me know if you like it."

He took his fork and cut through the eggs, bacon, cheese and onions and then put a forkful into his mouth. His eyebrows lifted and he got a very 'satisfied' expression on his face. "You have to keep this…. wonderful," he managed to say as he swallowed and took another mouthful. "Pure heaven," he said as she beamed at him and poured him a cup of coffee.

"I'm glad you like it. And since you were my guinea pig this morning… I'm not going to charge you for your meal."

"No…no…this is worth whatever you want to charge." He scooped another large forkful into his mouth. "I'll be...glad to…pay anything… for this," he said between chews. He soon finished his meal and over her objections, put a dollar on the counter. "Worth that and a lot more," he said as he left. When he got back to the office, he sat down at his desk and took a deep breath and patted his stomach.

"You look like the cat that swallowed the canary," Corey said as he sat down on the edge of Bill's desk.

"No….the marshal that ate the omelet."

"What?"

"Sally has a new menu item…absolutely heavenly. Uh…sorry," he said as he remembered Corey's 'condition'.

"That's OK…glad to see you happy for a change. See, just think how it would be to have her cooking for you every morning before you come to work. Not to mention all the other 'advantages'."

"Will you stop it!" Bill said, then stopped as there was a knock at the door. He went to open it and saw Sarah standing there.

"Good morning, Marshal, could I please see Pecos?"

"Sure, Miss Sarah. Come on in," he said, stepping back and allowing her to come inside. "I have moved Pecos to his own cell, so there should not be the problem we had the last time."

"Thank you, Marshal. You've been very kind to us about this."

"I know it must be hard for you. But don't you worry, I'm hoping this whole situation will be decided in a couple of days."

"I hope so," she said as she laid her bag on his desk and waited for him to open the door to the cells. Bill escorted her by Johnny's cell and stopped in front of Pecos.

"I'll be back in a few minutes," Bill told her and headed back to his office, but left the door open to the cell area.

"I'm glad to see you, Sarah…but you shouldn't have come."

"I had to, Pecos. The marshal said this should all be decided in a couple of days. Have they told you anything?"

"Not much, the judge appointed us a lawyer. I'm going to plead guilty and hope that I get a light sentence."

"But, Pecos…"

He put his finger over her lips. "It's best this way. You have to believe me."

"I'll try…it's just so hard knowing that you're locked up in here…and then to have to face you going to prison…"

"It'll be all right, Sarah. You'll see. We just have to have faith."

"Oh come on…" Johnny said from his cell. "Faith in what? Do you really think that there's some God that's going to protect you? You're worse off than I thought."

"You have to have something to believe in," Sarah came back at him. "If you don't, you don't have much of a life."

"My life is just fine the way it is."

"Well this sure shows it, doesn't it?" She responded.

"And Pecos is different? Give him the opportunity and he will be out of here as fast as I will."

"Why don't you just sit down and shut up?" Pecos told Johnny, who just snorted and went back to his cot. "I'm sorry, Sarah…it seems that we can't have a private conversation in here."

"It's all right, Pecos. The only thing important to me is being near you." She reached through the bars to touch his cheek. "Please make sure the marshal lets me know when the hearing will be…I want to be there."

"Are you sure? It might get kind of rough for you."

"I can handle it…especially if I know it will bring you back to me."

"I will come back for you…I would die before I would ever leave you."

"Oh, Brother…" Johnny said as Bill came back into the cell area.

"I'm sorry, Sarah, but the time's up." He watched as Pecos leaned over and gave her a kiss through the bars.

Sarah turned and started walking toward the door, preoccupied, and didn't notice how close she was to Johnny's cell. She screamed out as Johnny reached through and grabbed her arm, pulling her close to him as he brought a gun to her head.

"All right, Marshal…I'm calling the shots now…get the keys and unlock this cell, or do you want to be responsible for this little gal's brains being scattered across this floor?"

"LET HER GO, JOHNNY!!!" Pecos demanded.

"Not a chance! OK, Marshal, what's it going to be?"

"OK, Johnny…the keys are in the office…"

"Yeah…I saw where you keep them. First you drop your gun to the floor, and I happen to know you can reach those keys without going out of this room…I suggest you hurry it up. My trigger finger is starting to get real itchy."

Bill did what he was told and dropped his gun to the floor, not realizing it was within Pecos' reach. He went to the door and reached around and took the keys from the hook. "OK…unlock this cell and step back," Johnny ordered. Bill placed the key in the lock and slowly turned it, hoping that Johnny might let go of Sarah, but he didn't. Bill stepped back as Johnny pushed the door open while still holding onto Sarah. "OK, Marshall you're going to take my place in here…along with the little lady." He pushed Sarah toward Bill who had to grab her to keep her from falling. "Now…inside, both of you." He motioned them to go inside the cell, closed the door and reached for the key to lock it.

"I don't think so, Johnny," Pecos said and watched as Johnny glanced his way, then froze as he realized that Pecos was holding Bill's gun on him.

"That's more like, it Pecos. Let me lock this cell and I'll let you out and we'll get out of here together."

"Drop the gun, Johnny."

"Are you crazy?!!"

"No…just sensible…now drop the gun."

Johnny was still holding the gun on Bill when he swung around to fire at Pecos. Pecos fired, hitting Johnny in the chest just as Johnny pulled the trigger. Johnny's bullet penetrated Pecos arm and he fell back against the bars of his cell. Bill pushed Sarah down to the floor and charged the door of the cell kicking the gun away from Johnny. He felt for a heartbeat and found nothing. Johnny had died before he hit floor. Bill looked at Pecos who still had the gun in his hand. Cautiously Bill approached the cell, then stopped. Pecos flipped the gun in his hand, and pushed it between the bars to give it back to Bill who quickly grabbed the keys from the other cell and opened Pecos' cell and caught him, just as he started to sag to the floor. He lifted Pecos and helped him to his cot. "Pecos!" Sarah screamed and ran to his side. Bill touched her shoulder.

"I'll be right back…I'm going to send someone for the doctor." He smiled at her. "Don't worry, he'll be all right." When Bill turned around, he saw Corey standing in the door. He continued into the office and went to the door. He saw a couple of men walking toward the office and called out to them. "Hey…Andy…get the Doc over here…fast." Andy turned and ran toward the doctor's office. When Bill went back into his office Corey was still standing in the doorway.

"I couldn't do anything…I couldn't help you…"

"Corey...it's OK…"

"NO…it's not OK! Why did I stay here if I can't help you?"

"Look," Bill said softly, "you have helped…and will continue to help, but right now I have to take care of things back there. The door's not locked so the doctor should be able to come on in." He watched as Corey disappeared. Shaking his head, he went back to the cells and, grabbing a blanket, covered Johnny's lifeless body. He walked over to Sarah and Pecos. "I've sent for the doctor, he should be here in a couple of minutes."

"Thank you, Marshal…for everything," Sarah said as she stroked Pecos' forehead. "Look, Marshal, there's something I need to tell you…"

"Sarah…don't," Pecos said as he tried to sit up, but fell back onto the cot as the doctor suddenly appeared beside them.

"Why don't you two wait in the office," the doctor told Sarah and Bill. Bill nodded and led Sarah into the office.

"Don't worry, Miss Sarah, he'll be all right. From what I could tell the bullet went clean through. He'll be fine in a few days."

"I don't know what I would do without him," she said as Bill led her to a chair.

"Everything will be fine. I'll make sure the judge knows what he did in there. It will help a lot, I'm sure."

"Marshal…like I started to say…I was helping Pecos. I would tell him little things that I heard at the saloon. The things about you and Corey…"

"Sarah, listen to me…that's what Corey and I wanted. We needed to get someone on the inside. So, technically, you were helping us more than the outlaws."

"But…"

"No, Sarah…what you did was perhaps irresponsible, but you were in love and trying to help the man you loved. Ultimately, what you did turned out to do more good than harm. I'm not going to hold that against you… and neither will the judge."

"I don't know what to say."

"You don't have to say anything," he smiled at her. "Just make sure I get an invitation to the wedding."

"I don't know when that will be."

"It doesn't matter. I want to be there."

She smiled and dabbed at a tear that was falling down her cheek. They both looked up as the doctor came into the room. "He'll be all right. Lost a little blood, but he should be up and around in a day or two. I gave him something for the pain, but just keep him quiet right now, and I'll come back and check on him tomorrow."

"Thanks, Doc," Bill said as they shook hands and the doctor left the office. "See…I told you so," he smiled at Sarah. "Now, I'll let you see him again, but then I think you should go back and get some rest yourself. It's been an eventful morning."

She nodded and they went back to Corey's cell. Sarah went over and knelt beside him then kissed him. "Marshal said I should leave now, but I'll be back…I promise."

"You sure you're OK?" Pecos asked her.

"Fine…just worried about you."

"I'm OK…or will be soon," he smiled and looked into her eyes. "I love you."

"I love you too, Pecos," she leaned over and kissed him again as Bill touched her shoulder, letting her know it was time to leave.

"Come on, Sarah, I will walk you back to the saloon and then go have the undertaker come to 'collect' Johnny." Bill locked the cell and they left and headed over to the saloon. When they walked into the saloon Tom and Betty were both there. "Miss Betty," Bill said, "would you please take Sarah upstairs and make sure she lies down for a little while."

"What happened?" Tom asked him as Betty led Sarah up to her room.

"Chambers tried to break out, grabbed her and tried to use her as a shield. Everything's fine now, but she needs to rest for a little while."

"Pecos?"

"It's thanks to him that things are OK. He managed to get hold of my gun that I had to drop when Johnny grabbed Sarah. Johnny is dead and Pecos took a bullet in the arm, but he'll be all right."

"The main thing is that she's OK…she is a good girl," Tom told him.

"Yes, she is. And very much in love with Pecos."

"I know."

"I'll see you later…need to make arrangements with Horace to take care of Johnny." Bill left the saloon and headed over to the undertaker.

"Hi, Marshal, heard the gunshots…figured I would be seeing you eventually."

"One of my prisoners tried to escape. He didn't make it. Can you come get him and take care of the arrangements."

"Sure, I'll grab a couple of guys and be right there."

Bill left the building and headed back to his office. He went back to the cell area and saw that Pecos was now sleeping. He turned around as he heard Horace and two other men come in the door. "Back here," he said to them and watched as they carefully picked up the body and carried it out of the building. "I'll talk to the judge in a little while and let you know how he wants to proceed. As far as I know, there's no family, so we'll probably just have the town bury him in the cemetery."

An hour later, Bill went over to see Judge Cramer. "Hi, Bill," the judge said as he walked into the office. "Hear you had a little trouble over there this morning."

"Yeah…Chambers tried to escape. Somehow, he managed to get a gun and grabbed Sarah Riley when she came to visit Pecos. Tried to use her as a shield to get me to open the cell. I had to drop my gun and, somehow, Pecos was able to reach it and stop him. Johnny's dead, and Pecos has a bullet in his arm."

"So, Pecos had the chance to escape and didn't. Instead he stopped Chambers and took a bullet in the process."

"That's about it, Judge. From what I understand, he was going to plead guilty, do his time and come back so he could marry Sarah and get her out of the saloon. That's why he got involved in all of this in the first place. He need the cash for a 'stake' to get her out of here."

"Not exactly the right way to go about it."

"No…and he knows it. He's ready to do his time and put everything behind him. What I'm hoping, Judge, is that you'll take in to account what he did today. Maybe go a little easier on him."

"I'll think about it. Do you have any suggestions? After all you made the arrest."

"At no time did he give me any problems…he's been cooperative all the way."

"You know I can't just let him go."

"I know…it's just that, in the long run, I do owe him. I know that Johnny was going to lock Sarah and me in the cell, but I'm not sure that he wasn't going to put a bullet in our heads anyway."

"Cal told me how belligerent he was, so I wouldn't have been surprised. OK, let me talk to Cal, and I will schedule a hearing for tomorrow morning…providing Pecos is up to it."

"That seems reasonable. Why don't we have it in my office, he won't have to walk all the way over to the courthouse?"

"I can do that. Eleven o'clock sound good?"

"Works for me."

Bill got up and left the judge's office and stopped by the saloon on his way back to the office. "Hi, Tom," he said, "would you please tell Sarah that Pecos' hearing will be tomorrow morning in my office at eleven. She wanted me to let her know so she could be there."

"I'll let her know, Marshal, thanks."

Bill left the saloon and headed back to his office. When he went inside he saw Corey sitting at his desk, looking very dejected. "What's the matter with you? Oh, that," he said remembering what Corey had said earlier. "Look, there's only so much you can do. I need you as a consultant… someone to bounce ideas off and give me honest answers."

"A lot of good that is!"

"Yes! It is a lot of good. You've already put me on the track of who was behind this whole mess. But right now, I need to know how Johnny got that gun. Now, just saying Mrs. Mason is behind all of this…why would she want to bust him out?"

"To divert our attention away from her?"

"Probably, but think about this. She's probably, what…5'2" at the most?"

"Yeah…"

"That window is a good 6 feet off the ground…I don't think that she would be able to put a gun through that window without tossing it…and that would make a lot of noise."

"So…." Corey thought for a moment, "there's someone else involved."

"Yeah…and the answer has to be in the mail that is going back and forth between her and Wichita. Somehow, I have to get access to those letters."

"I'm beginning to gain more and more ability to move things. Maybe I should take another try at snooping around her house."

"Do it! Also, see if she has any new boarders."

"I'm on my way," Corey said as he disappeared.

It was almost noon when there was a knock at the door and Bill opened it to find Sally standing there with a tray. "I heard a little bit about what happened. Are you OK?"

"I'm fine…but it looks like we'll only need one meal instead of two."

"So I heard, but I figured with everything that's happening, you would probably forget that you have to eat, too. So, one of these is for you."

He smiled and shook his head. "Thanks, Mother."

She froze for a second and realizing what he was saying, started laughing. "OK…OK…guilty as charged, Marshal. But if I don't look out for you, who will?"

They both laughed as Bill checked the tray, put the plate and cup on his desk, then started to take the other back to the cell then sat it back down. "I will have to see if he's awake. The doctor gave him something for pain and the last time I was back there, he was asleep. I'll bring the tray over to you later…thanks again."

"Anytime, Marshal, anytime." She left as Bill closed and locked the door, then carried the tray to Pecos' cell.

"You awake, Pecos," he said as he sat the tray on the floor and slid it through the opening.

"Yeah…thanks, Marshal." He carefully got up and managed to pick up the tray and take it back to his cot.

"I talked with the judge a little while ago," Bill told him. "Your hearing is going to be tomorrow morning at eleven."

"Good, I'll be glad to get all of this over with. How's Sarah?"

"She's fine, just upset. Betty is looking after her. Look, Pecos, I know I've asked this before, but, have you remembered if Red said anything about who else was involved, other than the bunch you were with?"

"No…I just know he mentioned someone else, but that's it."

"OK…it was worth a try. Just trying to figure out how Johnny got that gun."

Pecos took a sip from the coffee cup. "Wait…last night…I heard something. I don't know what it was, but something woke me up. A noise of some kind, but when I sat up, I didn't see anything. Johnny seemed to be restless, but I didn't see anything else."

"By restless…could he have been just lying back down on his cot?"

Pecos thought for a few seconds. "Maybe…I was kind of out of it…you know the way you are when something wakes you up out of a deep sleep."

"Yeah, I know. OK, Pecos, if you remember anything else…"

"I'll let you know right away," Pecos said as Bill turned and went back to his desk and began to enjoy his lunch.

Chapter Twenty

The next morning, Bill went to check on Pecos and found him up, and sitting on the cot. "How are you feeling this morning?" He asked.

"My arm's a little stiff and sore, but otherwise, I'm OK, I guess."

"That's good to hear. You ready for the hearing?"

"I guess so. Not much I can do about it anyway." He stood up and went to look out the window. "Guess I'm going to be looking at the outside world like this for a long time."

"Just keep thinking about what you've got to come back to when you get out. Sarah's a great girl and seems to love you very much. Any man would be proud to have her as a wife. You're a very lucky man."

Pecos looked back at Bill and smiled. "I know. I just hope that she will wait for me."

"Oh, I wouldn't be too worried about that, from what I've seen." He thought for a moment and decided he needed to put Pecos' mind at ease about something else as well. "Pecos, Sarah and I had a little talk yesterday. She told me about her 'role' in all of this…"

"Marshal…!"

"Hold on, Pecos. I'm going to tell you, what I told her. There will be no, absolutely no charges against her. Inadvertently the information she supplied was what we needed to happen to get Corey on the inside." He paused as he thought about that part of the operation. "She actually did nothing wrong, just talking to her 'man' about her day at work. At least, that's the way I see it."

"Then she's not going…?"

"NO! Got that? Bill said as he watched Pecos take in a deep sigh of relief. He looked over his shoulder as he heard a knock at the door. "That's probably your breakfast. I'll be back in a couple of minutes." He went to the door and opened it. "'Morning, Sally."

"'Morning, Bill," she said as she came in and put the tray on the desk. "How is he this morning?"

"A little sore, but he'll be OK."

"That's good to hear."

"The hearing's at eleven this morning. When it's over, I'll bring this tray back and come to pick up his lunch."

"I hope everything will be work out for him.

"I think it will."

"Tom brought Sarah over to the café last evening, I think to just get her out of there and her mind on something else for a little while. She spent most of the time talking about Pecos and how much she cared for him. It's not often you see that kind of devotion between two people that are that young and not married yet."

"I know. Just between us, I don't think the judge will be too hard on him. A year or so, I'm guessing."

"That's still a long time."

"Yes, but, it could have been a lot worse."

"I see what you mean. Well, I'd better get back, I need to straighten up before the lunch time bunch comes in."

"OK…I'll be there as soon as the hearing is over and I have gotten Pecos back in there." He opened the door and she left, heading back toward the café.

When Bill checked the tray he found that she had made omelets for the both of them. He took Pecos' food back to him. "I think you're going to like what I have here. She made this for me yesterday and it is delicious."

Pecos lifted up the towel that was covering the dish. "What is it?"

"It's called an omelet. Try it. I think you'll be pleasantly surprised. I know I sure was."

"OK," Pecos said as he took the dish back to his cot and sat down. He put a forkful of the omelet into his mouth and Bill watched as he got that same satisfied look on his face. "Incredible."

"I know…you enjoy yours while I go into the office and devour mine."

"I will," Pecos said as he took another big bite.

An hour or so later, Bill was looking through some wanted posters that had come in the mail the day before when Corey suddenly appeared. "Took you an awful long time to check out the boarding house."

"Yeah, I know. I didn't find much. What I did find, that I didn't realize was there, is a small safe. She has it hidden in her bedroom closet."

"I don't suppose you were able to…."

"No…I don't have that kind of strength yet. I couldn't penetrate the wall."

"If you're right, everything we need is in that safe."

"We just have to figure out how to get at it."

"What we need is a court order to get her to open it, but before we can do that, we have to have some kind of proof we can show to the judge." He stopped as he heard a knock at the door. When he opened it, he saw the judge standing there. "You're early…it's only ten."

"I know, I thought we might talk for a little while."

"Sure…would you like some coffee? I just made a pot."

"That would be good, thanks."

Bill poured the judge a cup of coffee and they sat down, Bill behind his desk and the judge in the chair in front of his desk. "How's your prisoner this morning?"

"He said he was a little sore and stiff, but that's to be expected. I think he's just glad to be getting this whole thing over with."

"Probably, so. What is your opinion of the young man, Marshal?"

"Personally, I think he's a good kid. Got in with the wrong bunch, I guess. All he wanted was a quick stake to get his girl out of the saloon life."

"Oh?"

"Yes. Sarah Miles at the saloon…they're very much in love. He doesn't like her having to work there and wanted to get her out."

"Commendable, but not exactly the right way to go about it."

"I agree. But, I also have been asking myself, if I was his age, would I have acted any differently?"

"Ahhh youth…I remember a few of the antics I came up with," the judge chuckled. "Drove my father crazy."

"I think most of us did at that age," Bill agreed. "But now…what are you going to do about Pecos?"

"That's one reason I came over here early. I wanted to get a feel for the young man. I suppose you have checked on his background?"

"Yes…as much as I could. As far as I know, he has never been in any real trouble before this. A few bar fights that required the night in jail to sleep it off, but other than that…nothing. Of course, we don't know his real name so we can check that out."

"And he has refused to tell you?"

"Yes. I told him that you would probably require him to divulge that info at the hearing, and he seemed resigned to it."

"Very well, let me ask you this, Marshal. Would you have reservations about having Pecos living in Rio Madre after he has served his sentence?"

"Not at all…I think I would be at the train station to welcome him home."

"That's what I wanted to hear," Judge Cramer said as he stood up. "I think I'm going to take a little walk around town and think about what I'm going to do. I will be back in a few minutes." He left the office and walked down the street. He returned to Bill's office about five minutes to eleven and actually helped Bill as he rearranged the chairs. They had just finished when Tom and Sarah came in the door.

"Good morning, Marshal," Tom said as he came in. "I hope you don't mind me being here. I wanted to be here in case you needed a character witness for Pecos."

"Thank you, Tom. By all means, you're welcome to stay," Bill told him. "Good morning, Sarah, how are you feeling this morning?"

"OK, I guess. I'll let you know for sure after this is over," she said shakily.

"Why don't you have a seat over here?" Bill told her as he showed her where to sit. "I think we're about ready to start, aren't we, Judge?"

"Yes, Marshal. I think we can get started now, if you would please bring in the prisoner."

Bill went into the back and unlocked Pecos' cell. "I guess this is it? Huh?" Pecos said.

"Yes, the hearing is going to be here in the office. Since you've already declared that you don't want a trial and are pleading guilty, we saw no reason to go through the whole trial procedure. Easier for everyone."

Pecos nodded and allowed Bill to escort him into the office. Judge Cramer was sitting at Bill's desk, and Pecos was shown to the chair in front of the desk, while Bill stood behind him. Pecos was surprised to see Sarah and Tom there, but didn't say anything. He just wanted it over with.

"This hearing will now come to order," Judge Cramer said as he used a paperweight to tap on the desk. "We are here today to determine the sentence of one, 'Pecos Kid' on the charge of rustling. How do you plead, Young Man?"

"Guilty, Your Honor," Pecos said, then looked over at Sarah.

"Do you have anything to say in your defense?"

"No, Sir. I know what I did. I wasn't sure what they wanted me for in the beginning, but it dawned on me pretty fast what was up. I could have left, I guess. But, I needed the money."

"And this 'need' was enough to risk getting killed or going to jail?"

"Yes, Sir."

"Would you like to tell me what that need was?"

"I just wanted enough money to get Sarah out of the saloon and into a decent life, as my wife."

"I see. Well, you're not the first man to fall under the spell of a beautiful woman…and you probably won't be the last. Now…does anyone have anything to say on the young man's behalf before I pass sentence?"

"Your Honor," Tom said, stepping forward. "I don't know Pecos that well, but from what I've seen he's a good man. A bit young and impetuous, perhaps, but I believe that he has a lot of good in him." Tom stepped back and smiled down at Sarah, then at Pecos.

"OK, Pecos…I'm sorry, young man, before I pronounce sentence on you, I do need to know your real name."

Pecos hesitated for a long moment. "OK, Sir…" he looked around the room. "My real name is… Danny Wilde."

"Not Benjamin Wilde's son?" Bill said, surprised.

"Yes, Sir," Pecos said.

"Young man," Judge Cramer said, "your father was one of the most respected lawmen in the state of Texas.

"I know that, Sir."

"What do you think he would say about his son if he were alive today?"

"He would probably be very disappointed in me…and I would deserve it, Sir." Pecos took a deep breath and looked straight at the judge. "And he would probably tell you to throw the book at me."

Judge Cramer had a difficult time trying to hold back a smile as Bill put his hand over his mouth to keep from laughing. He glanced over at Corey's desk and saw him sitting on the edge of it laughing and shaking his head.

"OK…" the Judge said, "if there's no further input, I have something to say before I pass judgment. Daniel, the marshal has told me how you never offered any resistance the day that the posse caught up with the rustlers, and how, yesterday, you prevented the escape of the remaining rustler in custody and possibly saved the life of the marshal and Miss Riley. So, as of this day, I am sentencing you to one year in prison for your part in the rustling operation…" Everyone heard Sarah gasp and begin to cry as Tom put his hand on her shoulder again. "If I may continue," Judge Cramer said, as he knocked on the desk for order. "Thirty days of that sentence will be spent here in the Rio Madre jail. The other eleven months will be suspended…" Everyone in the room let out a collective breath, as Pecos couldn't believe what he had just heard. "But, Mr. Wilde, if at <u>any</u> point in those eleven months, you do anything out of line, you will go to the state prison to serve out the remaining eleven months of your sentence. Is that understood?"

"Yes, Sir…thank you, Sir," Pecos said as he turned and looked over at his shoulder at Sarah, whose crying had turned to a large smile.

"During those eleven months, you will report weekly to Marshal Raines and let him know how, and what, you are doing with your life."

"Yes, Sir. I can do that, Sir."

"I'm sure you can, Mr. Wilde. You seem to be an honorable young man, so let's hope that the faith that the Marshal and Mr. Lawson have in you is proven to be justified. Now, unless there is anything further anyone would like to say, this court is adjourned." He again knocked on the desk as everyone stood up and started to congratulate Pecos as Sarah gave him a huge hug, and kiss, while trying not to hurt his arm. Bill loudly cleared his throat and tapped Pecos on the shoulder and pointed toward the cells.

"Let's get this show on the road."

Chapter Twenty-One

Later that afternoon, Bill was at his desk when Corey made another appearance. "So, now that Pecos' future is settled, at least for the time being, what about our other little problem?" He asked Bill.

"I've been thinking about that. I'm going to have a talk with Mrs. Mason about any 'newcomers' to town that might have asked for a room at the boarding house. See if I get any kind of reaction from her. While I'm at it, I'll ask if she managed to find your mother's brooch anywhere."

"I told you she has it."

"I know that and you know that, but I can't go in there and accuse her on the word of a 'ghost'. The townsfolk would lock me up back there with Pecos. I've already had a couple of them ask me who I've been talking to when they passed by."

"There is one thing we could do," Corey said and hesitated for a moment.

"And that is?"

"See if Pecos would go along with a little charade."

"What do you mean?"

"Put out the word that he's started remembering some little things that Red said to him. Some things about the ring leader of the bunch. And those things, when they're put together, might lead to the identification of that person."

"In other words, see if Pecos would be willing to be a guinea pig to draw them out."

"Exactly. We know that Johnny had to have gotten that gun because someone handed it to him through the window. That same someone might try to use the window to silence Pecos."

"And just how do you intend to cover that window and the office here at the same time?"

"Well, there's two of us aren't there? I can wait out there, they're not going to see me. And I can pop back in here and let you know when they've taken the bait, and you can catch them in the act."

"And how do you propose that we explain this little plan to Pecos? How am I going to be in two places at the same time?"

"I guess I'll have to think about that one."

"Actually, Corey, it's a good plan. It will just take a little coordination. But, it just might work. Why don't I see if I can put the first part in motion and go have a little talk with Mrs. Mason?" He got out of his chair, grabbed his hat from the rack and headed out the door, locking it behind him. He walked down the street and over to the boarding house. He opened the door and went inside. "Mrs. Mason?" He called out and waited for a moment before she came from the back of the house.

"Hello, Marshal, what can I do for you today?"

"Well, I'm just looking for a little information. Has there been anyone new in town that has asked for a room in the last couple of days?"

"No, Marshal, there hasn't. I wish someone would…Corey's room is still empty and I need someone to come in and rent it."

"I see. Well, if someone new does approach you, would you please let me know?"

"Of course, Marshal. Is there a problem in town?"

"I'm not at liberty to say right now, Mrs. Mason. I'm just following up on a report that there may actually be members of the rustling gang still hanging around. Men we weren't aware of when we raided their camp."

"Oh, dear. I will certainly let you know, Marshal. I certainly wouldn't want someone like that living in my home. How did you find this out?"

"I can't tell you that right, now, Ma'am but it did come from a reputable source. Now, I'd better be going…oh, by the way, did you ever come across Corey's mother's brooch?"

"No…I haven't, Marshal. But I will keep an eye out for it, I promise you."

"I know you will, Ma'am. Thank you," Bill said, tipped his hat to her and left. He decided to make a tour around town and was walking by the hotel when he decided to go into the hotel and see if Wade had any new customers. "Afternoon, Wade," he said when he saw him at the desk.

"Hello, Marshal, what can I do for you today?"

"Just thought I would check and see if you had any new customers in the last day or so."

"No, Marshal. There hasn't been anybody new check in for at least a week. We have a few guests, but they have been here for a while."

"OK, Wade, thanks," Bill said as he turned and left the hotel. He was puzzled. If there were no new people in town, then someone locally must have gotten that gun to Johnny. But who? He was now in agreement with Corey that Mrs. Mason was involved. But there had to be someone else. He was walking by the mercantile when a shot rang out. He swung around toward the sound of the shot as the bullet flew passed his head and buried itself in the building. He searched the area visually, but couldn't see any sign of the shooter. He couldn't even be sure where the shot came from. Ok…that was it, he was definitely getting too close to something…and someone didn't like it. Corey's idea about using Pecos as 'bait' was beginning to look more and more favorable. Now, to find out if Pecos was willing to put his life on the line to help them. He headed back to his office without further incident.

*****

After Bill had left the boarding house, Molly had gone to the foot of the steps and called out, "Ryker! Get down here now!" A few seconds later a tall, dark, middle-aged man with a beard came hurrying down the steps and followed her into the parlor area. "We've got trouble," she said as she began pacing back and forth.

"What kind of trouble?"

"That marshal is getting too close to finding out that I'm involved in that rustling operation."

"Involved, isn't exactly accurate."

"Shut up and listen. I want you to get rid of him, and the sooner the better."

"You can't just go around shooting the local lawman and get away with it."

"Well, you'd better find a way, or you'll have more scars to match that one on your forehead."

He reached up and gingerly touched the old scar as she turned and walked toward the kitchen.

*****

A short time later he returned to the boarding house. "Well?" Molly said as he came into the room.

"I missed."

"You what!!" She almost shouted at him, afraid that if one of her boarders was in their room, that they might be heard. "You idiot, if he didn't know that there were others involved, he does now!"

"Not necessarily," Phil Ryker said. "He's a lawman. He must have made a lot of enemies by now."

"Well, I suggest you get rid of that lawman, and you might as well take care of Pecos, too. If he's the one that is the source of the info the marshal is getting, then he has to go too…"

"This is going to cost you."

"Excuse me!"

"Hey, I'm putting my life on the line too. I don't work for nothing." Ryker's tone was anything but friendly. "I think five thousand each should be quite sufficient."

"Ten thousand?! I don't have that kind of money. Maybe if that herd had gotten through, I would, but not now."

"Then I guess you're plumb out of luck, and accomplices."

"I don't think so…that marshal was over here asking if I had any new boarders…strangers in this town. I just might have to stop by his office and tell him about a new boarder that just came in."

"Not for long…I'm out of here."

"And how long do you think it will take him to catch up with you? We're in this together and there's nothing you can do about it."

Ryker knew he was not in a position to argue with her. She would make it look like he was guilty and she was trying to help the marshal out.

"OK…what do you want me to do?"

"GET RID OF THEM!"

*****

Later that night, Pecos had just lain down to try to go to sleep when he heard something in the alley outside the cell. Seconds later three sticks of dynamite, tied together with a lit fuse were thrown through the bars of the window in the adjoining cell. They landed just outside the bars in front of the cell. "MARSHAL!!! DYNAMITE!!!" Pecos yelled, then watched as the dynamite was lifted into the air and quickly moved through the bars and toward the window. It was thrown back through the window just as he heard a voice telling him to hit the floor. He did just that as the dynamite exploded outside. The heavy stone walls of the back of the jail, protected Pecos from the effects of the blast. He was getting to his feet when the marshal came running into the room.

"What happened?" Bill asked as he looked at the dirt and debris that had been thrown through the windows and into the cell.

Still shaken, Pecos got to his feet. "Dynamite…thrown through the window."

"That was quick thinking, throwing it back so fast."

"Not this window…that window," Pecos said pointing to the other cell.

"But how did it…?"

"It just lifted up and flew back through the window. Then I heard a voice tell me to hit the floor. I did, just as the explosion….Marshal…what's going on?"

Bill looked around the room and saw Corey leaning up against the bars in the other cell, wiggling his fingers at him. "I'm guessing that someone doesn't want us around anymore. This voice you heard…"

"It sounded like…Corey," Pecos said, suddenly not feeling so well. "Marshal…this place is haunted…he's still here!"

"I've had that feeling since the funeral," Bill said under his breath, but to Pecos he said. "Let's just consider that whatever is here, is a guardian angel."

"But…" Pecos started to say, not really knowing what to say next.

"Don't even try to figure it out. Just accept it."

Pecos shook his head, and sat back down on the cot. "I don't understand…I just don't understand."

"Try to get some rest Pecos, I'm going outside to see if whoever did this left anything to show who he was."

When he got outside, he found a crowd forming, drawn by the sound of the explosion. He went around to the dark alley and found that the boxes and barrels that had been stored there were now nothing but kindling. Bill turned to the crowd that had followed him into the alley. "Did any of you see anyone run from this alley right before the explosion?" There was a lot of shaking of heads but nobody stepped forward with any information.

The next morning Bill headed over to the mercantile as soon the doors were opened. "Hello, Burt."

"Marshal…what can I do for you?"

"Has anyone bought any dynamite from you in the last couple of days?"

"No, not from me. The last person to by any dynamite was old Joe. He said he wanted to open up a new shaft in his mine."

"When was that?"

"Oh, about a month ago, I guess. I haven't seen him since then. Must be pretty busy up there."

"Where is his claim, Burt?"

"Out on the west edge of the Pecos Mountains, I think."

"Thanks, Burt. Be seeing you." Bill turned and walked out and back toward his office. When he went inside, he saw Corey coming out of the cell area. "Corey…uh…thanks."

"What for?"

Bill just rolled his eyes and went back to check on Pecos. He found him asleep, so he went back to his desk. "Corey…what do you know about a guy named Joe who has a claim up on the west side of the mountains?"

"Old Joe Dice? A nice old man, I guess. Don't come to town very often except for supplies."

"Any place other than the mercantile that a man could get his hands on dynamite?"

"Not in town, some of the big mines have a cache, but they keep a tight guard on it." He stopped as there was a knock at the door. When Bill opened the door he saw Dean Gossett from the freight office standing there. "Morning, Dean." He stepped back and motioned for him to come inside.

"Morning, Marshal. I heard what happened and thought I should come right over."

"Oh?"

"A shipment of dynamite came in three days ago, waiting to be transferred to a train heading for Denver. When I heard what happened last night, I checked the crates and found that one of them had been broken into."

"Let me guess…three sticks were missing."

"Yes. Whoever did it, tried to hammer the crate lid back on, but you could still see where it had been pried open."

"Who knew about the shipment?"

"Well, it wasn't exactly a secret. But we didn't advertise it, if you know what I mean."

"Do you remember seeing anyone hanging around?" Bill asked him. "Someone that didn't belong there."

"There's always someone hanging around…come to think of it, there was a man hanging around a couple of days ago. I asked him if I could help him, but he said that he was just getting an idea of the way we operated. Had some freight coming in and wanted to make sure it would be handled in the right way. I asked him what he meant by it, but he didn't elaborate, just walked away."

"What did this man look like?"

"Tall, dark, beard…oh yeah, he had a small scar on his forehead."

"Thanks, Dean. I'll let you know if I need anything else from you."

"Wish I could be more help, Marshal. When I think what could have happened because my men and I were careless…"

Bill put his hand on his shoulder, "I'm not blaming you," he said as Dean took a deep breath. "Let me know if you remember anything else."

"Will do, Marshal. I'm sorry." With that he left the office as Bill turned to Corey.

"I think it's time I took another trip over to the boarding house. See if Mrs. Mason has any boarders by that description." Corey said and faded from sight just as Sarah came to the door.

"Hello, Marshal. Can I please see Pecos?"

"Of course, Miss Sarah." Bill stepped back to allow her to come in and then escorted her to Pecos' cell. "I'll be back in a few minutes."

"Pecos," Sarah said anxiously as he came to the bars and took her hand in his. "Are you all right? I heard about the explosion…"

"Sarah, I'm fine. See…look at me." He stepped back and turned around for her. Then went back to again take her hand as she couldn't help but give a little smile. "That's better," he said, "you're much prettier when you smile."

"Oh, Pecos," she said looking up at him, "I'm was so scared. I don't know what I would do if I lost you."

"You're not going to lose me. I'm yours, Sarah, completely." He leaned down and managed to kiss her through the bars. "When I'm out of here, I'll make all of this up to you. I promise."

"What are you going to do, Pecos? The judge said you will have to stay around here for the next year."

"I'll find a job. Whatever I have to do, I'll do." He touched her cheek. "Nothing is going to keep me from being with you. I guess you're stuck with me," he said, trying to lighten the conversation a little.

"I love you, Pecos," she said as they again kissed.....

Corey materialized in the living room of the house. He looked around to make sure she wasn't in sight and carefully opened the drawer in the table and realized that the brooch wasn't there. "Damn," he thought to himself. "She must have put it in that safe." He went up the stairs to the rented rooms to see if he could find anything incriminating. As he started up the steps, Molly was coming down. They met about halfway and Molly suddenly felt that cold sensation again. She shivered and then began trembling.

"He's here...he has to be here." She thought to herself. "Why won't you leave me alone?" She said out loud as she looked all around her.

Corey just smiled and continued up the steps. He hadn't intended for her to figure out he might still be around, but he kind of liked the idea of making her fidget. Just maybe it would distract her just enough to make her slip up. He again started searching the rooms. Over the last couple of days had had become more and more able to be able to pick up and move things, and not have to expend so much energy to do so. In one of the rooms, he opened the closet door to find a canvas bag containing fuse line and blasting caps. This had to be the room of the man that tossed the dynamite through the cell window. He decided to hang around for a little while and see just who came walking in that door.

An hour or so later Ryker came in the back door of the boarding house and headed into the parlor. "Hello, Molly," he said as he came into the room.

"Don't you 'hello Molly' me, you idiot. How could you mess up something as simple as tossing a couple of sticks of dynamite through those bars?"

"I did toss them in there," he said as he threw his hat on the table. "How do I know how they got back out the window. I even threw it into the empty cell. With that short fuse...there shouldn't have been more than a five second delay. Just enough time for me to get back out onto the street before it blew."

"Well, you did blow it…or should I say didn't blow it. We have to get rid of the marshal and Pecos if we're going to get out of this. They're getting too close."

"I know that…but what else can we do. It seems like that marshal leads a charmed life or something."

"Yeah…or something," Molly said with a quiver in her voice as Ryker just looked at her then decided that he had better head back to his room, grabbed his hat, and quickly went up the stairs. When he went inside he felt a slight chill in the room. He hung his hat on a peg beside the door and began taking his jacket off, but instead, put it back on and went to sit on the edge of the bed and take off his boots. Standing in the corner of the room, Corey watched the man trying to remember if he had seen him with any of the rustlers. Come to think of it, he might have seen him in the saloon in one of the poker games, just before he was approached about joining the gang. Ryker emptied his pockets and laid back to try to relax for a while before he went down to the dining room for supper.

Waiting to make sure that Ryker was asleep, Corey carefully tried to look through the man's wallet. He found a bank receipt made out to a Phil Ryker and smiled, then put everything back, left the boarding house, and went back to the office. He appeared at his desk as Bill was going back to his desk after showing Sarah out. "Well, you finally decided to come back, huh?"

"Now, Marshal, be nice or I won't tell you the name of the guy with the dynamite and where to find him."

"Oh?" He said as he sat down in his chair. "In that case, my apologies."

"His name is Phil Ryker. He's staying at the boarding house, 2nd room on the left, 2nd floor."

"How do you know it was him?"

"Found a canvas bag with blasting caps and fuse wire in the closet."

"Good work, I'd call that a pretty sure sign. Now, how do we get the judge to issue a search warrant. I think I'll go over to the telegraph office and have Paul send a telegram to see if this guy's wanted anywhere. Keep an eye on Pecos while I'm gone…make sure he stays in one piece." Corey nodded and disappeared to reappear in the cell area. Pecos was sitting on the cot, still trying to make sense of what had happened the night before.

He suddenly had a feeling that he was being watched and began looking around, even standing on his cot to see if he could see anyone out the window. Seeing that the alley was clear, he stepped down and sat back down on the cot.

"Corey…if you're here…at least DO something. Anything to let me know I'm not going crazy."

Corey knew that Pecos had seen what he had done with the dynamite, and that he would have to eventually reveal himself; but now he decided to just lie low on the other cot and wait, along with Pecos, until Bill got back. He realized that they had to come up with some viable evidence before this gunman actually completed his tasks. As he sat there, he began to think about something that Pecos just said. "Going crazy." Maybe that's what he would have to do. After all, Molly was already feeling his presence and getting very nervous. If he carried it a little further, just maybe, she would beg to tell Bill what she had been up to. "Hmmmm," he thought as a large smile came over his face, "this could end up being a lot of fun." Maybe he could play around a little with that Ryker fellow as well.

After he went to the telegraph office, Bill decided to stop by and have a little talk with the judge. "Hello, Judge," he said as he entered the office.

"Marshal, what can I do for you?"

"I've got a couple of leads on the identity of the leader of the rustler gang and I wanted to know what it would take to get a search warrant."

"What kind of leads?"

"Well, there were some letters seen on the table from Wichita, the destination of the rustled herd. Also, a canvas bag with blasting caps and fuse in it was found one of the rooms. Probably the source of the dynamite that was used to try and blow up my office last night."

"And just how did you come by this information? Have you seen it?"

"No, I haven't seen it, but it does come from a reliable source."

"And that would be?"

"I, uh, I can't tell you that right now, Your Honor."

"Let me get this straight, you want me to issue a search warrant on a couple of envelopes and a canvas bag, that you haven't even seen yourself, but have been told about by a 'reliable source'. Bill, you know I can't issue that kind of warrant without something a little more tangible, or at least a reliable witness that is willing to testify to what he saw."

"I kind of thought that would be the case," Bill said as he got up to leave.

"Marshal, this witness of yours…how come you can't tell me who it is?"

"Sorry, Judge, that will have to remain my secret…for now, anyway." When he got outside, Bill realized how late it was getting and stopped by the café to pick up supper for Pecos, then went back to his office.

He took the tray to the cells and saw Corey disappear when he entered. "Here, you go, Pecos," he said sliding the tray through the opening. "Did you have a nice visit with Sarah?"

"Yes. Thanks, Marshal, for letting her come here. It means a lot to both of us."

"Pecos, I know I'm prying, and you can tell me to mind my own business, but what happened with you? Your father was a good man. Died much too soon. Did the two of you have a falling out or something?"

"You're not prying. I guess I've always been a bit of a loner. Pa was away a lot and Ma had to handle a lot of things on her own. Don't get me wrong, now. Pa was a good man and provided well for us, but you know how the job of a lawman can be. He spent most of his time in his office, or escorting prisoners….whatever."

"Believe it or not, I can see a lot of him in you."

Pecos smiled and continued to eat his supper. "I guess so. He tried to teach me a lot about what he did. I guess I made a pest out of myself sometimes, just hanging around his office. When he didn't have any prisoners locked up, it was kind of fun. But when he did have someone there…it was like I wasn't welcome any more."

"That was for your safety, Pecos. A lot can happen under those circumstances."

"I realized that later on…after it was too late, I guess. By then, I just wanted to be out on my own. I cut out of there just after I hit sixteen. Been on my own ever since."

"Then you weren't there when he died?"

"No…I was a hundred miles away. I wanted to go home for Ma, but somehow I just couldn't. Didn't have the nerve, I guess. Figured that after I left like I did, she wouldn't want me around anymore."

"Oh, I wouldn't be too sure about that," Bill said.

"Well, I guess I'll never know, at least not for the next year."

"Never say 'never', Kid…" Bill got up and went back into his office to let Pecos finish his dinner in peace.

Chapter Twenty-Two

The next morning all of her boarders had left for their daily businesses and Molly was just finishing washing the breakfast dishes when Ryker came into the kitchen. "Well, have you figured out how you're going to get rid of our two 'problems'?" She asked him.

"Not yet."

"Don't you think you'd better get about it? Every day they're around is that much more dangerous for us."

"I know that. It's not that easy."

"I thought you were supposed to be the cream of the crop at what you do…right now all I see is the crumbs at the bottom of the bowl."

An hour later Molly was cleaning one of the rooms and had just finished making the bed and began to dust the furniture. When she turned around she saw that the bedspread had been pulled back away from the pillows and was now about halfway toward the foot of the bed. "No, it can't be…I know you're here. Stop it! Just stop it!" She hurried out of the room and went to her own room and closed and locked the door behind her. She walked over to the chest of drawers and poured some water from a pitcher into a wash bowl and splashed it onto her face. When she reached for a towel she saw it suspended in the air before her. She screamed as the towel fell to the floor.

Corey reappeared in Bill's office with a smug expression on his face. Actually he could hardly keep himself from bursting out laughing. "What's the matter with you?" Bill asked, then shook his head. "I know,

I know…someday I will get it through my head and quit asking. To rephrase, what have you been up to?"

"Just having a little fun at Mrs. Mason's expense."

Bill just sighed and leaned back in his chair. "What did you do?"

"Not much…unmade a bed. Offered her a towel after she washed her face…not much."

"Are you telling me she reached for a towel and saw it hanging in the air in front of her?"

"That's about it."

"And how is this going to help us?"

"Well…I was just thinking that she already suspects I'm hanging around…with a little 'encouragement', maybe she'll be willing to 'confess her sins' so to speak."

"Or run her out of town and then we get nothing."

"I don't think so, from what I've learned she doesn't have much of anything in the way of money right now. Just what she's bringing in from a couple of boarders. Not enough to do much travelling. The money she would have gotten from that herd was going to be her way out of here."

"Just be careful. We don't want to scare her to death."

"Why not? She's trying to kill you and Pecos, isn't she?"

Bill just shook his head, when they heard a knock at the door. He opened it and saw Paul standing there with a paper in his hand. "Marshal, here is the answer to that telegram you sent yesterday."

"Thanks, Paul," he said then handed him a tip and watched as Paul headed back toward the telegraph office. He looked up and down the street, then saw someone leaning against the wall outside the barber shop down the street. "Corey," he said softly. Then as Corey joined him, "is that the man you saw at the boarding house?"

"That's him," Corey said as he walked out onto the sidewalk. "Seems to be watching the office, doesn't he?"

"That's what I was thinking. This telegram should give us more info about him."

"I think I'll keep an eye on him for a little while," Corey said and headed down the street toward the barber shop as Bill went back to his desk. When he opened the telegram he read.

"Phillip Ryker, arrested in Oklahoma Territory for murder, released when only witness disappeared. No current warrants."

"Well, Mr. Ryker," Bill said, leaning back in his chair, "seems like Corey is on the right track. Now, how do we get you to give yourself away?" He got to his feet and went back to the cells. "How are you doing, Pecos?" He asked as he walked over to Pecos' cell.

"Not too bad, Marshal."

"How's the arm?"

"Pretty good. Just a little sore right now."

"That's good to hear. I have a question for you."

"Sure, Marshal," Pecos said as he got up and walked over to the cell door.

"Do you know anything about a guy named Phillip Ryker?"

"Ryker…." Pecos said as he thought about the name. "Name's familiar, but I don't know where I heard it."

"Could Red have mentioned it at any time?"

"Maybe…I'm sorry, Marshal, I just don't know right now. Let me think about it for a while."

"Sure, no problem. I just thought you might have heard of him."

"Any particular reason?"

Bill thought for a minute before he answered Pecos. "There's reason to believe he might have been the one that threw that dynamite in here."

"What? Why?"

"Right now, we don't know, except for the fact that just maybe someone thinks we're getting too close to finding out their role in the rustling."

"You mean the 'big boss' that Red mentioned."

"Exactly."

"But Red was the only one that knew who he was working for… wasn't he?"

"Let's just say we've come up with a couple of leads."

"We?"

"Yeah…I've made a few inquiries…found out a few things."

"But you said, 'we'." Pecos couldn't get what happened with the dynamite out of his mind. "It is Corey, isn't it? He is still hanging around."

"Now, Pecos…"

"I knew it! It had to be. It WAS his voice I heard that night."

"You keep talking like that and you will have people thinking you're as crazy as I am."

Pecos smiled, "You have a problem with that?"

"Not at all, Pecos…not at all," Bill said as he walked back to the office area and sat down.

Corey decided to stick with Ryker for a while longer and see what he was up to. Ryker had thought that if the marshal left the office, it might be the opportune time to try to get to Pecos. The problem was, he couldn't help feeling that he was the one being watched. He began looking around, but couldn't see anyone that seemed to be watching him. The longer he stood there, the stronger the feeling got. It got to the point that the hairs on the back of his neck seemed to be standing up…this was a feeling he didn't like…not one little bit. He decided that it might be a good time to head for the saloon and get a drink. He surely needed one right then. When he went into the saloon he went straight to the bar. "Whiskey," was all he said and laid a two-bit piece down. Jake placed a shot-glass on the bar and poured some whiskey into it, then picked up the coin and went back to the register. Ryker downed the drink in one gulp and stood there for a second.

"Anything wrong, Mister?" Jake asked him.

"Anything? Everything." Ryker said, then pulled out another two-bit piece and motioned for the glass to be filled again, which Jake obligingly did as he took that coin. Ryker looked at the glass for a moment, then downed it in one gulp again, then sat the glass down and looked around the room. For some reason, he still had that feeling. Corey couldn't help smiling as he leaned against the end of the bar just watching him. He was beginning to enjoy this to no end, but then he looked upward and shrugged, and faded away. A few moments later he appeared in Bill's office.

"I think Ryker's beginning to get the idea he's not alone anymore," he said to Bill.

"What?"

"Oh, just a feeling I'm getting. He's suddenly feeling that just maybe he's the one being watched instead of the other way around."

'You're having way too much fun with this."

"Hey, if they hadn't been rustling the ranchers' herds, I wouldn't have ended up like this. I think a little payback is not too much to ask."

"Then how come you're here and not tailing him now?"

"Didn't want to push him too hard…yet. But the more nervous they get, the more apt they'll be to mess up and give something away."

Bill thought for a few moments. "Knowing that Molly missed out on her payday from the herd, any sign that she might be ready to try something else?"

Corey shook his head. "Not that I know of. But, Ryker being here and staying at the boarding house has got to mean something. We just have to figure out what."

"I can't believe I'm saying this, but keep up what you're doing. Maybe we can push them into something, whether it's confessing, or making them desperate enough to try something they're not ready for." He pulled out his pocket watch. "It's after twelve, I think I'll go to the café and pick up lunch for me and Pecos."

"I'll check in on Mrs. Mason," Corey said and disappeared.

Bill entered the café and saw Sally wiping down the counter. "Hello, Bill," she said when she saw him. "Sorry I'm late getting lunch over to the office, but I was really swamped for a little while."

"That's all right, Sally. Besides, being swamped is a good thing, isn't it?"

"Yes, it is. Things have been picking up lately." She leaned on the counter as Bill sat down on one of the stools. "What would you and Pecos like today?"

"How about some roast beef sandwiches? Got any?"

"Sure…just give me five minutes." She headed back to the kitchen area as Bill looked around the café. He picked up the morning paper that was lying on the counter and began to read it while he waited. Most of it was just the same stuff as usual, until he saw a small article at the bottom of the page that was talking about the ranchers and the rustlers, and how the ranchers were now readying their herds for the actual drive to the railhead in Wichita.

*****

At the boarding house, Molly had been munching on some cookies and drinking a cup of coffee as she read the morning paper. She suddenly threw down the paper and looked at Ryker. "Those cattle going to the railhead should have been mine."

"You know," Ryker said, "with enough men, we might be able to take that whole herd away from them and still accomplish what we started."

"Yeah…and how do you propose we do that?" Molly said as she turned to him. "They're not just going to give them up that easily…we've already seen that."

"I agree…I was just thinking that maybe this time, we let them do all the hard work and we ambush the herd a few days out of Wichita. Take care of the drovers and take the herd in ourselves. I know a couple of buyers there that won't quibble about what brands they're wearing. We might not get as high a price, but….?"

"It'll take a lot of men and it won't be easy."

"I know that, but right now, they think they're home free. This will be the last thing they will expect," Ryker said as he got up from his chair and left the room.

"See what kind of force you can round up. It will take time for them to get to Wichita with the herd, just maybe you're right and we could intercept them."

"Some people just never learn," Corey thought to himself as he stood in the doorway listening to them. He watched as Molly again picked up the newspaper and began reading. Not being able to resist, he carefully changed the positions of the coffee and cookies and when Molly reached for another cookie, her hand went into the cup of hot coffee. She yelled out when she realized what had happened and saw that now the plate of cookies was on the far edge of the end table. She grabbed a small towel that she used for dusting and wiped her fingers as she jumped to her feet.

"Leave me alone…why can't you leave me alone?" She called out, but all she heard was what she thought was a very faint chuckle.

Chapter Twenty-Three

It had been almost three weeks since Corey had been killed. Bill had sent for Ken Harris and Bob Randall and they were now in his office. "Gentlemen," Bill said, "I'm very glad to hear that your roundup and preparations for the drive are almost complete. I am curious about any security measures you may have taken to insure that you are able to get your herds to Wichita."

"Security measures?" Randall guffawed. "I think our drovers are quite capable of handling anything thrown at them."

"Look, Gentlemen, I realize that the rustlers were taken care of…at least the ones we know about."

"The ones we know about?" Ken asked. "I thought we took care of all of them."

"I have been doing a little digging and I know that Red said that there was someone higher up that was running the whole operation. That person, or persons, is still out there…and we don't know if they are finished with their attempts to take the herds."

"You've got to be joking," Randall said, trying not to laugh. "There's no way that we are going to let anyone try anything now. Besides, you don't even know if there was a bigger boss."

"Let's just say I have it on good authority."

Ken had been sitting back listening to everything. "I have to agree with Bob on this one. We'll have enough hands to take on anything that anyone would want to throw at us."

Bill slightly shook his head. “OK, I just thought you would want to know that there is the possibility that someone might make a try to get the whole herd this time.”

Bob and Ken both got to their feet, shook hands with Bill and left his office. Bill watched them for a few seconds then decided to take a tour around town. He locked up the office and headed toward the barber shop. Rusty O’Hara was a red-headed Irishman, through and through. Nearly sixty years old, he had been a barber all his life, following in his father’s footsteps. “Hi, Rusty,” Bill said as he walked into the shop.

“And a good morning to you, Marshal. What can I do for you on this bright sunshiny day?”

“Just a trim.”

“Fine, Marshal, fine.” Rusty said as Bill sat down in the chair. He draped the smock over Bill’s chest and proceeded to begin trimming his hair. “And would you like a shave today, too?”

“No thanks, Rusty, just the trim. By the way…what’s the latest gossip in Rio Madre?”

“Gossip? Me? Now, Marshal, you don’t think that I would…?”

“Come on, Rusty, you know everything that happens in this town.”

“I do hear things occasionally, but…” he paused for a moment. “Seriously, Marshal, I haven’t heard anything unusual lately. Just the same old stuff. Who’s seeing who…what rancher is doing well while another isn’t.”

“Anything about the rustling situation we had?”

“No, Sir. I had heard some of the ranchers were having a problem, but it wasn’t until poor Corey got killed that I really knew anything about it. Oh, sorry, Marshal,” he said as he felt Bill tense up when he mentioned Corey. “Corey was a good lad. I really hated to hear what happened to him.”

“We all hated it, Rusty. We all did. Uh…have you noticed a new fellow in town lately, I’ve seen him hanging around your shop.”

“Come to think of it, I have seen a newcomer hanging around. He hasn’t been in…at least not yet. There you go, Marshal,” Rusty said as he finished and pulled the smock away.

“Thanks, Rusty. Look, if that fellow comes in and starts asking questions, or says anything unusual, would you let me know?” He paid Rusty and turned to leave.

“Sure, Marshal, be glad to. Always happy to be of service to the law.”

Bill continued his tour of the town, noting the comings and goings of the townsfolk. He hadn’t really been doing a regular tour since Corey died, and he knew he needed to get back into a normal routine. He also knew that Sally had been right…he was going to have to think about looking for a new deputy. The man would have to have that special quality…he stopped himself, realizing what he was doing. Trying to find someone just like Corey would be impossible. No, he would have to find someone with their own admirable qualities. Someone he could trust. But who? Oh well, he would have to cross that bridge when he came to it. He soon found that he had pretty much made a circuit of the town and was back in front of the saloon and decided to go inside. He noticed Sarah watering a potted plant near the window. “Good morning, Sarah,” he said as he walked over to her. “How are you doing this morning?”

“Pretty good, Marshal. Just trying to get some of the chores out of the way before we start getting busy.” She stopped for a moment and touched a leaf on the plant. “This is sure doing a lot better now. Corey was the one that suggested we put it by the window…it’s done beautifully since then…”

“I’m sure he would be glad to know that his advice helped it,” Bill told her and smiled as he remembered Corey telling him about getting that particular plant ‘drunk’ one night. “I’ll be heading back to the office in a few minutes if you want to visit Pecos.”

“Thanks, Marshal. Tell him I will be over in a little while.” She smiled and took the watering can back toward the storeroom.

*****

It was shortly after noon when Bill heard a knock at the door and opened it to find Sally there with a tray. “Hello, Bill,” she said as she came in and sat the tray on the desk. “I was getting worried about you when you didn’t come over for breakfast this morning.”

"Sorry, Sally…I just had a lot on my mind today and to tell the truth, I hadn't even thought about breakfast, 'til now, that is. That smells wonderful."

"It's not much, just some of that stew that Corey liked so much." She hesitated then continued. "You haven't slipped back into your 'I'm not hungry' ways, have you?"

"No…really. I was just busy this morning." He lifted up the corner of the towel covering the tray and inhaled the aroma.

"OK…for now, but just know that I'm keeping an eye on you."

"Yes, Ma'am," Bill said, saluting her then grinned big. "I'll bring his over later." She nodded at him and smiled, then left to go back to the café.

"You know, she is getting you wrapped around her little finger, or should I say 'ring finger'," Corey said as he sat down at his desk.

"What?" Bill said. "Oh, come on, Corey, give it a rest, OK?" He headed back to give Pecos his lunch, then returned a couple of minutes later and sat down at his desk to eat.

"Why should I give it a rest? You two were made for each other."

"Not to change the subject," Bill said in between bites, "but did you find out anything else this morning?"

"Not really," Corey said shaking his head. "Mrs. Mason knows I'm here and is getting really jumpy. I don't think it will be long before she caves in."

"She might, but what about Ryker?"

"I don't know about him. He's going to be tough to break. He also seems to be the schemer brains behind this whole thing. She tells him to come up with a solution and he does."

"I tried to warn Randall and Harris about the possibility that someone might make a try for the entire herd, but they didn't want to entertain the idea. Seems they think they have plenty of hands to take on whatever is thrown at them."

"My guess is that they probably do…under normal circumstances. But, given the right time and place…"

"I know what you mean," Bill said, nodding. "It's going to be our job to see that it doesn't get that far.

*****

Molly was in her kitchen preparing the evening meal for her boarders when Ryker came through the kitchen carrying a brick, a couple of bottles of whiskey and a couple of rags. "What are you going to do with those?" She asked him.

"I have a feeling things are going to get a little warm around the marshal's office tonight. Stick the rag in the whiskey bottle, throw brick through window, sit rag on fire, throw bottle through broken window…well, let's just say…roasted lawman. The marshal sleeps in a room to the right of the office. With just the right placement, he will be trapped by the fire…and Pecos…well, nobody will be able to get to him either."

"Not a bad plan…if it works. Right now the score seems to be Marshal 2, Ryker 0."

"It'll work…you'll see. And then there'll be nothing standing in our way of getting that herd."

"I've heard that before," Molly said as she went back to stirring the pot on the stove.

*****

That evening, Bill and Pecos were enjoying a game of checkers when Corey appeared to Bill and motioned toward the office area just as Pecos finished the current game by jumping Bill's three remaining checkers. Bill shook his head and stood up. "You're too good at this, Pecos. I've got to check things out front…be back in a couple of minutes." He followed Corey into the office.

"OK…what's up?"

"Ryker's up to something, Marshal. I'm not sure what, but I saw him heading toward the boarding house with his arms full of stuff and, well, I don't know, it just doesn't feel right."

"What was he carrying?"

"That's just it, I'm not sure. Mrs. Mason was cooking something and for some reason, I couldn't get near them to figure out what they were talking about."

"Excuse me…"

"I told you, I don't know what was happening. She had a lot of vegetables and stuff out on the counter and table. There must have been something there that repels spirits."

"Hmmm," Bill smiled, "maybe I should ask her for the recipe…might find a way to keep you out of my hair as well."

"That's not funny."

"Sorry, Corey. But you are right that we do need to keep an eye on them. It's been much too quiet around here for the last week or so."

"WILL YOU TWO COME BACK HERE AND LET ME IN ON THIS?" They heard Pecos call out from the cell area. Corey looked at Bill who just shook his head.

"Yes, he knows you're still around."

"I know…just didn't want to get him involved. He's in enough danger already locked up in there."

"I've been thinking about that. He's only got another couple of weeks or so before he'll be free…they're going to have to move soon if they're going to get both of us at the same time."

They both headed back toward the cells. Pecos looked up when he heard Bill and realized that he could see Corey standing there as well…at least it looked like Corey…just that he could see right through him. "Corey?" Pecos said, suddenly not so sure that he was ready for this.

"Hello, Pecos," Corey said as he smiled at him and watched as Pecos took a couple of steps back. "Sorry about keeping you in the dark, so to speak."

"No…no problem…." Pecos said, still not really sure he believed what he was seeing and hearing. "I knew it had to be you…but now…"

"Come on you two," Bill said, "we have to make plans. "Pecos…Corey thinks that Ryker and Mrs. Mason are planning something again. Something to take us both out of the picture…soon."

"And…?"

"That's just it, we don't know what."

"Isn't that what you're still here for?" He asked Corey.

"Supposedly…but not even I can know everything. I was told I was on my own, and to figure it out for myself."

"Oh, great." Pecos threw up his arms, turned and walked over to the window to look out.

"Look," Corey said, "I don't need sleep the way that you guys do, so I'll be keeping an eye on Ryker, especially at night."

"Let's hope that's enough," Bill said as he looked at both of them.

It was shortly after midnight when Ryker left his room and headed toward the Marshal's Office. He had already soaked the rags in the whiskey and was ready to light them as soon as he broke the window. Corey was sitting outside the office and saw Ryker heading down the street, keeping in the shadows close to the buildings. He watched as Ryker stopped in front of the office, then stepped away from the window and raised his hand as he got ready to throw the brick. Corey walked up behind him. "I don't think I would do that," he said, letting Ryker hear him. Ryker stopped and looked around, but didn't see anyone and raised his hand again. "I told you not to do that." Corey repeated, this time with an edge to his voice. Again Ryker stopped and looked around, but this time he felt what had to be a hand pulling his arm down. As much as he tried to lift his arm to throw the brick, he couldn't.

"Let me go," Ryker growled.

"I don't think so," Corey answered.

"Who are you? What are you?"

"Why, I'm your worst nightmare," Corey even more menacingly growled directly into his ear, then shifted and pushed Ryker, but kept hold of his arm, causing him to lose his balance and drop the whiskey bottle. Ryker had had enough. He dropped the brick and tried to pull away from whatever had him. Corey just laughed and released him, then watched as Ryker alternately ran and stumbled back toward the boarding house, looking over his shoulder all the way.

*****

The next morning Molly came down to the kitchen and found Ryker there…with what was left of a bottle of whiskey. "Well," she said. "I didn't hear any fire claxons last night."

"Oh, just shut up."

"Just a minute, Buster, you don't tell me to shut up. I thought you were going to take care of our little problem last night."

"Let's just say something got in my way."

"What?"

"If I told you, you wouldn't believe me."

"Try me."

"All right," Ryker said downing the last of the whiskey. "I got ready to break the window and this 'voice' told me not to. Then something grabbed my arm…"

"Voice? Now you're the one going crazy. You're starting to hear things." She said, more for her own good than his. This was confirming her own fears….Corey was back and he wasn't happy, with either of them.

"What do you mean that now I'm the one going crazy?"

"Let's just say that Deputy Hansen may be dead, but he hasn't left Rio Madre."

Ryker got to his feet and headed for the door and then turned around. "You know something, Molly, you had it right the first time…you're the one that's crazy around here. THERE'S NO SUCH THING AS GHOSTS!" They both watched as a butcher knife lying on the table suddenly lifted into the air and embedded itself in a cabinet door.

Corey was laughing as he appeared in Bill's office. Bill was getting used to things now and just shook his head at Corey. "Uh, that was an interesting little show you put on last night." Corey raised an eyebrow. "I heard something and went to look out the window just as our friend started to make his play."

"That was nothing compared to what just happened at the boarding house," Corey said and explained what had happened, including the bit with the knife. "They should both be wanting to confess, real soon. Especially Mrs. Mason."

"Just be careful. Like I said before, they could both just up and leave in the 'dead' of night and we wouldn't have anything. By the way, any sign that Ryker has called in any of his 'friends' to help to try to take that herd."

"Not that I know about. I think they've been too busy trying to figure out how to get rid of you first."

"Let's see if we can keep it that way. I saw Ken Harris briefly this morning. He said that they're pulling out tomorrow morning." Bill told him.

"If Ryker's going to try something, he's going to have to do it soon."

"It'll take a herd that size at least two to three weeks to get to Wichita, plenty of time for his gang to catch up to them," Bill said. "What I want is to keep Ryker from getting his gang together at all."

"Agreed, but to do that I guess I need to see what else I can do."

"What do you have in mind?" Bill asked as Corey got to his feet.

"I don't know. I guess I'll just have to wing it."

Bill did a double-take. "Wing it?"

"Well, that's what I'm trying to get isn't it?" Corey said as he motioned toward his back. Bill just shook his head in disbelief as Corey vanished from the room.

It was almost noon and Corey was watching the boarding house from across the street when he saw Ryker come out and head down the street. He followed him into the telegraph office and watched as he wrote out a message for Paul to send. As he looked over Ryker's shoulder he could see that he was contacting a man name 'Saunders' in Cactus Lake and asking that he and his friends join him in Rio Madre. Ryker waited until Paul had sent the telegram, then left and headed toward the saloon with Corey still following him. Somehow he couldn't shake that same feeling that he was being watched again. If Molly wasn't looney, Hansen was still there and following him around. But what could he do? How could he fight someone he couldn't see? And last night…what was that? Something had held onto his arm…something had spoken to him…it just wasn't in his mind…it happened. Right now, the only thing he could think of was to get his men together and go after that herd…get out of Rio Madre and NEVER come back. Besides, he could finish the deal for the herd, pay off his men and keep going. And Molly…let her fend for herself with Hansen. He had no intention of staying in that town any longer than he had to, much less come back to split the money with her. Saunders would be there by tomorrow and they would get the hell out of town and be waiting when the herd reached that gap in the mountains a couple of days ride from Wichita…the perfect spot to pull off the heist. When he got into the saloon, he got a bottle of whiskey from the bartender, paid for it and took it back to the boarding house. If he had to, he would hole up there until Saunders arrived and they could get out of that place.

Corey watched him go back to the boarding house and headed back to the office, getting there just as Sally was getting ready to leave after delivering the lunch tray for Pecos. "As you could see, I didn't bring your lunch, Bill. You need to get out of here more often. I'll see you at the café in a little while." She turned and left the office as Bill lifted the cover on the tray to do the inventory, although, at this point, he didn't think he really need to. He started to pick up the tray when he heard Corey's voice.

"Ryker has sent for his men."

"How many?"

"Don't really know. Just sent a telegram to a man named Saunders and told him to get the men together and come here. The message was sent to Cactus Lake, so they will probably get here in a couple of days. Any chance you could get their sheriff to detain them."

"Not without a warrant."

"You know," Corey said, "I'm beginning to think this lawman job has way too many restrictions."

"They're for the good of the people, Corey."

"Yeah, but what about the innocent people that get caught in the middle?"

"I agree with you, Corey, but we're sworn to uphold the law, even when it grates against us."

Chapter Twenty-Four

Two days later, Corey was again hanging out in the boarding house, trying to find out when, where and how Molly and Ryker were going to try to steal the herd. "Look, Ryker," Molly said, as they both sat in the parlor, talking, "you've got to get rid of the marshal and Pecos tonight. If your men are going to be here tomorrow like you say, you can bet that he's not going to sit still and watch as you all ride out of town after that herd."

"If you're so bright, how do you propose we get rid of him?"

"I don't know…look…he makes his final rounds about ten o'clock. Pick him off, get his keys to the jail and take care of Pecos."

"What about Hansen?"

"What about him? He's a ghost. Ignore him."

"Well, there is that alley next to the saddle shop…might be a good place to jump him." He pulled up his pants leg and drew a Bowie knife from the sheath and ran his finger along the side of it. "This should make it nice and quiet…won't wake anyone up."

"I don't care how you do it, just get it done!" Molly got up and headed upstairs to her room.

Corey left the boarding house and went back to the jail. "I think we got them this time," he said as he popped back in.

"Oh?" Bill said, as he looked up from his desk.

"He's going to make a try to knife you tonight on your final rounds. The alley by the saddle shop. Then get your keys, come here and take care of Pecos."

Bill just smiled. "You know, Corey, having you in this state is sure coming in handy. Let's see what little surprise we can set up for him this time. We play our cards right and we can get him for the attempted murder of a marshal and put him in the cell next to Pecos. Should put a kink in their plans for the herd."

Corey smiled at him. "I guess I do have my moments," he said then got real serious. "Look, Marshal, I know he said the saddle shop, but just in case…be real careful. He could change his mind and try it from anywhere."

Bill nodded in agreement. "I'll be on my toes…that's for sure."

"Why don't you get someone that can testify to shadow you tonight… just in case."

"Yeah…and just who do you think that should be?"

Corey grinned as he said, "Don't you worry…I'll take care of it." He disappeared from sight.

It was about 9:30 when Bill finally locked up the office and headed down the street to make his final rounds of the evening. He had decided to change his timing a little, just in case. As he walked he checked the doors of the businesses to make sure that everything was locked. His senses were super jumpy, causing him to double check every shadow that seemed to move. Meanwhile, Corey had reappeared in the office. He took the keys for the cells from the hook and went to see Pecos. "Hello, Pecos," he said as he got to his cell.

"Corey? What are you doing here?" He couldn't help it but a little chill went through his body. He would never get used to seeing Corey this way. What surprised him more, was when Corey used the keys to unlock his cell. "What are you doing?"

"Look, Pecos…I think Ryker is going to make another try at the Marshal tonight while he's on his rounds." He then explained what he had heard in the boarding house. "The marshal just left a couple of minutes ago. I want you to follow him…back him up if he needs it."

"Uh, Corey, I'm supposed to be in this cell, if someone else sees me and decides to take matters into his own hands, I might not be much help to the marshal."

"I know…it's a gamble either way. But you're the only one that knows about me, and that I would trust to do this."

"Thanks, Corey. OK…let's give it a shot." Probably a wrong choice of words he thought to himself as he followed Corey into the office and Corey showed him where his pistol was. Pecos checked to see that it was loaded and left the office, trying to stay in the shadows as he headed down the street. A few moments later he spotted Bill about a block ahead of him and watched as Bill checked out the bank, trying the door and looking through the windows. Pecos decided to cover him from across the street, so when Bill crossed the street Pecos stayed where he was. As he looked across the street, Pecos thought he saw movement in an alley beside the mercantile, two doors from where Bill was now. He slowly pulled his gun from the holster and waited until he could be sure there was someone there. Bill began to get the feeling that he wasn't alone. He knew that Corey had something about getting someone to shadow him, but that wasn't logical…no one knew Corey was here. As he got in front of the mercantile, he tried the door and found it was secure. He continued slowly walking down the sidewalk until he heard someone call out, "MARSHAL!" He dropped to the ground as Ryker lunged toward him with the knife, but instead, Ryker ended up tripping over Bill kicking him in the head and momentarily stunning him. Ryker rolled and came up with the knife, moving to stab Bill in the back, but a shot rang out and Ryker felt a burning pain in his forearm, causing him to drop the knife. Bill quickly regained his senses and rolled out of the way, coming up with his gun pointed at Ryker.

"Well, we finally meet, Mr. Ryker."

"You know, Marshal, you must have a guardian angel watching over you," Ryker said as he staggered back a step, holding a hand to his bleeding forearm.

"You might say that," Bill said as he picked up the knife and motioned Ryker toward the office. As soon as he saw that Bill had the situation in hand, Pecos hurried back to the office and into his cell as Corey locked it and put the keys back on the peg.

Moments later Bill brought Ryker into the office, took him back to the cells and locked him up next to Pecos. "Hey, Marshal, I need a doctor… I'm bleeding." Ryker said still holding his arm.

"Don't you worry, I'll get you a doctor," Bill said as he left the area.

Ryker sat down on his cot and looked over at Pecos who was lying on his cot with his hat over his face, seemingly trying to sleep. "I'm not done with you yet," he said as Pecos just smiled and turned onto his side facing away from him.

Bill went outside, locking the office behind him and walked down the street to the doctor's house and knocked on the door. "Sorry to bother you, Doc," he said as Doctor Russell opened the door. "I've got a prisoner that could use a little of your attention."

"Sure, Marshall, I'll be right there," he said as he turned to go back into his house. "Just let me get my bag."

"Thanks, Doc," Bill said as he turned and headed back to his office. When he got there, Corey was just coming back from the cell area. He smiled at Corey. "Well, I guess I have you to thank for that," he pointed at the cells.

"Me…I just told you what they were planning. I can't use a weapon, if you hadn't noticed."

"I don't suppose you want to tell me who my 'shadow' was tonight?"

"Oh…just a friend that suddenly had the idea that he might need to keep an eye on you," Corey said as he sat down at his desk and put his feet up.

"I see," Bill said, and got to his feet when he heard a knock at the door. He let the doctor in and led him into the cell where Ryker was being held. Bill stayed at the door, and watched as Doctor Randall bandaged the arm, then left the cell. Bill locked the cell again and followed the doctor back to the office.

"He should be fine in a couple of days," the doctor said. "I'll come back tomorrow afternoon and check the arm, just to make sure there's no infection."

"Thanks, Doc. Sorry to get you out so late."

"I'm used to it, believe me," he said to Bill and then headed back to his house.

Bill locked the door and went to sit at his desk. "Might as well do this paperwork now," he said to Corey. "I won't have to worry with it in the morning." He started writing and when he finished he went back to the cells to make sure his prisoners were 'tucked in', then decided it was time for him to get some shut-eye.

*****

Molly had heard the shot and waited for Ryker to return with the good news. When he hadn't come back an hour later, she couldn't help herself and threw the book she had been trying to read against the wall. "That idiot! I can't trust him to do anything right." With that she headed upstairs to her bed and tried to go sleep, but did not accomplish much until it was time to get up and fix breakfast for her boarders.

When Bill awoke the next morning, he checked on his prisoners and then headed over to the café, knowing he would have to let Sally know that she would need to fix an extra meal. "Good morning, Bill," she said as she saw him come in the door.

"Good morning, Sally. Just thought I would come over and pick up breakfast this morning and let you know that there's another mouth to feed."

"Oh?"

"It seems that we might have gotten the guy with the dynamite."

"That's a relief," Sally said as she poured him a cup of coffee. "I hope that's the last of it."

"Me too," he said, taking a sip of the coffee, "but I doubt it. I got reason to think there's still another one out there."

*****

Molly had begun cleaning up after breakfast and turned to wipe the flour off the counter where she had been making the biscuits, and stopped short. Written in the flour was "Just 1 more." She quickly wiped up the flour and threw the rag into the sink, then turned and just stood there trembling. "What am I going to do now?" She realized that it was only a matter of time before Marshal Raines came knocking at her door to arrest her. But what else could she do? The money she did have wouldn't last long if she tried to leave town. Then she suddenly remembered that Ryker's men were due to ride into town that afternoon. Even if she tried to get Ryker's men to take care of the marshal, she couldn't pay them. The boarding house was just barely helping her to make ends meet. Her future livelihood had been based on what they were going to get for the stolen cattle. These men of Ryker's…she didn't know them. Could she trust them? She doubted it. Even if she told them what Ryker had in mind, they would just go after the herd and then keep right on going and she would be right back where she started…. nowhere. Then it dawned on her…Ryker was in custody…would he talk? Would he tell them that she had been the one giving the orders? If it came down to it…yes he would. She had no choice, she would have to get out of town, fast. But how? She didn't have enough money to get very far….wait…maybe…if she could just get to a good sized town, she might be able to sell that brooch. After all, it was a ruby…had to be worth quite a bit. Yes…that's it. She would pack her things, and catch that late train tonight. By the time anyone missed her in the morning, she would be long gone. If Ryker's men came calling, she would tell them she didn't know anything about what Ryker wanted with them; and anyway, he was in jail, so they could just go somewhere else. Yes, that was it…that's what she would do.

Chapter Twenty-Five

Bill was outside Ryker's cell. "OK, Mr. Ryker, we've got you for attempted murder of a town marshal. There's no way out of it. We also know that you were involved with the cattle rustlers and that there is still one more person out there...the leader of the gang. It might go a lot easier for you if you told us who that person is."

"Dream on, Lawman," Ryker said sarcastically.

"OK...if that's the way you want it, you can take the fall for the whole thing...the rustling, accessory in the death of a lawman, at least three attempts on my life and...."

"What do you mean three?"

"Well, it only stands to reason that you were the one that threw the dynamite through the window and I also happened to see you running away from the front of this office two nights ago, after you tried to throw a brick through the window. I'd be willing to be you're the one that slipped that gun to Chambers, too, and you're probably the one that took a shot at me." Bill looked over at Corey who was standing beside Pecos' cell. He could also see Pecos intently listening to what was going on.

"You can't prove any of that without witnesses."

"Oh, but we do have witnesses..." Bill said, glancing over at Pecos, hoping he would pick up on what Bill was doing.

"Uh, Marshal," Pecos said, standing up. "When that dynamite came through the window, I yelled for you then tried to see who threw it...this man sure fits the bill."

"You'd be willing to testify to that?" Bill asked.

"I sure would, Marshal." Pecos said as he looked at Ryker. "You know, his voice sounds like someone I heard talking to Red at the hideout. It was dark, but it sure sounds like his voice."

"You're lying!" Ryker shouted. "I was never at that cabin."

"Tell me, Mr. Ryker," Bill said, "How do you know the hideout was in a cabin?"

Ryker stood there for a long moment. "I just guessed…seemed logical, where else would they be?."

"There are a lot of caves up there in those mountains…"

"Hey…ain't I supposed to have a lawyer before you start asking me anything?"

"OK, Ryker, we'll see if we can find you a lawyer. But, if I were you I would come clean and tell us about your boss…could be a lot easier for you especially if you were just following orders..."

"I'm not telling you anything." Ryker said as he laid back down on his cot and put his hat over his face.

Bill walked over to Pecos' cell. "Thanks, Pecos. I'm sure your testimony will be a big help. Too bad he's going to have to take the fall for this while his boss gets off scot free. With Ryker in here, I'd be willing to bet he's packing his bags right now for a quick escape." He winked at Pecos and walked back to his office.

A short time later there was a knock at the door and when Bill opened it he saw Sally there with the lunch tray. "Hello, Sally. Come on in."

"Hello, Bill. Hope you and your 'charges' are ready for lunch."

"We sure are, Sally," he said as he took the tray from her and sat it on the desk. He thought for a moment. "You know, you have been a real trooper, taking care of us like you have," he smiled at her. "How would you like to go to a late supper tonight at the hotel, after you close your café?"

"I would like that very much, Bill. Thank you."

"I'll pick you up about eight o'clock at the café…that OK?"

"That will be wonderful. I'll be ready."

"Good. I'll bring the tray over this evening when I pick up supper for those guys." He nodded toward the cells.

"That will be fine, Bill. I'll see you then." She left his office and headed back to the café, but decided to make a quick detour to her house to pick up something nice that she could slip into before he picked her up that evening.

About mid-afternoon, Jake was cleaning the saloon's bar when two strangers walked up to him. "Howdy," one of the men said.

"Afternoon, Gents, what can I get for you?"

"A beer and a little information."

"Sure," Jake said as he turned to get their beers. When he handed the men their beers, they paid for them, then started looking around the room.

"You know a man named Ryker," the man asked.

"Ryker?" Jake thought for a moment. "Oh, yeah…don't know him, but hear the marshal's got someone by that name locked up in his jail. Seems he tried to knife the marshal last night, and that doesn't go well with folks around here."

The two men looked at each other. "Thanks," the man said and they finished their beers and left the saloon. As they reached their horses, the first man looked at the other. "Let's let the other guys know and get out of here. Whatever Ryker has gotten himself into, I want no part of it." The other man nodded and they mounted and rode out of town.

That evening, after the prisoners had eaten their supper, Bill went into his room and changed into a clean shirt and pants. He splashed on a bit of cologne and combed his hair before putting on his hat and walking back into his office where he found Corey sitting at his desk. Corey looked at Bill and whistled. "Looks like you have a date tonight," he said as Bill just smiled at him.

"I'm just taking some of your advice."

"Oh, ho…you're finally taking Miss Sally out to dinner….it's about time."

"Hold on, Corey, let's not blow this all out of proportion. She's gone above and beyond the call of duty when it comes to delivering meals over here. That's the job of the marshal or the deputy. I just thought I should show her a little appreciation for her efforts."

"Uh huh." Corey was doing everything he could not to burst out laughing. "A 'little appreciation' doesn't mean you have to get all gussied up, or does it?"

"It does. At least in my book it does."

"Well, pardon me. You two have a good time tonight…and try not to get into too much trouble. This is one time I don't think I should play bodyguard, or should it be 'chaperone'?"

Bill just glared at him. Corey was having much too much fun with this. "Just keep an eye on our 'friends' back there. If you need me, we'll be at the hotel."

"Oh, that's convenient," Corey couldn't help himself. "Have you booked the room yet?"

"Will you stop it!? We'll be in the restaurant, and then I'll walk her home. Nothing more." With that Bill left the office, locking the door behind him. He stood on the sidewalk for a few moments, shook his head, and then went over to the café. He stopped short when he saw Sally dressed in a dark blue dress with lace trim around the low cut, v-neck collar and long sleeves. She was also wearing a cream colored shawl and her hair was loose and flowing around her shoulders, with just a white ribbon tied in a bow on top of her head to hold it back from her face.

"Hello, Bill," she said as she grabbed her reticule and keys from a table and walked out as he held the door for her.

"May I," he asked, then took her keys and locked the door. He handed her the keys and offered her his arm, which she took as they walked to the hotel. "You look lovely this evening, Sally."

"Thank you, Bill," she said slightly blushing. "You're looking right handsome, yourself."

He smiled at her, realizing that he was feeling something he hadn't felt in a long time. Just maybe Corey was right, and it was time he should start thinking about letting himself fall in love again…that is, if he hadn't already. When they arrived at the hotel restaurant, they were met by Jenny Oliver, one of the waitresses who showed them to a table. "It's nice to see you two in here. What can I get for you this evening?"

"What would you recommend?" Bill asked her.

"Well, the chef has some really nice steaks."

Bill looked at Sally, who nodded. "Then steaks it is," Bill told Jenny. "Both medium, and you can bring us coffee, and a bottle of red wine."

"Coming right out," Jenny said then leaned down to whisper into Sally's ear. "You'd better hang on to him. He's a keeper." Jenny then turned and headed toward the kitchen as Sally stifled a chuckle.

"Woman talk?" Bill asked as Sally just nodded her head and then started looking around the room.

"It's been a long time since I was in here," she said. "I believe they've redecorated since I was here last."

"The café keeps you busy, I know that." Then he chuckled a little. "Especially when my little 'hotel' is full. It's about time you let someone else cook a meal for you." He looked up as Jenny came back to the table with coffee cups for both of them, as well as a bottle of wine and two glasses. She poured their coffee and then went back to the kitchen. A short time later Jenny returned with their meal and as they ate, they talked about their lives and began to get to know each other better. After they finished their dinner, Bill paid Jenny and they began walking toward Sally's house near the edge of town. They were nearing the house as they heard the train whistle, signaling the arrival of the 10:00 train. By habit, Bill looked over at the train depot and saw Molly standing there, with two large suitcases. "Sally, I want you to go home and lock your doors. I've got something to take care of."

"Bill, what's wrong?"

"Maybe nothing, maybe everything. Just do as I say....please. Now scoot." He watched her turn and head toward her house and then he headed toward the depot. Bill got there, just as the train was pulling in. "Hello, Mrs. Mason," he said as he walked up beside her."

"Why...uh..hello, Marshal."

"You're leaving town kind of sudden, aren't you?"

"I got a letter from my aunt today. She lives in Laramie, you know. She's taken a turn for the worse and I really need to be with her at this time." Molly was getting very nervous and it was beginning to show as she fiddled with her small reticule.

"I'm sorry to hear about your aunt. Who's going to be taking care of the boarding house?"

"I've made arrangements."

"I see." He pointed to the two large suitcases. "It looks like you might not be planning on coming back for some time."

"Well, you never know how these things turn out. She could live for a few days, or weeks…who knows."

"You do know that one of your tenants, a Mr. Ryker, is now occupying a cell in my jail, don't you?"

"Ryker…no…I don't know him, never heard of him. He's not one of my boarders. Now if you don't mind, I really must get on the train."

Bill knew he couldn't take a chance and let her get on that train. "I don't think so, Mrs. Mason. In fact, I think you need to come with me." He took her by the arm.

"You can't do this…you have no right!" She said as she began trying to pull away from him.

"Oh, but I do have the right, Mrs. Mason. As marshal of Rio Madre, I have every right to believe that you have been 'involved' with the gang of rustlers that had been plaguing the area."

"What!? You have no proof of that…whatever Ryker said is a lie. I…" At that point she knew she had said the wrong thing, her hand was already in her reticule and she pulled out a small derringer. Bill had seen the movement and grabbed her other arm, but not before she had pulled the trigger. A shot rang out and Bill eased his grip on her for a split second as a burning pain shot through his left side. She pulled away from him for a moment but was grabbed from behind by depot manager, Carl Gray. "Let me GO!" Molly screamed at him, but he held tight to her arms. Gray was about five feet 10 inches tall and almost sixty years old, but still strong and dependable, and prided himself on being able to take care of any situation that might disrupt his station and this definitely fit the bill.

"You OK, Marshal?" Carl asked.

"Yeah…just a flesh wound. Would you mind helping me get her back to the office and then send her belongings over there?" Bill motioned toward the office with his left hand as he placed his right hand over the wound.

"Be glad to, Marshal. Come on, Mrs. Mason," he said as he led her toward Bill's office. When they got there, Bill unlocked the door and led them back to the cell area, grabbing the key from the hook.

"Hello, Boys," Bill said as he came into the area. "I have a roommate for you." He walked over to the third and last cell and opened the door allowing Carl to gently push Molly inside.

Pecos jumped to his feet when he saw who was brought in, then noticed the blood on Bill's shirt. "You OK?" He asked Bill who was standing in front of his cell as Carl locked Molly into her cell.

"Yeah…I'm fine," Bill said as he started back to the office area.

Pecos reached through the bars and barely touched Carl's arm causing him to turn. "Make sure he sees a doctor."

Carl smiled. "I will, Son. I'll send Doc over here on my way back to the depot." He went into the office and saw Bill leaning against his desk. "Look, Marshal…why don't you just sit down before you fall down. I'll go get the Doc and send him over here."

Bill nodded and gingerly sat down in the chair. "Don't forget…"

"I know…I'll send her bags right over." Carl left the office as Corey suddenly appeared.

"I guess I should have played bodyguard tonight."

"Oh, don't start in on me." Bill was hurting and embarrassed. He knew he had underestimated Molly and he was paying for it. "Carl's going to bring her things over here in a few minutes. My bet is we'll find that brooch of yours all polished and ready to sell."

"To hell with the brooch! She could have killed you."

"Naaah. It's just a little scratch." He stopped when he saw the doctor come in the door. "Hi, Doc."

"Hi yourself. You know, Marshal, it seems that lately, I can't get a decent night's sleep because of you."

"Sorry, Doc. Just doing my job."

"So, let me do mine. Let's get you onto your bed so I can look at that." He helped Bill get to his feet and led him into the small sleeping quarters of the jail.

The doctor was just coming into the office area when Carl and one of his helpers brought Molly's bags into the office. "How's he doing?" Carl asked.

"Oh, he's fine. Just a deep gash. He'll be fine in a few days."

They all looked at the door as an out of breath Sally came rushing in. "Is Bill OK?"

"He's fine, Sally. Don't worry. I've got him patched up and told him to stay in bed for the rest of the night. He's right in there," he pointed to the sleeping quarters, "if you want to see for yourself."

She quickly hurried into the room, sat down beside the bed and brushed a stray lock of hair off Bill's forehead. He opened his eyes and looked at her. "Sally…what are you doing here?"

"Shhhh," she told him. "Just lie there and rest. I'll look after you."

"Sally…you have a café to open in the morning…"

"I'll post a sign…people will just have to go somewhere else for breakfast."

"Not that easy…I have 3 prisoners that…"

"Hush…I'll take care of them, and you."

"But…."

She leaned over and gently kissed him. "Now…see if that will shut you up. Get some sleep…that's an order." She leaned in to kiss him again, but this time he reached up and pulled her in for a longer embrace. When she straightened up, she just smiled at him, stroked his forehead and watched as he closed his eyes and relaxed into sleep.

*****

The next morning Bill awoke and started to sit up but was caught by a sharp pain in his side. "Oh yeah…that's right," he said as he slowly, this time, sat up and looked around the room. He managed to make it to the latrine to take care of his bodily needs, and when he walked into the office, he found Sally there, taking the towel off the tray with the prisoners' breakfast. "Sally?" He was a little confused. "How did you get in here?"

"I never left…correction, I went to the café to fix these meals and came back here."

"You stayed here all night…by yourself?" Bill couldn't believe what he was hearing.

"Oh, I wasn't really alone…I knew I could get Pecos to help if I really needed him, besides, Corey was keeping an eye on me."

"Corey? Uh, Sally, he's…"

"Dead? Yeah, I know, I was at the funeral, remember. But he's still here… maybe not in a solid form, but he's here. I spent the night on your bench over there," she pointed to a long bench with a back and cushions, "and, I think Corey spent most of the night at his desk, or in the cell area. I heard him moving around a couple of times."

Bill had walked over to his desk and sat down, not quite knowing what to say or do. "Now," she said as she got everything arranged, "do you want me to deliver these alone or do you want to accompany me?" He didn't say anything in response, just got up and showed her into the cell area. He gave everyone their instructions about stepping back and let Sally slide the plates and cups through the slots. When they got back to his desk, Bill didn't say anything, just stared at her for a few seconds. "What's wrong?" She asked him as she walked up to him.

"Nothing…nothing at all." He bent down and gently brushed her lips with his. "Uh, you know this could get a little complicated," he said smiling.

"Life gets boring when there are no complications," she said, then pointed to his chair. "Sit."

"Yes, Ma'am." Bill went and sat down at his desk. He didn't know whether it was his wound, or her, but he was actually feeling a little giddy. Out of the corner of his eye he could see Corey sitting at his desk, laughing heartily.

"Good morning, Corey," Sally said and Corey stopped laughing and sat straight up. "I may not be able to see you right now, but I know you're here. Now, I have a few things to take care of, but I'm warning you, take it easy. I know there's going to be a lot of traffic in here this morning but that's no excuse for not taking care of yourself. Corey," she turned to look at his desk. "I'm holding you responsible for taking care of him today."

Bill was looking around the room and saw Molly's bags sitting in a corner. "Sally," he said, suddenly serious, making her turn to him. "I'm going to need you to come by here later. I want to go through Molly's stuff and see what evidence I can find, but I think there should be a woman present when I do."

"We can do it when I bring lunch back for them. How's that?"

"That's fine," Bill said as he watched her walk out of the office. "Morning, Corey."

"How does she...?" Corey was still confused.

"Don't ask me. You're the expert in all of this."

"Who me? I've only been this way for a month..."

"Time flies, doesn't it?" Bill said. "Hey, wait a minute...you're right, it is almost a month now. Pecos is due to be released on...let's see...Friday." He reached into a desk drawer and pulled out a file of papers and began to read. A short time later he went back to the cell area and unlocked Pecos' cell. He had his gun ready, but knew that he wouldn't have to use it. It was mainly for show for Ryker and Molly. "Pecos, come with me." Pecos got up from his cot and preceded the Bill into his office.

"Anything wrong, Marshal?"

"No, Pecos. I just wanted to have a little talk with you in private. Mainly, I realized that your month as my 'guest' here is up on Friday. Have you thought about what you are going to do? The judge has stipulated that you can't leave the area."

"Yes, Marshal, I have been thinking about it. I'm going to try to get a job somewhere. Maybe one of the ranchers will be willing to hire me on, even after what I did."

"I will put in a good word for you with Ken Harris if you would like."

Pecos smiled. "That would great, Marshal. I would really appreciate it."

"Now, one more thing," Bill said. "You know now that Molly and Ryker were both involved with the rustlers. We have reason to believe that Molly was actually the one giving the orders. At any time while you were with Red and his gang, did you ever hear anything that might help us convict them? I know I've asked this before, but now that we have someone in custody, I was hoping something might ring a bell with you."

"Like I said before, Red didn't say anything other than there was someone higher up giving the orders. But I can tell you that those two have been throwing looks at each other. It's probably a good thing there's a cell between them, otherwise, they would probably kill each other. They haven't said anything to each other, but you could cut the tension between them with a knife, if you know what I mean."

"I think I do," Bill said smiling. "I would be willing to bet that if either one of them said just one thing against the other, they would both be falling head over heels to put the blame on the other…giving us just what we need."

"You're probably right," Pecos said. "I just hope it's before I get out of here. I would like to see the show. Besides, when it comes down to it, they're the reason I'm in here."

Bill looked him straight in the eyes. "Pecos…Danny, the only one to blame for you being here is you. You didn't have to take them up on their offer of a job."

Pecos looked down at the floor. "I know that. It's just that…."

"I know why you said you did it," Bill admonished him. "But it was still against the law."

"Yes, Sir."

"Now, if you do want to do something else to help…try to get them started."

"Sir?"

"You're quite good at coming up with the stray comment, I've seen it. Maybe you could say something to get the ball rolling. You've already planted the seed with Ryker. See if you can push it just a bit further."

"I'll see what I can do."

"OK, let's get you back in there. But don't say anything right away, we don't want them to suspect that what we were setting up out here. I'll let you know when."

"I'll just tell them that we were discussing what I can and can't do when I get released on Friday."

"Perfect." Bill looked at him. "Sorry, Danny....let's go back in there. You know...I do think 'Danny' suits you a lot better than 'Pecos'."

Pecos just smiled, "We'll see." Then he got to his feet and preceded Bill back to the cell. Bill locked him back into the cell and left as Pecos laid down on the cot.

"What was that all about?" Ryker asked, curious.

"Oh, I'm due to get out of here on Friday. The marshal was just giving me a little lecture on what I can and can't do after that."

"Such as?"

"Can't leave the area, have to check in with him every week, that kind of stuff. Mainly I have to find a respectable job and be an upright citizen for the next year."

"Could be worse, I guess," Ryker said then got up to look out the window at the town, at least what he could see of it. "I have a feeling I won't be as lucky," he thought to himself. He looked back at Pecos. "How come you got off so easy?"

"Didn't fight back when the posse showed up...why bother, they had us dead to rights. I told them what I knew, which wasn't a whole lot. After they put us in here, Johnny was being a pain in the ass, and when he tried to break out, he tried to use my girl as a hostage when she came to visit...I didn't appreciate it and helped the Marshal to stop him. I rather think that you might know something about how he got that gun. Anyway, I think cooperation was the key."

"I see," Ryker said thoughtfully as Molly sat in her cell, fuming. Things were looking worse and worse for her all the time. She suddenly looked around as she heard a little chuckle right next to her. Pecos thought he heard something and looked over at Molly to see Corey standing over her. He couldn't help himself and pulled his hat over his face to hide a huge smile.

Chapter Twenty-Six

After lunch, Sally and Bill began going through Molly's things, looking for anything that would point to her involvement in the rustling operation. In a pocket of the suitcase Bill pulled out an envelope that had a return address from Wichita. "This must be one of the envelopes that Corey saw on the table."

"Before…or after?" Sally asked.

"After," Bill responded, "he tried to tell me then that she was involved, but, at the time, I didn't think it was possible."

"Next time you will listen to me," Corey said as he appeared beside them.

"What's in it?" Sally asked him.

Bill opened the envelope and scanned through the papers. "Looks like it's a letter from a cattle dealer in Wichita. Making her an offer on 'her' herd, if she can get them there before the major drives begin."

"That's what you said from the beginning," Corey said as he smiled at Bill. "You nailed it."

"Comes from a long history of dealing with riffraff like this."

"Let's see if we find anything else," Sally said as she began sifting through some of Molly's clothing. She pulled out a heavy woolen jacket and as she folded it to lay it aside she felt something in the pocket. "Oh, my," she said as she pulled out the ruby brooch.

"My mother's brooch," Corey said angrily. "She found it all right…right where I had it in the dresser drawer."

"Easy Corey…we have it back now. I'll make sure that this is in my report to the judge. Rustling and petty theft, the charges just keep mounting."

"Don't forget murder," Sally said.

"And attempted murder," Corey injected.

"Don't worry, it'll all be in the report to the judge." He took the brooch from Sally. "Right now I'm going to put this in my safe with your other stuff," Bill said to Corey who nodded.

"Thanks."

They then continued going through the suitcases but didn't find anything else incriminating and repacked Molly's belongings, keeping out the envelope. "Well, if you two don't mind, I guess I'd better get busy writing this up so I can present it to the judge." Corey slowly faded from sight as Sally placed her hand on Bill's arm.

"At least you're finally safe."

"A lawman is never totally safe, Sally. If we're going to try to make this work, it's something you're going to have to accept. Being a lawman's wife is not an easy life."

"Why, Marshal Raines, is that a proposal?" She was hoping it was, but decided that she would try to tease him a little bit first.

Bill suddenly realized what he had said. He also realized that it was exactly what he wanted and put his hands on her shoulders. "It may not be the most romantic proposal ever, but…" he pulled her a little closer. "Sally Roberts, I do love you…will you marry me?"

She began trembling. She had never thought she would hear those words again. "Yes…yes, Bill Raines, I will marry you." He leaned down and they brought their lips together in a long, passionate kiss.

*****

The following morning, Bill took all of his evidence and reports and headed over to see Judge Cramer. "Good Morning, Your Honor," he said as he entered the office.

"'Morning, Marshal. Thought I might be seeing you today. From what I hear, you've been quite busy lately. I also heard what happened a couple of nights ago. I take it you're all right?"

"Yes, I'm fine." He placed a file on the desk. "This is what I've got on my two 'guests' over there." He explained everything to the judge about his suspicions about Molly and Ryker and showed him the letter from Wichita and brooch that were found in Molly's bag.

"I take it they're not going to be very cooperative and this will have to go to trial?"

"No, Judge, they're neither one saying a thing. But the way they look at each other from their cells, it may only be a matter of time before one of the decides to come clean and implicate the other."

Judge Cramer began looking through the file. "How has your other prisoner been doing? I take it he has been behaving himself."

"Model prisoner, Judge. He's also keeping an eye on those two and agreed to report to me anything that they say to each other."

Judge Cramer raised an eyebrow. "That's not totally ethical, Marshal."

"I know, but the way it looks, Ryker is the one that threw the dynamite in the window and tried to burn the office down a few nights ago. That incident I witnessed myself. So Pecos has a 'vested' interest in this, since he is also one of the targets."

"I see. Now what's this about burning the place down?"

Bill explained what he could about the situation without mentioning Corey. "Why didn't he throw the brick?" The judge asked.

"I can't say for sure. Except that it seemed like his arm didn't want to complete the throw…very strange."

"Uh-huh, very strange. You know, Bill," he said sitting back in his chair, "things have been a little weird around here lately. Several people, including Tom Lawson at the saloon, have had the feeling that something wasn't right. Any idea what that something could be?"

"No…" Bill said hesitantly. He didn't want to lie to the judge, but he also didn't want to sound like he was crazy. "I've sensed it too, Your Honor, but I really can't say."

"OK, Marshal, I'll look through this and set a court date. Let me know if they have a lawyer. If not, I'll assign Cal to look at their cases."

"Thanks, Judge. I'll talk with both of them in a little while." He got up and started walking to the door.

"Oh, Bill…." Judge Cramer said with a big smile on his face. "Say 'hi' to Corey for me and tell him not to scare too many people. We don't want this to become a real 'ghost town'."

Bill had gotten about half-way out the door and froze, then looked back at the Judge, who just gave him a two fingered salute and went back to reviewing the file. Bill continued out and walked down the street, shaking his head. He stopped by the saloon to see how things had been going. "Morning, Marshal," Jake called out as Bill came through the door. "Heard what happened. You OK?"

"Fine, Jake, thanks." He looked around the room. "Looks like things have been quiet around here. No broken furniture in sight," he smiled as he looked at Jake.

"Real quiet, Seems like folks haven't been in the mood to get real rowdy." He shook his head. "Can't figure it out…not that I am complaining."

"Let's just hope it stays this way. I like a nice peaceful little town. Makes my job a lot easier."

"Especially when you have to do everything yourself." He watched as Bill tensed up for a moment. "I know how you felt about Corey, Marshal, but maybe it's time you thought about hiring a new deputy. Give yourself some deserved time off."

"I've been thinking about it, Jake. Really. Just have to make sure I choose the right guy." He looked around the room. "Sarah around?"

"I think she went to run a couple of errands before it gets too busy. Any message for her?"

"Just tell her that she can stop by and see Pecos anytime today. Things were a little crazy over there yesterday."

"I'll let her know, Marshal." He paused for a second. "Thanks for being so understanding 'bout them."

"Who am I to stand in the way of young love?" Bill just chuckled, slapped the bar and headed back out to the street. He walked around town for a few minutes and as he passed by the doctor's office, he heard Dr. Russell call for him to come inside. "Hi, Doc," he said as he walked through the door.

"I saw you passing by and thought it might be a good time to see how that wound is healing."

"It's doing fine, Doc," Bill said as he walked over to the examining table. "Still a little sore, but other than that, no problems."

"Why don't you let me be the judge of that?" The doctor said as he motioned for Bill to pull his shirt up and show him the wound area. A few minutes later, the doctor had applied a fresh dressing and let Bill stand up and adjust his clothing. "You're a lucky man, Marshal. You know if that bullet had gone in at another angle, it could have been real bad."

Bill was suddenly very serious. "I know, Doc. I guess I had someone up there," he pointed to the ceiling, "looking over me that night."

"After the other night, I would say you have someone looking after you down here." He just smiled at Bill, waiting for a reaction.

Bill couldn't help but shake his head. "Yeah, I guess I do," he said. "And it looks like that's going to be a permanent situation."

"Well, well, congratulations."

"That's not for public knowledge right now, Doc. Let us get used to the idea for a few days."

"Sure, Marshal." They shook hands as Bill got ready to leave. "Just make sure I get an invitation to the wedding."

"You will, Doc. Don't worry." Bill left and continued down the street to his office. He was about to unlock the door, when he heard Sally call out to him.

"Hi, Bill. Your 'guests' ready for some lunch?"

"Probably." He held the door open and she carried the tray inside. "You know, Marshal, if you get any more prisoners, I'm not going to be able to carry this thing…it's getting heavy. I could only bring over enough for them." She pointed to the cells. "I guess you're just going to have to come over to my establishment for lunch." She smiled up at him as he looked around and then gave her a quick kiss. "That would be my pleasure. I'll wait until they're finished and bring the tray over and grab my lunch then."

"OK…oh, I saw you come out of the Doc's office. You OK?"

"Oh, sure. He saw me going by and pulled me inside to check my side. Said everything was fine."

"That's good. I was a little worried there for a minute."

"The only thing you have to worry about," he said softly as he tapped her on the nose with his index finger, "is finding yourself a wedding dress."

"That's at the top of my list," she said, then stood on her tiptoes to kiss him before she hurried back to the café.

Bill turned to go back to his desk. "Am I invited?" He heard Corey say.

"Could I keep you away?"

"Nope. After all, it was me that said you should marry her in the beginning."

"Oh, yeah…take all the credit." Bill said, chuckling. A few minutes later he went back to the cells and gathered the empty dishes and placed them back on the tray. He looked at Ryker and Molly. "I had a talk with the judge this morning. If you don't have a lawyer, he will assign Cal Stafford to represent you. I'll let you know about the court date as soon as he sets it."

"You can't do it, Marshal," Molly began to plead with him. "You can't put me on trial."

"Unless you want to confess everything, Mrs. Mason, that's exactly what we're going to do."

"But I didn't do anything!"

"Then, that will be decided in court, won't it?" Bill said as he went back into the office as Molly glared at Ryker and Pecos.

Pecos just looked at her and said, "Hey, what did I do?"

"Just what DID you tell them?" Molly asked him.

Pecos just shrugged at her. "Only what I knew. But I don't think I'm the one you need to be worried about." He glanced at Ryker, then relaxed back onto his cot as Molly started pacing in her cell. A short time later, Bill came back, escorting Sarah to Pecos' cell.

"Hi, Honey," Pecos said as he took her hand in his. "Only a couple more days and I will be out of here and we can start planning what to do with the rest of our lives."

"I can't wait for you to be out of here, Pecos," she said looking up at him. "I don't care what we do, as long as we're together."

"Oh, please," Molly said sarcastically.

"Just ignore, her, Sarah. That's what I try to do." Pecos said, smiling at Sarah. "The first thing I have to do is find a job. It will have to be in this area, so I'm hoping I might be able to get one of the ranchers to give me a chance. The marshal said he would put in a good word for me with Mr. Harris."

"That would be wonderful…even if I would only get to see you on the weekends, at least I'll know you're safe."

"Well, as safe as any cowboy is. But don't you worry, we'll work everything out…together. Besides, it will give you plenty of time to make that wedding dress you're always talking about." She blushed and raised up on her toes to kiss him.

*****

It was the next afternoon when Judge Cramer sent word for Bill to come to his office. "Hello, Marshal," he said when Bill came in the door.

"Judge, what can I do for you?"

"I've gone over these papers. It seems like you have a pretty cut and dried case against both of them. Has either of them asked for an attorney?"

"No, I think Ryker is pretty resigned as to what is going to happen. Mrs. Mason just keeps saying she hasn't done anything."

"Shooting an officer of the law and stealing property…I'd say that was something," the Judge said. "I'm going to set the hearing date for 9:00AM on Monday. I'll send Cal over to talk to them this afternoon and apprise them of what is going to happen. After he reports back to me, I'll decide then whether to try them together, or separately."

“Thanks, Your Honor,” Bill said as he got to his feet. “Oh, since Pecos’ thirty days are up tomorrow, I’m going to release him first thing if that’s all right with you.”

“Sure…has he said what his intentions are?”

“He wants to find a job, first. I told him I would put a good word in with Ken Harris, but I also have something else I’m thinking about if that doesn’t work out.”

Judge Cramer just grinned and shook his head. “If I know you, I wouldn’t even think about talking to Harris…just go with the backup plan.”

“You know, Judge, I’m beginning to think you’re clairvoyant. You always seem to be one step ahead of me.”

“Practice, Bill, practice.”

*****

The next morning, after breakfast, Bill unlocked Pecos’ cell and told him he was releasing him. When they got to the office Bill handed him his gun and other personal items. “I’m giving you your gun, Pecos, hoping that you will act responsibly from this point forward.”

“I will, Marshal, don’t worry.” He paused for a few seconds. “Marshal Raines, I want to thank you. I know that you had a big part in the judge’s decision, and I promise I won’t make you sorry that you supported me the way you did. I really do appreciate it.”

Bill looked at Pecos for a long moment. “Have you thought any more on what you want to do now?”

“Find me a job. I need to support myself and try to put something aside if I intend to have a future with Sarah.”

“I don’t believe I’m going to say this, Pecos…Danny…” he hesitated, just looking at Danny. “Daniel Wilde, would you be interested in becoming Rio Madre’s new deputy?” At that point, Danny had to sit down.

“Are you serious, Marshal?” He couldn’t believe what he had just heard.

“Yes, Danny, very serious. I’ve been watching you over the last few weeks and listening to you when we would have our little talks. You proved yourself when you kept Johnny from escaping that day…and again a few nights ago when Ryker played his hand." Danny stiffened, realizing that Bill knew that it was him that had fired the shot at Ryker.

"But…"

"Yes, I figured out that it was you…that is you and Corey backing me up that night. How he got you out of that cell and then back in before I got back…? Well, I don't think I want to know. You've pulled my hide out of the fire twice. I think I can trust you to keep doing it, and let me back you up when you need it. What about it Danny?" He pulled a deputy's badge out of the drawer and put in on the desk. "Feel like following in your father's footsteps."

Danny picked up the badge, gently fingering it. "I think I would like that very much, Marshal."

"Raise your right hand, Danny." Danny held up his hand. "Do you swear to uphold the laws of the town of Rio Madre?"

"Yes, Sir, I do." Danny said as he took a deep breath. He smiled at Bill, "I guess you figured out a way to keep an eye on me for the next year."

"And for a whole lot longer, I hope," Bill said as they shook hands and Danny pinned the badge onto his shirt. "Now, as far as a place for you to live…temporarily. There's a sleeping room back there." He pointed to a door. "I use it when I have prisoners here….which means I haven't seen my own bed in over a month. I would like to do that tonight. You can bunk here until you and Sarah find your own place."

Danny's face lit up as he realized that, just maybe, he and Sarah would have a life together sooner than they expected.

"Now for the not so good part," Bill said to him, "we're going to have to take care of those two until they go to trial, which will probably be next week. Which means, with you 'living' back there for the time being, you're going to be responsible for keeping an eye on them at night. Think you can handle it?"

"Yes, Sir."

"OK…as your first duty as my deputy, let's take a walk around town and give the townsfolk a formal introduction to their new lawman." They walked out of the office together and Bill locked the door as a smiling Corey appeared sitting at his desk. "How about we make the first introduction to a certain young lady at the saloon?" A few moments later the two lawmen walked into the saloon. Danny looked around the room for Sarah, but didn't see her. They walked over to the bar. "Hi Jake," Bill said.

"Marshal," Jake said as he looked at Bill then Danny, "what can I do for you?"

"Well, first, I would like to introduce you to my new deputy, Danny Wilde."

Danny and Jake just looked at each other for a minute. "Hi, Jake," Danny said. "Bet you didn't think you would see me in here again this soon."

"Well, uh…" Jake wasn't sure what to say. "I guess I hadn't thought about it, Pecos…uh Danny?"

"It's all right, Jake…I wasn't expecting this either. But, when Marshal Raines asked me if I was interested, I couldn't say no. It just felt like the right thing to do."

"I'm happy for you, Danny. And I know Sarah is going to be thrilled."

"Is she here?"

"Yes, she's in the back with Betty doing an inventory. Just a minute I'll get her." Jake walked to the back of the establishment and through a door. A few seconds later Sarah came into the bar area and saw Danny standing there…wearing a badge.

"Pecos…what?" She couldn't believe what she was seeing.

"It's real, Honey. I'm the new deputy. Looks like I'm going to be staying here in town after all." She jumped up and threw her arms around his neck and kissed him.

"I can't believe it! Deputy?"

"Believe it, Miss Sarah," Bill said as he walked over to them. "I happen to think he's going to be a good one, too." He just looked at Danny for a moment then grinned. "Just one thing, Danny, I know the view is good in here," he looked at Sarah, "but you will have to spend the majority of your time doing your duties as a deputy. Think you can do that?"

"I can do that, Marshal. Just knowing that I can be close in case she needs me….that's all I want."

"Sarah," Bill said, "think you can deal with this? It won't be easy for you either."

"Yes, Marshal…I believe I can. Like he said, just knowing he's close… that's all I need."

"Good…OK, Deputy…let's finish making our rounds." Danny gave Sarah a quick kiss and followed Bill out of the saloon. An hour or so later they had completed the rounds and were headed back to the office when they saw Cal Stafford coming toward them.

"Morning, Marshal," he said, then saw the badge on Danny's chest and grinned, big. "Well, well, he's hornswaggled you already, huh?" Danny just smiled but didn't say anything. "I'm happy for you Pecos, really. I hope everything works out."

"Thanks, Cal. I think it will. I just hope I can be half the deputy that Corey was. If anyone was born to the job, he was."

"I think we can call him 'Danny' now, Cal," Bill said.

"Danny, it is. Marshal, I would like to talk with your prisoners if it's all right?"

"Sure, come on inside." They entered the office and Bill took Cal back to the cells. Corey was sitting at his desk and got up when Danny looked over at him.

"It's all yours, Danny," Corey said as he stepped away from the desk.

Danny walked over to the desk and touched it, but somehow, couldn't sit down in the chair. "Corey…"

"Come on, Danny, you deserve it."

"But, you didn't deserve what happened to you."

"Stop it right there, Danny." Corey had heard enough from everyone about what had happened to him. "It happened. I didn't want to die, but I did. The only one to blame was Red. He's the one that went for his gun and started the fight."

Danny looked at Corey and then went and sat down in the chair as Corey smiled at him. "What now Corey?"

"I don't know really. I'm not ready to go on to the so called 'other side'. I really want to stay around and help out whenever I can. Talk about someone that can really go undercover." They both started laughing as Bill came back into the office.

"Well you two are really cheerful. Corey, I take it you're satisfied with my decision."

"No complaints from me." He walked over to Bill's desk. "We were just talking…I think I'm going to hang around for a little while. Not really ready to go yet. That is, unless you have some objections."

"Never. But, Corey, maybe you should think about…"

"I will…when I'm ready." He faded from view.

A few minutes later, Cal came into the office. "I think we'll be ready to go to trial next week," he said. "I tried to convince them that a confession might be easier for them, but they didn't seem to be very receptive, especially Mrs. Mason. She says she hasn't done anything wrong."

"I guess we'll just have to wait and see. Thanks, Cal," Bill said as they shook hands and Cal left the office.

"Do you want me to talk to them?" Danny asked.

"No. Right now, I think we should let the court handle things. Judge Cramer has all of the evidence and we'll just have to go by his call."

"Uh…might be a good idea if I was brought up to date on everything." Danny said as he got up and walked over to Bill's desk.

"Sorry, Danny…you're right." Bill went on to explain about the letter, the brooch and exactly what had happened the night he arrested her.

"Seems pretty clear to me," Danny said.

"Look, Danny…why don't you go get some lunch and then bring back something for our guests, then I'll go?"

"I'll do that. Besides, my stomach is starting to complain a little."

"Oh, Danny…I didn't pay much attention to how much money you have…if you need an advance until payday…"

He double checked his wallet. "No, thanks, Marshal. I have about ten dollars on me, and since I probably won't be getting into any card games now, it should get me through."

Bill grinned at him. "Just let me know…" Danny left the office and headed over to the café.

"Hello, Mrs. Roberts," Danny said as he went into the café.

"Hello, Pecos. Well, well, I see congratulations are in order."

"Thank you, Ma'am. And I guess you can call me 'Danny' now. Seems I've put the Pecos Kid behind me."

"I'm glad, Danny, real glad. When did all this happen?" She pointed to the badge.

"This morning. The marshal took me on a tour earlier, but you were really busy when we went by so we didn't want to bother you."

"Bill could never be a bother to me…and neither could you. Now, what can I get for you?"

"I'm pretty hungry…how about a bowl of stew and some coffee?"

"Stew coming up."

"Also, the marshal asked me to bring back lunch for the prisoners."

"I'll have it ready for you in a few minutes."

"Thanks, Mrs. Roberts," Danny said, then dug into his meal.

"Oh, we must do something about that," Sally said as he looked up at her. She smiled at him. "Why don't you just call me Sally?"

"Thank you, Mrs…uh…Miss Sally…is that all right? I just don't know if I could call you by your first name yet."

"You're a fine young gentleman, Danny. 'Miss Sally' it is."

Later that afternoon, Danny made his first solo tour as the town deputy. Most of the people were very friendly and accepted him right away, but a few others were obviously skeptical. He vowed to himself that he would prove those skeptics wrong. He made the saloon his last stop and when he walked in he saw Sarah standing by one of the tables where a poker game was going on. He walked over to the bar where Jake had just drawn a beer for one of the poker players. "Sarah," Jake called and put the mug on the bar. She turned and smiled when she saw Danny standing there. She took the beer, put it on a tray and delivered it to the table, then came back and gave Danny a quick kiss.

"Hi, Pecos…"

"Huh-uh, Honey. From now on it's 'Danny'."

"That may take some getting used to." She smiled at him. "But I think I could get used to it."

"Look, I'm going to be bunking at the office, at least until the trial is over," he said to her. "But I would like to sit down and have a talk with you about our future plans. How about having breakfast with me in the morning?"

"That sounds wonderful, Pec....Danny. About nine o'clock OK?"

"Perfect. We'll have breakfast and then I can make my rounds."

"You're really happy about this, aren't you?"

Danny nodded his head. "Six months ago I would have scoffed at the idea, but now...I don't know what it is, Sarah, but I want this to succeed more than anything...anything that is except marrying you."

"I accept, Danny, I would love to be your wife."

Danny froze for a second as he realized what he had just done. Then a huge smile lit up his face as he picked her up and swung her around. Jake had been watching, and listening. "Hey Everyone...drinks on the house...Sarah's getting married!"

Chapter Twenty-Seven

At nine o'clock on Monday morning, the trial for Molly and Ryker began. Because of the connection between the events, the judge had decided to try them together. The prosecuting attorney, Alfred Gray, assisted by Marshal Raines, presented the evidence that they had against the two defendants. Alfred was fifty-five years old with brown hair that was beginning to turn gray around temples. He had started out as a practicing attorney in the area and had grown into the position of prosecuting attorney through astute insight into people and situations. By the time he had presented the letter to Molly quoting a price for 'her' herd, as well as the brooch belonging to Corey that was found in her suitcase, there hadn't been much doubt as to her involvement. Along with the rustling charges, both of the defendants were also charged with the attempted murder of Marshal Raines. Bill had wanted to charge Molly as an accessory to Corey's murder, but Judge Cramer had been reluctant to press that charge since she had not been physically at the scene at the time. Cal was asked to present his defense of his clients, and put Ryker on the stand first. Ryker knew that there was little chance that he could dodge the charge of trying to kill the marshal since he was caught in the act, but he also didn't want to go down alone and finally, under cross-examination, admitted that all of his orders, from the rustling to the attempts on Marshal Raines, had come from Molly. When it was her turn on the stand, Molly tried to deny everything, even saying that the brooch must have fallen into her pocket when she was packing up Corey's room. To which Alfred asked her if she normally packed up a boarder's room while wearing a heavy wool coat, in the summer. At that point

Molly broke down and began crying, knowing that there was nothing she could do.

It took the jury about a half hour to come back with a guilty conviction on all charges against both of the defendants. Three days later two U.S. Marshals arrived in Rio Madre with a prison wagon to escort the Molly and Ryker to the State Institution in Huntsville, where they would stay for the next five years.

Over the next few days, both Bill and Danny took a collective breath, as they tried to put the stress of the past few weeks behind them. Bill had continued to show Danny 'the ropes' of being a town marshal. They were both also trying to cope with the women in their lives as they prepared for their weddings. There were times when both of them sought refuge in the office to escape the two women as they tried to make all of the needed arrangements.

"You know, Marshal," Danny said one afternoon, "I almost wish we had eloped."

"I totally agree with you," Bill said as he grinned at Danny. "Those two women are something else on their own…and when you put them together. But, you know, I don't think I would have it any other way."

Danny nodded in agreement. "I just wish there was a way to just sit back and then show up on the appointed day."

"It will never happen, Son," Bill laughed. Then they both looked up as the two excited women came bouncing into the office. Both Bill and Danny looked at each other and shook their heads.

"Bill…we just came up with a wonderful idea," Sally said, looking at Sarah. "Why don't we have a double wedding!" The men almost fell out of their chairs.

"Really," Sarah said, "it will definitely save on expenses with a combined reception. We all have about the same friends. We would have to stagger the honeymoons, of course…"

"WHOA…."Bill called out, momentarily silencing the excited girl. "One thing at a time. There are still a few roadblocks that have to be worked out," he looked at Danny. "Unless I'm missing something, you and Danny don't have a place to live yet. And…" he put up his hand to stop her from saying anything, "I don't think it would be appropriate for the town deputy to be living over the saloon…even if he is married."

Corey was standing over in the corner watching and listening to everything. He motioned to Bill for them to huddle at Danny's desk. Although Sally knew about Corey, Sarah did not and was momentarily confused. "Let's let the menfolk talk this over for a few minutes," she said to Sarah. "Bill, why don't you and Danny come over to the café when you've figured things out?"

"Thanks, Sally…we'll be over in a few minutes," Bill said then watched as the women, slightly subdued, left the office.

"OK, Corey, what's up?" Bill asked him.

"Marshal, would you please open the safe and get my mother's jewelry?"

Bill hesitated, but opened the safe and got out a pouch containing the jewelry and laid it on Danny's desk. Corey looked at both of them very seriously. "I have no family left. You two and Peggy were the closest people to me. I have entrusted Peggy with Sunny, but I think this jewelry may solve a lot of problems for both of you." Bill and Danny looked at each other, then back at Corey. "Marshal, I want you to have my mother's ring and locket…for Sally. The ring was her wedding ring and now I want you to give it to Sally….No…don't stop me," he said as Bill started to interrupt. "It's what I want. That's what I had in mind when I had you to put them in the safe. Now, Danny, I know you and Sarah are starting out with pretty much nothing right now," and smiled as Danny nodded. "I want you to take this brooch to the bank and see if you can use it as collateral for enough money to buy Sally a ring…and the boarding house." Danny's mouth dropped open and he turned 'white as a ghost'. "You two need a place to live, and you want to get Sarah out of the saloon. Let her run the boarding house. Molly lost all claims to any of her property here in Rio Madre as part of her sentence, so right now, it needs an owner. You'll both have a source of money coming in. It might be tough for a little while, but I think you can do it. I don't know what the balance was on Molly's mortgage, but that brooch should be worth enough to cover you taking over that mortgage. You can use it for collateral, or sell it and buy the boarding house, outright…your choice."

"Corey…I can't…it's too much…how would I explain?"

"Danny, Corey had given me a power of attorney when he became my deputy. He knew something could happen, and he wanted to make sure these," he motioned to the jewelry, "were taken care of. That signed paper is in a deposit box at the bank…there will be no questions."

"Well, Danny, what do you say?" Corey asked him.

There was moisture in his eyes as Danny touched the brooch and looked up at Corey. "Thank you, Corey…I don't know how I will ever be able to repay you…" Corey chuckled.

"There's not a whole lot that I need at this point in time," Corey replied. "What I do need is to know that those that I leave behind are taken care of. Now why don't you go over to the café, set a wedding date and see what Sarah has to say about our idea?"

Bill carefully placed the jewelry back into the pouch and locked it back into the safe. Then the three left the office. Bill glanced back as he realized Corey was following them. "You don't think I'm going miss out on seeing her reaction, do you?" Corey said to them. They got to the café and went inside to see the two women sitting at one of the tables drinking a cup of coffee. The two men went to sit down beside their future brides.

"Well, have you two ladies decided on a wedding date yet?" Bill asked them.

"Well, uh…we sort of were waiting to see what you two decided," Sally said. Bill and Danny could both see that the two women had both come down off the clouds they had been riding a short time before.

Danny put his arm around Sarah and turned her toward him. "Sarah, what would you say if I told you that we could buy the boarding house, live there, and you could run it, instead of having to work at the saloon?"

Sarah began crying as she put her head on Danny's chest. "But….how?"

"Let's just say we have a benefactor that wants us to make a good life for ourselves."

Sally looked over her shoulder. "Thank you, Corey," she said softly and watched as he smiled and placed his hand on her shoulder.

"Cuh..Corey?" Sarah said between happy sobs.

"Yes, Honey," Danny said. "Corey had left some of his mother's valuables in the Marshal's possession and Marshal Raines thinks that Corey would be very happy if we put them to use to give us our start together."

"Thank you, Marshal," Sarah said. "We won't let you…or Corey down, I promise."

"I know you won't, Sarah. Now…about that wedding date?" He looked at Sally as he raised an eyebrow.

Epilogue

The wedding was scheduled for Saturday of the following week, giving them about ten days to make the final arrangements. The two couples went over to the saloon to give Tom the bad news that he was going to be losing one of his employees. Although he was not happy about losing Sarah, he was very happy for her. "Mr. Lawson," Sarah said to him, "I don't have any family anywhere, so, would you do me the honor of walking me down the aisle?"

A huge smile came over Tom as he took Sarah in his arms and gave her a big hug. "Honey, I would be the one to be honored to give you away. And as for you, young man," he looked at Danny, "you'd better take good care of her."

"I will, Sir…you don't have to worry about that."

Once all the arrangements were in place, Bill, Danny and Sarah went to the bank to see Henry Cole, the manager. Bill had the brooch with him and showed it to Henry when they all sat down. "Henry, these young people would like to use this brooch as collateral to take over the mortgage on the boarding house. Since Mrs. Mason lost all claims to her property in court, Danny and Sarah, who are getting married next week, would like to buy the boarding house and keep the business open."

Henry took the brooch and examined it. "This is a fine piece of jewelry, Marshal. Do you mind if I ask where you got it?"

"Not at all. It belonged to Corey Hansen's mother. Corey gave me the power of attorney over his possessions in case anything happened to him, and I have had that in my safe since it was recovered from Mrs. Mason's luggage. I think you probably heard all of that at the trial?"

"Yes, Marshal, I did. Well," he pulled a ledger out of his drawer and scanned through a few pages, "it looks like the balance on the boarding house is two hundred and twenty dollars. If this is as valuable as I think it is, I don't see why we can't use it as collateral. If you will give me a couple of hours, I will get all of the paperwork done and you can sign this afternoon." He looked up at the clock on the wall. "Why don't you come back here about one o'clock and we'll get everything signed and you can take possession of the building today? How's that?"

"That's wonderful, Mr. Cole, but one other thing…could I please get a few extra dollars with the loan…I need to buy Sarah a wedding ring?"

"I think that can be arranged, Deputy. What say we make the loan for an even three hundred? Enough to take over the mortgage, a ring, and a few dollars to help you get started out."

Danny and Sarah were beaming. "Thank you, Mr. Cole. Thank you so much," Sarah said to him. "You don't know what this means to us."

"I think I do, Miss Riley. I wish you and Mr. Wilde all the best in your marriage and in your new business." They shook hands and Danny and Sarah told him they would be there at one o'clock sharp.

After Danny and Sarah met with Mr. Cole and signed the papers they went over to the boarding house where they were met by Mrs. Johannsen who had volunteered to look after the establishment until the trial was over and other arrangements had been made. "I want to thank you for what you have done, Mrs. Johannsen," Sarah said to her. "This has been such a whirlwind the last few days…"

"I want to thank you, too," Danny told her. "Your stepping in and taking over meant that we still have boarders."

"It was nothing, Deputy. Since Mr. Johannsen passed, I have been very lonely, and this gave me the opportunity to be out and do something again. I've been thinking about selling the house, anyway, it's just too much for me now."

"What would you do then?" Sarah asked her.

"Oh, I don't know. Find some other place smaller. I guess."

Sarah looked up at Danny who nodded. "Mrs. Johannsen, would you be interested in staying here? In exchange for your room and board, you could help me take care of the place. I'm afraid I don't know a whole lot about things right now. It's going to be a learning experience and you would be a big help. If I'm not mistaken this place has eight or ten rooms…"

"Eight," Mrs. Johannsen said.

"Danny and I will only need one and with you staying and helping, that would still leave six rooms that can be rented. Oh, dear, am I making any sense at all?" Sarah said excited at the thought of what was happening with her life.

"You're making a lot of sense, My Dear. And I think I would be interested…in fact, your offer is most appreciated."

"Then it's settled," Danny said. "Why don't you sit down with us this evening after dinner, and we can decide what we can do to make this place the best boarding house in the state of Texas?"

"Thank you, Mr. Wilde, thank you."

"Now, about the Mr. Wilde…" Danny smiled at her. "Why don't you call us Danny and Sarah?"

"You're so sweet, Danny, and you can call me Annie. Now, why don't I show you around your new home?"

*****

On the day before the wedding, Bill and Danny were doing the town tour together, when the noon train pulled in. "Come on, Deputy, let's see who's arriving in our fine town."

They went across the street to the station and waited as the passengers began to exit the train. Danny had been looking toward the engine when he heard his name called and turned around. He stood there in shock. "Momma?" She held out her arms and Danny walked to her and threw his arms around her. "Oh Momma, I'm so sorry…."

"Hush, hush, Danny…you don't have anything to apologize for. And from what I hear, you've become a fine young man. You're even following in your father's footsteps." She touched his badge. "I'm so proud of you." She stepped back from him and gave him a good looking over. "Marshal, what is this boy eating? He's skin and bones."

Bill burst out laughing and slapped Danny on the back. "Well, Belle, I think his new wife will probably take care of that."

"Momma…how did you get here?"

"The train of course," she said, teasing him.

"I mean…how did you know…" Danny stopped when he saw her look at Bill. "Marshal?"

"You didn't seriously think I would let you get married without inviting your mother, did you?"

With that Bill picked up Belle's bags and they headed toward the boarding house to introduce Belle to her new soon-to-be daughter-in-law.

The next morning, both brides were in a room at the church putting on the final touches before the ceremony. They heard a knock at the door and Betty, who had been helping them, went to the door. She saw Tom there and stepped back letting him in. He let out a slow whistle. "Oh my, such beauty, all in one room."

"Why thank you, Mr. Lawson," Sally said, blushing. "You know, we've been talking, and since you're walking Sarah down the aisle, how about walking both of us?"

"Sally, it would be my pleasure."

A few minutes later, Bill and Danny were talking with their guests in the church. Ken and Peggy were there and for the first time in what seemed like a long time, Peggy felt happy. As the music started, Bill and Danny joined Father Michael at the altar as Ken and Peggy took their seats. The two grooms-to-be watched the father and daughter as, unbeknownst to them, Corey sat down beside Peggy to watch the ceremony. As the sound of the wedding march began, the two lawmen looked to the back of the church and watched as Betty, acting as a bridesmaid to both brides, walked down the aisle. Behind her they saw two beautiful visions, walking toward them on the arms of Tom Lawson.

THE END…